THE COLOUR OF MAGIC

Terry Pratchett

CORGI BOOKS

TRANSWORLD PUBLISHERS
61-63 Uxbridge Road, London W5 5SA
A Random House Group Company
www.rbooks.co.uk

THE COLOUR OF MAGIC
A CORGI BOOK: 9780552166591

Originally published in Great Britain in 1983 by Colin Smythe Ltd
Corgi edition published 1985
Copyright © Dunmanifestin Ltd 1983

Discworld ® is a trademark registered by Dunmanifestin Ltd

Addresses for Random House Group Ltd companies outside the UK
can be found at: www.randomhouse.co.uk
The Random House Group Ltd Reg. No. 954009

Penguin Random House is committed to a sustainable future for
our business, our readers and our planet. This book is made from
Forest Stewardship Council® certified paper.

MIX
Paper from
responsible sources
FSC® C018179

Typeset in Minion by Falcon Oast Graphic Art Ltd

Printed in the UK by Clays Ltd, Elcograf S.p.A.

Contents

THE COLOUR OF MAGIC

· Prologue ·

IN A DISTANT AND second-hand set of dimensions, in an astral plane that was never meant to fly, the curling star-mists waver and part . . .

See . . .

Great A'Tuin the Turtle comes, swimming slowly through the interstellar gulf, hydrogen frost on his ponderous limbs, his huge and ancient shell pocked with meteor craters. Through sea-sized eyes that are crusted with rheum and asteroid dust He stares fixedly at the Destination.

In a brain bigger than a city, with geological slowness, He thinks only of the Weight.

Most of the weight is of course accounted for by Berilia, Tubul, Great T'Phon and Jerakeen, the four giant elephants upon whose broad and star-tanned shoulders the disc of the World rests, garlanded by the long waterfall at its vast circumference and domed by the baby-blue vault of Heaven.

Astropsychology has been, as yet, unable to establish what they think about.

The Great Turtle was a mere hypothesis until the day the small and secretive kingdom of Krull, whose rim-most mountains project out over the Rimfall, built a gantry and pulley arrangement at the tip of the most precipitous crag and lowered several observers over the Edge in a quartz-windowed brass vessel to peer through the mist veils.

The early astrozoologists, hauled back from their long dangle by enormous teams of slaves, were able to bring back much information about the shape and nature of A'Tuin and the elephants but this did not resolve fundamental questions about the nature and purpose of the universe.

For example, what was A'Tuin's actual sex? This vital question, said the astrozoologists with mounting authority, would not be answered until a larger and more powerful gantry was constructed for a deep-space vessel. In the meantime, they could only speculate about the revealed cosmos.

There was, for example, the theory that A'Tuin had come from nowhere and would continue at a uniform crawl, or steady gait, into nowhere, for all time. This theory was popular among academics.

An alternative, favoured by those of a religious persuasion, was that A'Tuin was crawling from the Birthplace to the Time of Mating, as were all the stars in the sky which were, obviously, also carried by giant turtles. When they arrived they would briefly and passionately mate, for the first and only time, and from that fiery union new turtles would be born to carry a new pattern of worlds. This was known as the Big Bang hypothesis.

Thus it was that a young cosmochelonian of the Steady Gait faction, testing a new telescope with which he hoped to make measurements of the precise albedo of Great A'Tuin's right eye, was on this eventful evening the first outsider to see the smoke rise hubward from the burning of the oldest city in the world.

Later that night he became so engrossed in his studies he completely forgot about it. Nevertheless, he was the first.

There were others . . .

THE COLOUR
OF MAGIC

FIRE ROARED THROUGH THE bifurcated city of Ankh-Morpork. Where it licked the Wizards' Quarter it burned blue and green and was even laced with strange sparks of the eighth colour, octarine; where its outriders found their way into the vats and oil stores all along Merchants Street it progressed in a series of blazing fountains and explosions; in the streets of the perfume blenders it burned with a sweetness; where it touched bundles of rare and dry herbs in the storerooms of the drugmasters it made men go mad and talk to God.

By now the whole of downtown Morpork was alight, and the richer and worthier citizens of Ankh on the far bank were bravely responding to the situation by feverishly demolishing the bridges. But already the ships in the Morpork docks – laden with grain, cotton and timber, and coated with tar – were blazing merrily and, their moorings burnt to ashes, were breasting the river Ankh on the ebb tide, igniting riverside palaces and bowers as they drifted like drowning fireflies towards the sea. In any case, sparks were riding the breeze and touching down far across the river in hidden gardens and remote rickyards.

The smoke from the merry burning rose miles

high, in a wind-sculpted black column that could be seen across the whole of the discworld.

It was certainly impressive from the cool, dark hilltop a few leagues away, where two figures were watching with considerable interest.

The taller of the pair was chewing on a chicken leg and leaning on a sword that was only marginally shorter than the average man. If it wasn't for the air of wary intelligence about him it might have been supposed that he was a barbarian from the Hubland wastes.

His partner was much shorter and wrapped from head to toe in a brown cloak. Later, when he has occasion to move, it will be seen that he moves lightly, cat-like.

The two had barely exchanged a word in the last twenty minutes except for a short and inconclusive argument as to whether a particularly powerful explosion had been the oil bond store or the work-shop of Kerible the Enchanter. Money hinged on the fact.

Now the big man finished gnawing at the bone and tossed it into the grass, smiling ruefully.

'There go all those little alleyways,' he said. 'I liked them.'

'All the treasure houses,' said the small man. He added thoughtfully, 'Do gems burn, I wonder? 'Tis said they're kin to coal.'

'All the gold, melting and running down the gutters,' said the big one, ignoring him. 'And all the wine, boiling in the barrels.'

'There were rats,' said his brown companion.

'Rats, I'll grant you.'

'It was no place to be in high summer.'

'That, too. One can't help feeling, though, a – well, a momentary—'

He trailed off, then brightened. 'We owed old Fredor at the Crimson Leech eight silver pieces,' he added. The little man nodded.

They were silent for a while as a whole new series of explosions carved a red line across a hitherto dark section of the greatest city in the world. Then the big man stirred.

'Weasel?'

'Yes?'

'I wonder who started it?'

The small swordsman known as the Weasel said nothing. He was watching the road in the ruddy light. Few had come that way since the Deosil Gate had been one of the first to collapse in a shower of white-hot embers.

But two were coming up it now. The Weasel's eyes, always at their sharpest in gloom and half-light, made out the shapes of two mounted men and some sort of low beast behind them. Doubtless a rich merchant escaping with as much treasure as he could lay frantic hands on. The Weasel said as much to his companion, who sighed.

'The status of footpad ill suits us,' said the barbarian, 'but as you say, times are hard and there are no soft beds tonight.'

He shifted his grip on his sword and, as the leading rider drew near, stepped out onto the road with a hand held up and his face set in a grin nicely calculated to reassure yet threaten.

'Your pardon, sir—' he began.

The rider reined in his horse and drew back his hood. The big man looked into a face blotched with superficial burns and punctuated by tufts of singed beard. Even the eyebrows had gone.

'Bugger off,' said the face. 'You're Bravd the Hublander,[1] aren't you?'

Bravd became aware that he had fumbled the initiative.

'Just go away, will you?' said the rider. 'I just haven't got time for you, do you understand?'

He looked around and added: 'That goes for your shadow-loving fleabag partner too, wherever he's hiding.'

The Weasel stepped up to the horse and peered at the dishevelled figure.

'Why, it's Rincewind the wizard, isn't it?' he said in

---

[1] The shape and cosmology of the disc system are perhaps worthy of note at this point.

There are, of course, two major directions on the disc: Hubward and Rimward. But since the disc itself revolves at the rate of once every eight hundred days (in order to distribute the weight fairly upon its supportive pachyderms, according to Reforgule of Krull) there are also two lesser directions, which are Turnwise and Widdershins.

Since the disc's tiny orbiting sunlet maintains a fixed orbit while the majestic disc turns slowly beneath it, it will be readily deduced that a disc year consists of not four but eight seasons. The summers are those times when the sun rises or sets at the nearest point on the Rim, the winters those occasions when it rises or sets at a point around ninety degrees along the circumference.

Thus, in the lands around the Circle Sea, the year begins on Hogs' Watch Night, progresses through a Spring Prime to its first mid-summer (Small Gods' Eve) which is followed by Autumn Prime and, tones of delight, meanwhile filing the wizard's description of him in his memory for leisurely vengeance. 'I thought I recognized the voice.'

Bravd spat and sheathed his sword. It was seldom worth tangling with wizards, they so rarely had any treasure worth speaking of.

'He talks pretty big for a gutter wizard,' he muttered.

'You don't understand at all,' said the wizard wearily. 'I'm so scared of you my spine has turned to jelly, it's just that I'm suffering from an overdose of terror right now. I mean, when I've got over that then I'll have time to be decently frightened of you.'

The Weasel pointed towards the burning city.

'You've been through that?' he asked.

The wizard rubbed a red-raw hand across his eyes. 'I was there when it started. See him? Back there?' He pointed back down the road to where his travelling

straddling the half-year point of Crueltide, Winter Secundus (also known as the Spindlewinter, since at this time the sun rises in the direction of spin). Then comes Secundus Spring with Summer Two on its heels, the three quarter mark of the year being the night of Alls Fallow – the one night of the year, according to legend, when witches and warlocks stay in bed. Then drifting leaves and frosty nights drag on towards Backspindlewinter and a new Hogs' Watch Night nestling like a frozen jewel at its heart.

Since the Hub is never closely warmed by the weak sun the lands there are locked in permafrost. The Rim, on the other hand, is a region of sunny islands and balmy days.

There are, of course, eight days in a disc week and eight colours in its light spectrum. Eight is a number of some considerable occult significance on the disc and must never, ever, be spoken by a wizard.

Precisely why all the above should be so is not clear, but goes some way to explain why, on the disc, the Gods are not so much worshipped as blamed.

companion was still approaching, having adopted a method of riding that involved falling out of the saddle every few seconds.

'Well?' said Weasel.

'He started it,' said Rincewind simply.

Bravd and Weasel looked at the figure, now hopping across the road with one foot in a stirrup.

'Fire-raiser, is he?' said Bravd at last.

'No,' said Rincewind. 'Not precisely. Let's just say that if complete and utter chaos was lightning, then he'd be the sort to stand on a hilltop in a thunderstorm wearing wet copper armour and shouting "All gods are bastards". Got any food?'

'There's some chicken,' said Weasel. 'In exchange for a story.'

'What's his name?' said Bravd, who tended to lag behind in conversations.

'Twoflower.'

'Twoflower?' said Bravd. 'What a funny name.'

'You,' said Rincewind, dismounting, 'do not know the half of it. Chicken, you say?'

'Devilled,' said Weasel. The wizard groaned.

'That reminds me,' added the Weasel, snapping his fingers, 'there was a really big explosion about, oh, half an hour ago—'

'That was the oil bond store going up,' said Rincewind, wincing at the memory of the burning rain.

Weasel turned and grinned expectantly at his companion, who grunted and handed over a coin from his pouch. Then there was a scream from the roadway, cut off abruptly. Rincewind did not look up from his chicken.

'One of the things he can't do, he can't ride a horse,' he said. Then he stiffened as if sandbagged by a sudden recollection, gave a small yelp of terror and dashed into the gloom. When he returned, the being called Twoflower was hanging limply over his shoulder. It was small and skinny, and dressed very oddly in a pair of knee length britches and a shirt in such a violent and vivid conflict of colours that Weasel's fastidious eye was offended even in the half-light.

'No bones broken, by the feel of things,' said Rincewind. He was breathing heavily. Bravd winked at the Weasel and went to investigate the shape that they assumed was a pack animal.

'You'd be wise to forget it,' said the wizard, without looking up from his examination of the unconscious Twoflower. 'Believe me. A power protects it.'

'A spell?' said Weasel, squatting down.

'No-oo. But magic of a kind, I think. Not the usual sort. I mean, it can turn gold into copper while at the same time it is still gold, it makes men rich by destroying their possessions, it allows the weak to walk fearlessly among thieves, it passes through the strongest doors to leach the most protected treasuries. Even now it has me enslaved – so that I must follow this madman willynilly and protect him from harm. It's stronger than you, Bravd. It is, I think, more cunning even than you, Weasel.'

'What is it called then, this mighty magic?'

Rincewind shrugged. 'In our tongue it is called

reflected-sound-as-of-underground-spirits. Is there any wine?'

'You must know that I am not without artifice where magic is concerned,' said Weasel. 'Only last year did I – assisted by my friend there – part the notoriously powerful Archmage of Ymitury from his staff, his belt of moon jewels and his life, in that approximate order. I do not fear this *reflected-sound-of-underground-spirits* of which you speak. However,' he added, 'you engage my interest. Perhaps you would care to tell me more?'

Bravd looked at the shape on the road. It was closer now, and clearer in the pre-dawn light. It looked for all the world like a—

'A box on legs?' he said.

'I'll tell you about it,' said Rincewind. 'If there's any wine, that is.'

Down in the valley there was a roar and a hiss. Someone more thoughtful than the rest had ordered to be shut the big river gates that were at the point where the Ankh flowed out of the twin city. Denied its usual egress, the river had burst its banks and was pouring down the fire-ravaged streets. Soon the continent of flame became a series of islands, each one growing smaller as the dark tide rose. And up from the city of fumes and smoke rose a broiling cloud of steam, covering the stars. Weasel thought that it looked like some dark fungus or mushroom.

The twin city of proud Ankh and pestilent Morpork, of which all the other cities of time and space are, as it were, mere reflections, has stood many assaults in its long and crowded history and has always risen to flourish again. So the fire and its subsequent flood, which destroyed everything left that was not flammable and added a particularly noisome flux to the survivors' problems, did not mark its end. Rather it was a fiery punctuation mark, a coal-like comma, or salamander semi-colon, in a continuing story.

Several days before these events a ship came up the Ankh on the dawn tide and fetched up, among many others, in the maze of wharves and docks on the Morpork shore. It carried a cargo of pink pearls, milknuts, pumice, some official letters for the Patrician of Ankh-Morpork, and a man.

It was the man who engaged the attention of Blind Hugh, one of the beggars on early duty at Pearl Dock. He nudged Cripple Wa in the ribs, and pointed wordlessly.

Now the stranger was standing on the quayside, watching several straining seamen carry a large brass-bound chest down the gangplank. Another man, obviously the captain, was standing beside him. There was about the seaman – every nerve in Blind Hugh's body, which tended to vibrate in the presence of even a small amount of impure gold at fifty paces, screamed into his brain – the air of one anticipating imminent enrichment.

Sure enough, when the chest had been deposited on the cobbles, the stranger reached into a pouch and there was the flash of a coin. Several coins. Gold. Blind Hugh, his body twanging like a hazel rod in the presence of water, whistled to himself. Then he nudged Wa again, and sent him scurrying off down a nearby alley into the heart of the city.

When the captain walked back onto his ship, leaving the newcomer looking faintly bewildered on the quayside, Blind Hugh snatched up his begging cup and made his way across the street with an ingratiating leer. At the sight of him the stranger started to fumble urgently with his money pouch.

'Good day to thee, sire,' Blind Hugh began, and found himself looking up into a face with four eyes in it. He turned to run.

'!' said the stranger, and grabbed his arm. Hugh was aware that the sailors lining the rail of the ship were laughing at him. At the same time his specialized senses detected an overpowering impression of money. He froze. The stranger let go and quickly thumbed through a small black book he had taken from his belt. Then he said 'Hallo'.

'What?' said Hugh. The man looked blank.

'Hallo?' he repeated, rather louder than necessary and so carefully that Hugh could hear the vowels tinkling into place.

'Hallo yourself,' Hugh riposted. The stranger smiled widely then fumbled yet again in the pouch. This time his hand came out holding a large gold coin. It was in fact slightly larger than an 8,000-dollar Ankhian crown and the design on it was unfamiliar, but it spoke inside Hugh's mind in a language he understood perfectly. My current owner, it said, is in need of succour and assistance; why not give it to him, so you and me can go off somewhere and enjoy ourselves?

Subtle changes in the beggar's posture made the

stranger feel more at ease. He consulted the small book again.

'I wish to be directed to an hotel, tavern, lodging house, inn, hospice, caravanserai,' he said.

'What, all of them?' said Hugh, taken aback.

'?' said the stranger.

Hugh was aware that a small crowd of fishwives, shellfish diggers and freelance gawpers were watching them with interest.

'Look,' he said, 'I know a good tavern, is that enough?' He shuddered to think of the gold coin escaping from his life. He'd keep that one, even if Ymor confiscated all the rest. And the big chest that comprised most of the newcomer's luggage looked to be full of gold, Hugh decided.

The four-eyed man looked at his book.

'I would like to be directed to an hotel, place of repose, tavern, a—'

'Yes, all right. Come on then,' said Hugh hurriedly. He picked up one of the bundles and walked away quickly. The stranger, after a moment's hesitation, strolled after him.

A train of thought shunted its way through Hugh's mind. Getting the newcomer to the Broken Drum so easily was a stroke of luck, no doubt of it, and Ymor would probably reward him. But for all his new acquaintance's mildness there was something about him that made Hugh uneasy, and for the life of him he couldn't figure out what it was. Not the two extra eyes, odd though they were. There was something else. He glanced back.

The little man was ambling along in the middle of

the street, looking around him with an expression of keen interest.

Something else Hugh saw nearly made him gibber.

The massive wooden chest, which he had last seen resting solidly on the quayside, was following on its master's heels with a gentle rocking gait. Slowly, in case a sudden movement on his part might break his fragile control over his own legs, Hugh bent slightly so that he could see under the chest.

There were lots and lots of little legs.

Very deliberately, Hugh turned around and walked very carefully towards the Broken Drum.

'Odd,' said Ymor.

'He had this big wooden chest,' added Cripple Wa.

'He'd have to be a merchant or a spy,' said Ymor. He pulled a scrap of meat from the cutlet in his hand and tossed it into the air. It hadn't reached the zenith of its arc before a black shape detached itself from the shadows in the corner of the room and swooped down, taking the morsel in mid-air.

'A merchant or a spy,' repeated Ymor. 'I'd prefer a spy. A spy pays for himself twice, because there's always the reward when we turn him in. What do you think, Withel?'

Opposite Ymor the second greatest thief in Ankh-Morpork half-closed his one eye and shrugged.

'I've checked on the ship,' he said. 'It's a freelance trader. Does the occasional run to the Brown Islands. People there are just savages. They don't understand about spies and I expect they eat merchants.'

'He looked a bit like a merchant,' volunteered Wa. 'Except he wasn't fat.'

There was a flutter of wings at the window. Ymor shifted his bulk out of the chair and crossed the room, coming back with a large raven. After he'd unfastened the message capsule from its leg it flew up to join its fellows lurking among the rafters. Withel regarded it without love. Ymor's ravens were notoriously loyal to their master, to the extent that Withel's one attempt to promote himself to the rank of greatest thief in Ankh-Morpork had cost their master's right-hand man his left eye. But not his life, however. Ymor never grudged a man his ambitions.

'B12,' said Ymor, tossing the little phial aside and unrolling the tiny scroll within.

'Gorrin the Cat,' said Withel automatically. 'On station up in the gong tower at the Temple of Small Gods.'

'He says Hugh has taken our stranger to the Broken Drum. Well, that's good enough. Broadman is a – friend of ours, isn't he?'

'Aye,' said Withel. 'If he knows what's good for trade.'

'Among his customers has been your man Gorrin,' said Ymor pleasantly, 'for he writes here about a box on legs, if I read this scrawl correctly.' He looked at Withel over the top of the paper.

Withel looked away. 'He will be disciplined,' he said flatly. Wa looked at the man leaning back in his chair, his black-clad frame resting as nonchalantly as a Rimland puma on a jungle branch, and decided that Gorrin atop Small Gods temple would soon be joining those little deities in the multifold dimensions of Beyond. And he owed Wa three copper pieces.

Ymor crumpled the note and tossed it into a corner. 'I think we'll wander along to the Drum later on, Withel. Perhaps, too, we may try this beer that your men find so tempting.'

Withel said nothing. Being Ymor's right-hand man was like being gently flogged to death with scented bootlaces.

The twin city of Ankh-Morpork, foremost of all the cities bounding the Circle Sea, was as a matter of course the home of a large number of gangs, thieves' guilds, syndicates and similar organizations. This was one of the reasons for its wealth. Most of the humbler folk on the widdershins side of the river, in Morpork's mazy alleys, supplemented their meagre incomes by filling some small role for one or other of the competing gangs. So it was that by the time Hugh and Twoflower entered the courtyard of the Broken Drum the leaders of a number of them were aware that someone had arrived in the city who appeared to have much treasure. Some reports from the more observant spies included details about a book that told the stranger what to say, and a box that walked by itself. These facts were immediately discounted. No magician capable of such enchantments ever came within a mile of Morpork docks.

It still being that hour when most of the city was just rising or about to go to bed there were few people in the Drum to watch Twoflower descend the stairs. When the Luggage appeared behind him and started to lurch confidently down the steps the customers at the rough wooden tables, as one man, looked suspiciously at their drinks.

Broadman was browbeating the small troll who swept the bar when the trio walked past him. 'What in hell's that?' he said.

'Just don't talk about it,' hissed Hugh. Twoflower was already thumbing through his book.

'What's he doing?' said Broadman, arms akimbo.

'It tells him what to say. I know it sounds ridiculous,' muttered Hugh.

'How can a book tell a man what to say?'

'I wish for an accommodation, a room, lodgings, the lodging house, full board, are your rooms clean, a room with a view, what is your rate for one night?' said Twoflower in one breath.

Broadman looked at Hugh. The beggar shrugged.

'He's got plenty money,' he said.

'Tell him it's three copper pieces, then. And that Thing will have to go in the stable.'

'?' said the stranger. Broadman held up three thick red fingers and the man's face was suddenly a sunny display of comprehension. He reached into his pouch and laid three large gold pieces in Broadman's palm.

Broadman stared at them. They represented about four times the worth of the Broken Drum, staff included. He looked at Hugh. There was no help there. He looked at the stranger. He swallowed.

'Yes,' he said, in an unnaturally high voice. 'And then there's meals, o'course. Uh. You understand, yes? Food. You eat. No?' He made the appropriate motions.

'Fut?' said the little man.

'Yes,' said Boardman, beginning to sweat. 'Have a look in your little book, I should.'

The man opened the book and ran a finger down one page. Broadman, who could read after a fashion, peered over the top of the volume. What he saw made no sense.

'Fooood,' said the stranger. 'Yes. Cutlet, hash, chop, stew, ragout, fricassee, mince, collops, souffle, dumpling, blancmange, sorbet, gruel, sausage, not to have a sausage, beans, without a bean, kickshaws, jelly, jam. Giblets.' He beamed at Broadman.

'All that?' said the innkeeper weakly.

'It's just the way he talks,' said Hugh. 'Don't ask me why. He just does.'

All eyes in the room were watching the stranger – except for a pair belonging to Rincewind the wizard, who was sitting in the darkest corner nursing a mug of very small beer.

He was watching the Luggage.

Watch Rincewind.

Look at him. Scrawny, like most wizards, and clad in a dark red robe on which a few mystic sigils were embroidered in tarnished sequins. Some might have taken him for a mere apprentice enchanter who had run away from his master out of defiance, boredom, fear and a lingering taste for heterosexuality. Yet around his neck was a chain bearing the bronze octagon that marked him as an alumnus of Unseen University, the high school of magic whose time-and-space transcendent campus is never precisely Here or There. Graduates were usually destined for mageship at least, but Rincewind – after an unfortunate event – had left knowing only one spell and made a living of sorts around the town by capitalizing on an innate gift for languages. He avoided work as a rule, but had a quickness of wit that put his acquaintances in mind of a bright rodent. And he knew sapient pearwood when he saw it. He was seeing it now, and didn't quite believe it.

An archmage, by dint of great effort and much expenditure of time, might eventually obtain a small staff made from the timber of the sapient peartree. It grew only on the sites of ancient magic. There were probably no more than two such staffs in all the cities of the Circle Sea. A large chest of it ... Rincewind tried to work it out, and decided that even if the box were crammed with star opals and sticks of auricholatum the contents would not be worth one-tenth the price of the container. A vein started to throb in his forehead.

He stood up and made his way to the trio.

'May I be of assistance?' he ventured.

'Shove off, Rincewind,' snarled Broadman.

'I only thought it might be useful to address this gentleman in his own tongue,' said the wizard gently.

'He's doing all right on his own,' said the innkeeper, but took a few steps backward.

Rincewind smiled politely at the stranger and tried a few words of Chimeran. He prided himself on his fluency in the tongue, but the stranger only looked bemused.

'It won't work,' said Hugh knowledgeably. 'It's the book, you see. It tells him what to say. Magic.'

Rincewind switched to High Borogravian, to Vanglemesht, Sumtri and even Black Oroogu, the language with no nouns and only one adjective, which is obscene. Each was met with polite incomprehension. In desperation he tried heathen Trob, and the little man's face split into a delighted grin.

'At last!' he said. 'My good sir! This is remarkable!' (Although in Trob the last word in fact became 'a thing which may happen but once in the usable lifetime of a canoe hollowed diligently by axe and fire from the tallest diamondwood tree that grows in the noted diamondwood forests on the lower slopes of Mount Awayawa, home of the firegods or so it is said.')

'What was all that?' said Broadman suspiciously.

'What did the innkeeper say?' said the little man.

Rincewind swallowed. 'Broadman,' he said. 'Two mugs of your best ale, please.'

'You can understand him?'

'Oh, sure.'

'Tell him – tell him he's very welcome. Tell him breakfast is – uh – one gold piece.' For a moment Broadman's face looked as though some vast internal struggle was going on, and then he added with a burst of generosity, 'I'll throw in yours, too.'

'Stranger,' said Rincewind levelly. 'If you stay here you will be knifed or poisoned by nightfall. But don't stop smiling, or so will I.'

'Oh, come now,' said the stranger, looking around. 'This looks like a delightful place. A genuine Morporkian tavern. I've heard so much about them, you know. All these quaint old beams. And so reasonable, too.'

Rincewind glanced around quickly, in case some leakage of enchantment from the Magicians' Quarter across the river had momentarily transported them to some other place. No – this was still the interior of the Drum, its walls stained with smoke, its floor a compost of old rushes and nameless beetles, its sour beer not so much purchased as merely hired for a while. He tried to fit the image around the word 'quaint', or rather the nearest Trob equivalent, which was 'that pleasant oddity of design found in the little coral houses of the sponge-eating pygmies on the Orohai peninsula'.

His mind reeled back from the effort. The visitor went on, 'My name is Twoflower,' and extended his hand. Instinctively, the other three looked down to see if there was a coin in it.

'Pleased to meet you,' said Rincewind. 'I'm Rincewind. Look, I wasn't joking. This is a tough place.'

'Good! Exactly what I wanted!'

'Eh?'

'What is this stuff in the mugs?'

'This? Beer. Thanks, Broadman. Yes. Beer. You know. Beer.'

'Ah. The so-typical drink. A small gold piece will be sufficient payment, do you think? I do not want to cause offence.'

It was already half out of his purse.

'Yarrt,' croaked Rincewind. 'I mean, no, it won't cause offence.'

'Good. You say this is a tough place. Frequented, you mean, by heroes and men of adventure?'

Rincewind considered this. 'Yes?' he managed.

'Excellent. I would like to meet some.'

An explanation occurred to the wizard. 'Ah,' he said. 'You've come to hire mercenaries ("warriors who fight for the tribe with the most milknut-meal")?'

'Oh no. I just want to meet them. So that when I get home I can say that I did it.'

Rincewind thought that a meeting with most of the Drum's clientele would mean that Twoflower never went home again, unless he lived downriver and happened to float past.

'Where is your home?' he enquired. Broadman had slipped away into some back room, he noticed. Hugh was watching them suspiciously from a nearby table.

'Have you heard of the city of Bes Pelargic?'

'Well, I didn't spend much time in Trob. I was just passing through, you know—'

'Oh, it's not in Trob. I speak Trob because there are many beTrobi sailors in our ports. Bes Pelargic is the major seaport of the Agatean Empire.'

'Never heard of it, I'm afraid.'

Twoflower raised his eyebrows. 'No? It is quite big. You sail turnwise from the Brown Islands for about a week and there it is. Are you all right?'

He hurried around the table and patted the wizard on the back. Rincewind choked on his beer.

The Counterweight Continent!

Three streets away an old man dropped a coin into a saucer of acid and swirled it gently. Broadman waited impatiently, ill at ease in a room made noisome by vats and bubbling beakers and lined with shelves containing shadowy shapes suggestive of skulls and stuffed impossibilities.

'Well?' he demanded.

'One cannot hurry these things,' said the old alchemist peevishly. 'Assaying takes time. Ah.' He prodded the saucer, where the coin now lay in a swirl of green colour. He made some calculations on a scrap of parchment.

'Exceptionally interesting,' he said at last.

'*Is it genuine?*'

The old man pursed his lips. 'It depends on how you define the term,' he said. 'If you mean: is this coin the same as, say, a fifty-dollar piece, then the answer is no.'

'I *knew* it,' screamed the innkeeper, and started towards the door.

'I'm not sure that I'm making myself clear,' said the alchemist. Broadman turned round angrily.

'What do you mean?'

'Well, you see, what with one thing and another our coinage has been somewhat watered, over the years. The gold content of the average coin is barely four parts in twelve, the balance being made up of silver, copper—'

'What of it?'

'I said this coin isn't like ours. It is *pure* gold.'

After Broadman had left, at a run, the alchemist spent some time staring at the ceiling. Then he drew out a very small piece of thin parchment, rummaged for a pen amongst the debris on his workbench, and wrote a very short, small message. Then he went over to his cages of white doves, black cockerels and other laboratory animals. From one cage he removed a glossy coated rat, rolled the parchment into the phial attached to a hind leg, and let the animal go.

It sniffed around the floor for a moment, then disappeared down a hole in the far wall.

At about this time a hitherto unsuccessful fortune-teller living on the other side of the block chanced to glance into her scrying bowl, gave a small scream and, within the hour, had sold her jewellery, various magical accoutrements, most of her clothes and almost all her other possessions that could not be conveniently carried on the fastest horse she could buy. The fact that later on, when her house collapsed in flames, she herself died in a freak landslide in the Morpork Mountains, proves that Death, too, has a sense of humour.

Also at about the same moment as the homing rat disappeared into the maze of runs under the city, scurrying along in faultless obedience to an ancient instinct, the Patrician of Ankh-Morpork picked up the letters delivered that morning by albatross. He looked pensively at the topmost one again, and summoned his chief of spies.

And in the Broken Drum Rincewind was listening open-mouthed as Twoflower talked.

'So I decided to see for myself,' the little man was saying. 'Eight years' saving up, this has cost me. But worth every half-*rhinu*. I mean, here I am. In Ankh-Morpork. Famed in song and story, I mean. In the streets that have known the tread of Heric Whiteblade, Hrun the Barbarian, and Bravd the

Hublander and the Weasel ... It's all just like I imagined, you know.'

Rincewind's face was a mask of fascinated horror.

'I just couldn't stand it any more back in Bes Pelargic,' Twoflower went on blithely, 'sitting at a desk all day, just adding up columns of figures, just a pension to look forward to at the end of it . . . where's the romance in that? Twoflower, I thought, it's now or never. You don't just have to listen to stories. You can go there. Now's the time to stop hanging around the docks listening to sailors' tales. So I compiled a phrase book and bought a passage on the next ship to the Brown Islands.'

'No guards?' murmured Rincewind.

'No. Why? What have I got that's worth stealing?'

Rincewind coughed. 'You have, uh, gold,' he said.

'Barely two thousand *rhinu*. Hardly enough to keep a man alive for more than a month or two. At home, that is. I imagine they might stretch a bit further here.'

'Would a *rhinu* be one of those big gold coins?' said Rincewind.

'Yes.' Twoflower looked worriedly at the wizard over the top of his strange seeing-lenses. 'Will two thousand be sufficient, do you think?'

'Yarrrt,' croaked Rincewind. 'I mean, yes – sufficient.'

'Good.'

'Um. Is everyone in the Agatean Empire as rich as you?'

'Me? Rich? Bless you, whatever put that idea into your head? I am but a poor clerk! Did I pay the innkeeper too much, do you think?' Twoflower added.

'Uh. He might have settled for less,' Rincewind conceded.

'Ah. I shall know better next time. I can see I have a lot to learn. An idea occurs to me. Rincewind, would you perhaps consent to be employed as a, I don't know, perhaps the word "guide" would fit the circumstances? I think I could afford to pay you a *rhinu* a day.'

Rincewind opened his mouth to reply but felt the words huddle together in his throat, reluctant to emerge in a world that was rapidly going mad. Twoflower blushed.

'I have offended you,' he said. 'It was an impertinent request to make of a professional man such as yourself. Doubtless you have many projects you wish to return to – some works of high magic, no doubt . . .'

'No,' said Rincewind faintly. 'Not just at present. A *rhinu*, you say? One a day. Every day?'

'I think perhaps in the circumstances I should make it one and one-half *rhinu* per day. Plus any out-of-pocket expenses, of course.'

The wizard rallied magnificently. 'That will be fine,' he said. 'Great.'

Twoflower reached into his pouch and took out a large round gold object, glanced at it for a moment, and slipped it back. Rincewind didn't get a chance to see it properly.

'I think,' said the tourist, 'that I would like a little rest now. It was a long crossing. And then perhaps you would care to call back at noon and we can take a look at the city.'

'Sure.'

'Then please be good enough to ask the innkeeper to show me to my room.'

Rincewind did so, and watched the nervous Broadman, who had arrived at a gallop from some back room, lead the way up the wooden steps behind the bar. After a few seconds the Luggage got up and pattered across the floor after them.

Then the wizard looked down at the six big coins in his hand. Twoflower had insisted on paying his first four days' wages in advance.

Hugh nodded and smiled encouragingly. Rincewind snarled at him.

As a student wizard Rincewind had never achieved high marks in precognition, but now unused circuits in his brain were throbbing and the future might as well have been engraved in bright colours on his eyeballs. The space between his shoulder-blades began to itch. The sensible thing to do, he knew, was to buy a horse. It would have to be a fast one, and expensive – offhand, Rincewind couldn't think of any horse-dealer he knew who was rich enough to give change out of almost a whole ounce of gold.

And then, of course, the other five coins would help him set up a useful practice at some safe distance, say two hundred miles. That would be the sensible thing.

But what would happen to Twoflower, all alone in a city where even the cockroaches had an unerring instinct for gold? A man would have to be a real heel to leave him.

* * *

The Patrician of Ankh-Morpork smiled, but with his mouth only.

'The Hub Gate, you say?' he murmured.

The guard captain saluted smartly. 'Aye, lord. We had to shoot the horse before he would stop.'

'Which, by a fairly direct route, brings you here,' said the Patrician, looking down at Rincewind. 'And what have you got to say for yourself?'

It was rumoured that an entire wing of the Patrician's palace was filled with clerks who spent their days collating and updating all the information collected by their master's exquisitely organized spy system. Rincewind didn't doubt it. He glanced towards the balcony that ran down one side of the audience room. A sudden run, a nimble jump – a sudden hail of crossbow quarrels. He shuddered.

The Patrician cradled his chins in a beringed hand, and regarded the wizard with eyes as small and hard as beads.

'Let me see,' he said. 'Oathbreaking, the theft of a horse, uttering false coinage – yes, I think it's the Arena for you, Rincewind.'

This was too much.

'I didn't steal the horse! I bought it fairly!'

'But with false coinage. Technical theft, you see.'

'But those *rhinu* are solid gold!'

'*Rhinu?*' The Patrician rolled one of them around in his thick fingers. 'Is that what they are called? How interesting. But, as you point out, they are not very similar to dollars . . .'

'Well, of course they're not—'

'Ah! you admit it, then?'

Rincewind opened his mouth to speak, thought better of it, and shut it again.

'Quite so. And on top of these there is, of course, the moral obloquy attendant on the cowardly betrayal of a visitor to this shore. For shame, Rincewind!'

The Patrician waved a hand vaguely. The guards behind Rincewind backed away, and their captain took a few paces to the right. Rincewind suddenly felt very alone.

It is said that when a wizard is about to die Death himself turns up to claim him (instead of delegating the task to a subordinate, such as Disease or Famine, as is usually the case). Rincewind looked around nervously for a tall figure in black (wizards, even failed wizards, have in addition to rods and cones in their eyeballs the tiny octagons that enable them to see into the far octarine, the basic colour of which all other colours are merely pale shadows impinging on normal four-dimensional space. It is said to be a sort of fluorescent greenish-yellow purple).

Was that a flickering shadow in the corner?

'Of course,' said the Patrician, 'I could be merciful.'

The shadow disappeared. Rincewind looked up, an expression of insane hope on his face.

'Yes?' he said.

The Patrician waved a hand again. Rincewind saw the guards leave the chamber. Alone with the overlord of the twin cities, he almost wished they would come back.

'Come hither, Rincewind,' said the Patrician. He indicated a bowl of savouries on a low onyx table by the throne. 'Would you care for a crystallized jellyfish? No?'

'Um,' said Rincewind, 'no.'

'Now I want you to listen very carefully to what I am about to say,' said the Patrician amiably, 'otherwise you will die. In an interesting fashion. Over a period. Please stop fidgeting like that.

'Since you are a wizard of sorts, you are of course aware that we live upon a world shaped, as it were, like a disc? And that there is said to exist, towards the far rim, a continent which though small is equal in weight to all the mighty landmasses in this hemi-circle? And that this, according to ancient legend, is because it is largely made of gold?'

Rincewind nodded. Who hadn't heard of the Counterweight Continent? Some sailors even believed the childhood tales and sailed in search of it. Of course, they returned either empty handed or not at all. Probably eaten by giant turtles, in the opinion of more serious mariners. Because, of course, the Counterweight Continent was nothing more than a solar myth.

'It does, of course, exist,' said the Patrician. 'Although it is not made of gold, it is true that gold is a very common metal there. Most of the mass is made up by vast deposits of octiron deep within the crust. Now it will be obvious to an incisive mind like yours that the existence of the Counterweight Continent poses a deadly threat to our people here—' he paused, looking at Rincewind's open mouth. He sighed. He said, 'Do you by some chance fail to follow me?'

'Yarrg,' said Rincewind. He swallowed, and licked his lips. 'I mean, no. I mean – well, gold . . .'

'I see,' said the Patrician sweetly. 'You feel, perhaps,

that it would be a marvellous thing to go to the Counterweight Continent and bring back a shipload of gold?'

Rincewind had a feeling that some sort of trap was being set.

'Yes?' he ventured.

'And if every man on the shores of the Circle Sea had a mountain of gold of his own? Would that be a good thing? What would happen? Think carefully.'

Rincewind's brow furrowed. He thought. 'We'd all be rich?'

The way the temperature fell at his remark told him that it was not the correct one.

'I may as well tell you, Rincewind, that there is some contact between the Lords of the Circle Sea and the Emperor of the Agatean Empire, as it is styled,' the Patrician went on. 'It is only very slight. There is little common ground between us. We have nothing they want, and they have nothing we can afford. It is an old Empire, Rincewind. Old and cunning and cruel and very, very rich. So we exchange fraternal greetings by albatross mail. At infrequent intervals.

'One such letter arrived this morning. A subject of the Emperor appears to have taken it into his head to visit our city. It appears he wishes to look at it. Only a madman would possibly undergo all the privations of crossing the Turnwise Ocean in order to merely *look* at anything. However.

'He landed this morning. He might have met a great hero, or the cunningest of thieves, or some wise and great sage: he met you. He has employed you as a guide. You will be a guide, Rincewind, to this *looker*, this Twoflower. You will see that he returns home with a good report of our little homeland. What do you say to that?'

'Er. Thank you, lord,' said Rincewind miserably.

'There is another point, of course. It would be a tragedy should anything untoward happen to our little visitor. It would be dreadful if he were to die, for example. Dreadful for the whole of our land, because the Agatean Emperor looks after his own and could certainly extinguish us at a nod. A mere nod. And that would be dreadful for you, Rincewind, because in the weeks that remained before the Empire's huge mercenary fleet arrived certain of my servants would occupy themselves about your person in the hope that the avenging captains, on their arrival, might find their anger tempered by the sight of your still-living body. There are certain spells that can prevent the life departing from a body, be it never so abused, and – I see by your face that understanding dawns?'

'Yarrg.'

'I beg your pardon?'

'Yes, lord. I'll, er, see to it, I mean, I'll endeavour to see, I mean, well, I'll try to look after him and see he comes to no harm.' And after that I'll get a job juggling snowballs through Hell, he added bitterly in the privacy of his own skull.

'Capital! I gather already that you and Twoflower are on the best of terms. An excellent beginning. When he returns safely to his homeland you will not find me ungrateful. I shall probably even dismiss the charges against you. Thank you, Rincewind. You may go.'

Rincewind decided not to ask for the return of his five remaining *rhinu*. He backed away, cautiously.

'Oh, and there is one other thing,' the Patrician said, as the wizard groped for the door handles.

'Yes, lord?' he replied, with a sinking heart.

'I'm sure you won't dream of trying to escape from your obligations by fleeing the city. I judge you to be a born city person. But you may be sure that the lords of the other cities will be apprised of these conditions by nightfall.'

'I assure you the thought never even crossed my mind, lord.'

'Indeed? Then if I were you I'd sue my face for slander.'

Rincewind reached the Broken Drum at a dead run, and was just in time to collide with a man who came out backwards, fast. The stranger's haste was in part accounted for by the spear in his chest. He bubbled noisily and dropped dead at the wizard's feet.

Rincewind peered around the doorframe and jerked back as a heavy throwing axe whirred past like a partridge.

It was probably a lucky throw, a second cautious glance told him. The dark interior of the Drum was a broil of fighting men, quite a number of them – a third and longer glance confirmed – in bits. Rincewind swayed back as a wildly thrown stool sailed past and smashed on the far side of the street. Then he dived in.

He was wearing a dark robe, made darker by constant wear and irregular washings. In the raging gloom no-one appeared to notice a shadowy shape that shuffled desperately from table to table. At one point a fighter, staggering back, trod on what felt like fingers. A number of what felt like teeth bit his ankle. He yelped shrilly and dropped his guard just sufficiently for a sword, swung by a surprised opponent, to skewer him.

Rincewind reached the stairway, sucking his bruised hand and running with a curious, bent-over gait. A crossbow quarrel thunked into the banister rail above him, and he gave a whimper.

He made the stairs in one breathless rush, expecting at any moment another, more accurate shot.

In the corridor above he stood upright, gasping, and saw the floor in front of him scattered with bodies. A big black-bearded man, with a bloody sword in one hand, was trying a door handle.

'Hey!' screamed Rincewind. The man looked around and then, almost absent-mindedly, drew a short throwing knife from his bandolier and hurled it. Rincewind ducked. There was a brief scream behind him as the crossbow man, sighting down his weapon, dropped it and clutched at his throat.

The big man was already reaching for another knife. Rincewind looked around wildly, and then with wild improvisation drew himself up into a wizardly pose.

His hand was flung back. 'Asoniti! Kyorucha! Beazleblor!'

The man hesitated, his eyes flicking nervously from side to side as he waited for the magic. The conclusion that there was not going to be any hit him at the same time as Rincewind, whirring wildly down the passage, kicked him sharply in the groin.

As he screamed and clutched at himself the wizard dragged open the door, sprang inside, slammed it behind him and threw his body against it, panting.

It was quiet in here. There was Twoflower, sleeping peacefully on the low bed. And there, at the foot of the bed, was the Luggage.

Rincewind took a few steps forward, cupidity moving him as easily as if he were on little wheels. The chest was open. There were bags inside, and in one of them he caught the gleam of gold. For a moment greed overcame caution, and he reached out gingerly . . . but what was the use? He'd never live to enjoy it. Reluctantly he drew his hand back, and was surprised to see a slight tremor in the chest's open lid. Hadn't it shifted slightly, as though rocked by the wind?

Rincewind looked at his fingers, and then at the lid. It looked heavy, and was bound with brass bands. It was quite still now.

What wind?

'Rincewind!'

Twoflower sprang off the bed. The wizard jumped back, wrenching his features into a smile.

'My dear chap, right on time! We'll just have lunch, and then I'm sure you've got a wonderful programme lined up for this afternoon!'

'Er—'

'That's great!'

Rincewind took a deep breath. 'Look,' he said desperately, 'let's eat somewhere else. There's been a bit of a fight down below.'

'A tavern brawl? Why didn't you wake me up?'

'Well, you see, I – *what*?'

'I thought I made myself clear this morning, Rincewind. I want to see genuine Morporkian life – the slave market, the Whore Pits, the Temple of Small Gods, the Beggars' Guild . . . and a genuine tavern brawl.' A faint note of suspicion entered Twoflower's voice. 'You *do* have them, don't you? You know, people swinging on chandeliers, swordfights over the table, the sort of thing Hrun the Barbarian and the Weasel are always getting involved in. You know – *excitement*.'

Rincewind sat down heavily on the bed.

'You *want* to see a fight?' he said.

'Yes. What's wrong with that?'

'For a start, people get hurt.'

'Oh, I wasn't suggesting we get involved. I just want to see one, that's all. And some of your famous heroes. You do have some, don't you? It's not all dockside talk?' And now, to the wizard's astonishment, Twoflower was almost pleading.

'Oh, yeah. We have them all right,' said Rincewind hurriedly. He pictured them in his mind, and recoiled from the thought.

All the heroes of the Circle Sea passed through the gates of Ankh-Morpork sooner or later. Most of them were from the barbaric tribes nearer the frozen Hub, which had a sort of export trade in heroes. Almost all of them had crude magic swords, whose unsuppressed harmonics on the astral plane played hell with any delicate experiments in applied sorcery for miles around, but Rincewind didn't object to them on that score. He knew himself to be a magical dropout, so it didn't bother him that the mere appearance of a hero at the city gates was enough to cause retorts to explode and demons to materialize all through the Magical Quarter. No, what he didn't like about heroes was that they were usually suicidally gloomy when sober and homicidally insane when drunk. There were too many of them, too. Some of the most notable questing grounds near the city were a veritable hub-bub in the season. There was talk of organizing a rota.

He rubbed his nose. The only heroes he had much time for were Bravd and the Weasel, who were out of town at the moment, and Hrun the Barbarian, who was practically an academic by Hub standards in that he could think without moving his lips. Hrun was said to be roving somewhere Turnwise.

'Look,' he said at last. 'Have you ever met a barbarian?'

Twoflower shook his head.

'I was afraid of that,' said Rincewind. 'Well, they're—'

There was a clatter of running feet in the street outside and a fresh uproar from downstairs. It was followed by a commotion on the stairs. The door was flung open before Rincewind could collect himself sufficiently to make a dash for the window.

But instead of the greed-crazed madman he expected, he found himself looking into the round red face of a Sergeant of the Watch. He breathed again. Of course. The Watch were always careful not to intervene too soon in any brawl where the odds were not heavily stacked in their favour. The job carried a pension, and attracted a cautious, thought-ful kind of man.

The sergeant glowered at Rincewind, and then peered at Twoflower with interest.

'Everything all right here, then?' he said.

'Oh, fine,' said Rincewind. 'Got held up, did you?'

The sergeant ignored him. 'This the foreigner, then?' he enquired.

'We were just leaving,' said Rincewind quickly, and switched to Trob. 'Twoflower, I think we ought to get lunch somewhere else. I know some places.'

He marched out into the corridor with as much aplomb as he could muster. Twoflower followed, and a few seconds later there was a strangling sound from the sergeant as the Luggage closed its lid with a snap, stood up, stretched, and marched after them.

Watchmen were dragging bodies out of the room downstairs. There were no survivors. The Watch had ensured this by giving them ample time to escape via the back door, a neat compromise between caution and justice that benefited all parties.

'Who are all these men?' said Twoflower.

'Oh, you know. Just men,' said Rincewind. And before he could stop himself some part of his brain that had nothing to do took control of his mouth and added, 'Heroes, in fact.'

'Really?'

When one foot is stuck in the Grey Miasma of H'rull it is much easier to step right in and sink rather than prolong the struggle. Rincewind let himself go.

'Yes, that one over there is Erig Stronginthearm, over there is Black Zenell—'

'Is Hrun the Barbarian here?' said Twoflower, looking around eagerly. Rincewind took a deep breath.

'That's him behind us,' he said.

The enormity of this lie was so great that its ripples did in fact spread out on one of the lower astral planes as far as the Magical Quarter across the river, where it picked up tremendous velocity from the huge standing wave of power that always hovered there and bounced wildly across the Circle Sea. A harmonic got as far as Hrun himself, currently fighting a couple of gnolls on a crumbling ledge high in the Caderack Mountains, and caused him a moment's unexplained discomfort.

Twoflower, meanwhile, had thrown back the lid of the Luggage and was hastily pulling out a heavy black cube.

'This is fantastic!' he said. 'They're never going to believe this at home!'

'What's he going on about?' said the sergeant doubtfully.

'He's pleased you rescued us,' said Rincewind. He looked sidelong at the black box, half expecting it to explode or emit strange musical tones.

'Ah,' said the sergeant. He was staring at the box, too.

Twoflower smiled brightly at them.

'I'd like a record of the event,' he said. 'Do you think you could ask them all to stand over by the window, please? This won't take a moment. And, er, Rincewind?'

'Yes?'

Twoflower stood on tiptoe to whisper.

'I expect you know what this is, don't you?'

Rincewind stared down at the box. It had a round

glass eye protruding from the centre of one face, and a lever at the back.

'Not wholly,' he said.

'It's a device for making pictures quickly,' said Twoflower. 'Quite a new invention. I'm rather proud of it but, look, I don't think these gentlemen would – well, I mean they might be – sort of apprehensive? Could you explain it to them? I'll reimburse them for their time, of course.'

'He's got a box with a demon in it that draws pictures,' said Rincewind shortly. 'Do what the madman says and he will give you gold.'

The Watch smiled nervously.

'I'd like you in the picture, Rincewind. That's fine.' Twoflower took out the golden disc that Rincewind had noticed before, squinted at its unseen face for a moment, muttered, 'Thirty seconds should about do it,' and said brightly, 'Smile please!'

'Smile,' rasped Rincewind. There was a whirr from the box.

'Right!'

High above the disc the second albatross soared; so high in fact that its tiny mad orange eyes could see the whole of the world and the great, glittering, girdling Circle Sea. There was a yellow message capsule strapped to one leg. Far below it, unseen in the clouds, the bird that had brought the earlier message to the Patrician of Ankh-Morpork flapped gently back to its home.

Rincewind looked at the tiny square of glass in astonishment. There he was, all right – a tiny figure, in perfect colour, standing in front of a group of Watchmen whose faces were each frozen in a terrified rictus. A buzz of wordless terror went up from the men around him as they craned over his shoulder to look.

Grinning, Twoflower produced a handful of the smaller coins Rincewind now recognized as quarter-*rhinu*. He winked at the wizard.

'I had similar problems when I stopped over in the Brown Islands,' he said. 'They thought the iconograph steals a bit of their souls. Laughable, isn't it?'

'Yarg,' said Rincewind and then, because somehow that was hardly enough to keep up his side of the conversation, added, 'I don't think it looks *very* like me, though.'

'It's easy to operate,' said Twoflower, ignoring him. 'Look, all you have to do is press this button. The iconograph does the rest. Now, I'll just stand over here next to Hrun, and you can take the picture.'

The coins quietened the men's agitation in the way that gold can, and Rincewind was amazed to find, half a minute later, that he was holding a little glass portrait of Twoflower wielding a huge notched sword and smiling as though all his dreams had come true.

They lunched at a small eating-house near the Brass Bridge, with the Luggage nestling under the table. The food and wine, both far superior to Rincewind's normal fare, did much to relax him. Things weren't going to be too bad, he decided. A bit of invention and some quick thinking, that was all that was needed.

Twoflower seemed to be thinking too. Looking

reflectively into his wine cup he said, 'Tavern fights are pretty common around here, I expect?'

'Oh, fairly.'

'No doubt fixtures and fittings get damaged?'

'Fixt— oh, I see. You mean like benches and what-not. Yes, I suppose so.'

'That must be upsetting for the innkeepers.'

'I've never really thought about it. I suppose it must be one of the risks of the job.'

Twoflower regarded him thoughtfully.

'I might be able to help there,' he said. 'Risks are my business. I say, this food is a bit greasy, isn't it?'

'You did say you wanted to try some typical Morporkian food,' said Rincewind. 'What was that about risks?'

'Oh, I know all about risks. They're my business.'

'I thought that's what you said. I didn't believe it the first time either.'

'Oh, I don't *take* risks. About the most exciting thing that happened to me was knocking some ink over. I *assess* risks. Day after day. Do you know what the odds are against a house catching fire in the Red Triangle district of Bes Pelargic? Five hundred and thirty-eight to one. I calculated that,' he added with a trace of pride.

'What—' Rincewind tried to suppress a burp – 'what for? 'Scuse me.' He helped himself to some more wine.

'For—' Twoflower paused. 'I can't say it in Trob,' he said. 'I don't think the beTrobi have a word for it. In my language we call it—' he said a collection of out-landish syllables.

'*Inn-sewer-ants*,' repeated Rincewind. 'That's a funny word. Wossit mean?'

'Well, suppose you have a ship loaded with, say, gold bars. It might run into storms or be taken by pirates. You don't want that to happen, so you take out an *inn-sewer-ants-polly-sea*. I work out the odds against the cargo being lost, based on weather reports and piracy records for the last twenty years, then I add a bit, then you pay me some money based on those odds—'

'—and the bit—' Rincewind said, waggling a finger solemnly.

'—and then, if the cargo *is* lost, I reimburse you.'

'Reeburs?'

'Pay you the value of your cargo,' said Twoflower patiently.

'I get it. It's like a bet, right?'

'A wager? In a way, I suppose.'

'And you make money at this *inn-sewer-ants*?'

'It offers a return on investment, certainly.'

Wrapped in the warm yellow glow of the wine, Rincewind tried to think of *inn-sewer-ants* in Circle Sea terms.

'I don't think I unnerstan' this *inn-sewer-ants*,' he said firmly, idly watching the world spin by. 'Magic, now. Magic I unnerstan'.'

Twoflower grinned. 'Magic is one thing, and *reflected-sound-of-underground-spirits* is another,' he said.

'Wha'?'

'What?'

'That funny wor' you used,' said Rincewind impatiently.

'*Reflected-sound-of-underground-spirits*?'

'Never heard o' it.'

Twoflower tried to explain.

Rincewind tried to understand.

In the long afternoon they toured the city turnwise of the river. Twoflower led the way, with the strange picturebox slung on a strap round his neck. Rincewind trailed behind, whimpering at intervals and checking to see that his head was still there.

A few others followed, too. In a city where public executions, duels, fights, magical feuds and strange events regularly punctuated the daily round, the inhabitants had brought the profession of interested bystander to a peak of perfection. They were, to a man, highly skilled gawpers. In any case, Twoflower was delightedly taking picture after picture of people engaged in what he described as typical activities, and since a quarter-*rhinu* would subsequently change hands 'for their trouble' a tail of bemused and happy *nouveaux-riches* was soon following him in case this madman exploded in a shower of gold.

At the Temple of the Seven-Handed Sek a hasty convocation of priests and ritual heart-transplant artisans agreed that the hundred-span-high statue of Sek was altogether too holy to be made into a magic picture, but a payment of two *rhinu* left them astoundedly agreeing that perhaps He wasn't as holy as all that.

A prolonged session at the Whore Pits produced a number of colourful and instructive pictures, a number of which Rincewind concealed about his person for detailed perusal in private. As the fumes cleared from his brain he began to speculate seriously as to how the iconograph worked.

Even a failed wizard knew that some substances were sensitive to light. Perhaps the glass plates were treated by some arcane process that froze the light that passed through them? Something like that, anyway. Rincewind often suspected that there was something, somewhere, that was better than magic. He was usually disappointed.

However, he soon took every opportunity to operate the box. Twoflower was only too pleased to allow this, since that enabled the little man to appear in his own pictures. It was at this point that Rincewind noticed something strange. Possession of the box conferred a kind of power on the wielder – which was that anyone, confronted with the hypnotic glass eye, would submissively obey the most peremptory orders about stance and expression.

It was while he was thus engaged in the Plaza of Broken Moons that disaster struck.

Twoflower had posed alongside a bewildered charm-seller, his crowd of new-found admirers watching him with interest in case he did something humorously lunatic.

Rincewind got down on one knee, the better to arrange the picture, and pressed the enchanted lever.

The box said, 'It's no good. I've run out of pink.'

A hitherto unnoticed door opened in front of his eyes. A small, green and hideously warty humanoid figure leaned out, pointed at a colour-encrusted palette in one clawed hand, and screamed at him.

'No pink! See?' screeched the homunculus. 'No good you going on pressing the lever when there's no pink, is there? If you wanted pink you shouldn't of took all those pictures of young ladies, should you? It's monochrome from now on, friend. Alright?'

'Alright. Yeah, sure,' said Rincewind. In one dim corner of the little box he thought he could see an easel, and a tiny unmade bed. He hoped he couldn't.

'So long as that's understood,' said the imp, and shut the door. Rincewind thought he could hear the muffled sound of grumbling and the scrape of a stool being dragged across the floor.

'Twoflower—' he began, and looked up.

Twoflower had vanished. As Rincewind stared at the crowd, with sensations of prickly horror travelling up his spine, there came a gentle prod in the small of his back.

'Turn without haste,' said a voice like black silk. 'Or kiss your kidneys goodbye.'

The crowd watched with interest. It was turning out to be quite a good day.

Rincewind turned slowly, feeling the point of the sword scrape along his ribs. At the other end of the blade he recognized Stren Withel – thief, cruel swordsman, disgruntled contender for the title of worst man in the world.

'Hi,' he said weakly. A few yards away he noticed a couple of unsympathetic men raising the lid of the Luggage and pointing excitedly at the bags of gold. Withel smiled. It made an unnerving effect on his scar-crossed face.

'I know you,' he said. 'A gutter wizard. What is that *thing*?'

Rincewind became aware that the lid of the Luggage was trembling slightly, although there was no wind. And he was still holding the picturebox.

'This? It makes pictures,' he said brightly. 'Hey, just hold that smile, will you?' He backed away quickly and pointed the box.

For a moment Withel hesitated. '*What*?' he said.

'That's fine, hold it just like that . . .' said Rincewind.

The thief paused, then growled and swung his sword back.

There was a *snap*, and a duct of horrible screams. Rincewind did not glance around for fear of the terrible things he might see, and by the time Withel looked for him again he was on the other side of the Plaza, and still accelerating.

The albatross descended in wide, slow sweeps that ended in an undignified flurry of feathers and a thump as it landed heavily on its platform in the Patrician's bird garden.

The custodian of the birds, dozing in the sun and hardly expecting a long-distance message so soon after this morning's arrival, jerked to his feet and looked up.

A few moments later he was scuttling through the palace's corridors holding the message capsule and – owing to carelessness brought on by surprise – sucking at the nasty beak wound on the back of his hand.

* * *

Rincewind pounded down an alley, paying no heed to the screams of rage coming from the picturebox, and cleared a high wall with his frayed robe flapping around him like the feathers of a dishevelled jackdaw. He landed in the forecourt of a carpet shop, scattering the merchandise and customers, dived through its rear exit trailing apologies, skidded down another alley and stopped, teetering dangerously, just as he was about to plunge unthinkingly into the Ankh.

There are said to be some mystic rivers one drop of which can steal a man's life away. After its turbid passage through the twin cities the Ankh could have been one of them.

In the distance the cries of rage took on a shrill note of terror. Rincewind looked around desperately for a boat, or a handhold up the sheer walls on either side of him.

He was trapped.

Unbidden, the spell welled up in his mind. It was perhaps untrue to say that he had learned it; it had learned him. The episode had led to his expulsion from Unseen University, because, for a bet, he had dared to open the pages of the last remaining copy of the Creator's own grimoire, the Octavo (while the University librarian was otherwise engaged). The spell had leapt out of the page and instantly burrowed deeply into his mind, from whence even the combined talents of the Faculty of Medicine had been unable to coax it. Precisely which one it was they were also unable to ascertain, except that it was one of the eight basic spells that were intricately interwoven with the very fabric of time and space itself.

Since then it had been showing a worrying tendency, when Rincewind was feeling rundown or especially threatened, to try to get itself said.

He clenched his teeth together but the first syllable forced itself around the corner of his mouth. His left hand raised involuntarily and, as the magical force whirled him round, began to give off octarine sparks . . .

The Luggage hurtled around the corner, its several hundred knees moving like pistons.

Rincewind gaped. The spell died, unsaid.

The box didn't appear to be hampered in any way by the ornamental rug draped roguishly over it, nor by the thief hanging by one arm from the lid. It was, in a very real sense, a dead weight. Further along the lid were the remains of two fingers, owner unknown.

The Luggage halted a few feet from the wizard and, after a moment, retracted its legs. It had no eyes that Rincewind could see, but he was nevertheless sure that it was staring at him. Expectantly.

'Shoo,' he said weakly. It didn't budge, but the lid creaked open, releasing the dead thief.

Rincewind remembered about the gold. Presumably the box had to have a master. In the absence of Twoflower, had it adopted him?

The tide was turning and he could see debris drifting downstream in the yellow afternoon light towards the River Gate, a mere hundred yards downstream. It was the work of a moment to let the dead thief join them. Even if it was found later it would hardly cause comment. And the sharks in the estuary were used to solid, regular meals.

Rincewind watched the body drift away, and considered his next move. The Luggage would probably float. All he had to do was wait until dusk, and then go out with the tide. There were plenty of wild places downstream where he could wade ashore, and then – well, if the Patrician really *had* sent out word about him then a change of clothing and a shave should take care of that. In any case, there were other lands and he had a facility for languages. Let him but get to Chimera or Gonim or Ecalpon and half a dozen armies couldn't bring him back. And then – wealth, comfort, security . . .

There was, of course, the problem of Twoflower. Rincewind allowed himself a moment's sadness.

'It could be worse,' he said by way of farewell. 'It could be *me*.'

It was when he tried to move that he found his robe was caught on some obstruction.

By craning his neck he found that the edge of it was being gripped firmly by the Luggage's lid.

'Ah, Gorphal,' said the Patrician pleasantly. 'Come in. Sit down. Can I press you to a candied starfish?'

'I am yours to command, master,' said the old man calmly. 'Save, perhaps, in the matter of preserved echinoderms.'

The Patrician shrugged, and indicated the scroll on the table.

'Read that,' he said.

Gorphal picked up the parchment and raised one eyebrow slightly when he saw the familiar ideograms of the Golden Empire. He read in silence for perhaps a minute, and then turned the scroll over to examine minutely the seal on the obverse.

'You are famed as a student of Empire affairs,' said the Patrician. 'Can you explain this?'

'Knowledge in the matter of the Empire lies less in noting particular events than in studying a certain cast of mind,' said the old diplomat. 'The message is curious, yes, but not surprising.'

'This morning the Emperor *instructed*,' the Patrician allowed himself the luxury of a scowl, '*instructed* me, Gorphal, to protect this Two Flower person. Now it seems I must have him killed. You don't find that surprising?'

'No. The Emperor is no more than a boy. He is – idealistic. Keen. A god to his people. Whereas this afternoon's letter is, unless I am very much mistaken, from Nine Turning Mirrors, the Grand Vizier. He has grown old in the service of several Emperors. He regards them as a necessary but tiresome ingredient in the successful running of the Empire. He does not like things out of place. The Empire was not built by allowing things to get out of place. That is his view.'

'I begin to see—' said the Patrician.

'Quite so.' Gorphal smiled into his beard. 'This tourist is a thing that is out of place. After acceding to his master's wishes Nine Turning Mirrors would, I am quite sure, make his own arrangements with a view to ensuring that one wanderer would not be allowed to return home bringing, perhaps, the disease of dissatisfaction. The Empire likes people to stay where it puts them. So much more convenient, then, if this

Two Flower disappears for good in the barbarian lands. Meaning here, master.'

'And your advice?' said the Patrician.

Gorphal shrugged.

'Merely that you should do nothing. Matters will undoubtedly resolve themselves. However,' he scratched an ear thoughtfully, 'perhaps the Assassins' Guild . . . ?'

'Ah yes,' said the Patrician. 'The Assassins' Guild. Who is their president at the moment?'

'Zlorf Flannelfoot, master.'

'Have a word with him, will you?'

'Quite so, master.'

The Patrician nodded. It was all rather a relief. He agreed with Nine Turning Mirrors – life was difficult enough. People ought to stay where they were put.

Brilliant constellations shone down on the discworld. One by one the traders shuttered their shops. One by one the gonophs, thieves, finewirers, whores, illusionists, backsliders and second-storey men awoke and breakfasted. Wizards went about their poly-dimensional affairs. Tonight saw the conjunction of two powerful planets, and already the air over the Magical Quarter was hazy with early spells.

'Look,' said Rincewind, 'this isn't getting us any-where.' He inched sideways. The Luggage followed faithfully, lid half open and menacing. Rincewind briefly considered making a desperate leap to safety. The lid smacked in anticipation.

In any case, he told himself with sinking heart, the damn thing would only follow him again. It had that dogged look about it. Even if he managed to get to a horse, he had a nasty suspicion that it would follow him at its own pace. Endlessly. Swimming rivers and oceans. Gaining slowly every night, while he had to stop to sleep. And then one day, in some exotic city and years hence, he'd hear the sound of hundreds of tiny feet accelerating down the road behind him . . .

'You've got the wrong man!' he moaned. 'It's not my fault! I didn't kidnap him!'

The box moved forward slightly. Now there was just a narrow strip of greasy jetty between Rince-wind's heels and the river. A flash of precognition told him that the box would be able to swim faster than he could. He tried not to imagine what it would be like to drown in the Ankh.

'It won't stop until you give in, you know,' said a small voice conversationally.

Rincewind looked down at the iconograph, still hanging around his neck. Its trapdoor was open and the homunculus was leaning against the frame, smoking a pipe and watching the proceedings with amusement.

'I'll take you in with me, at least,' said Rincewind through gritted teeth.

The imp took the pipe out of his mouth. 'What did you say?' he said.

'I said I'll take you in with me, dammit!'

'Suit yourself.' The imp tapped the side of the box meaningfully. 'We'll see who sinks first.'

The Luggage yawned, and moved forward a fraction of an inch.

'Oh all right,' said Rincewind irritably. 'But you'll have to give me time to think.'

The Luggage backed off slowly. Rincewind edged his way back onto reasonably safe land and sat down with his back against a wall. Across the river the lights of Ankh city glowed.

'You're a wizard,' said the picture imp. 'You'll think of some way to find him.'

'Not much of a wizard, I'm afraid.'

'You can just jump down on everyone and turn them into worms,' the imp added encouragingly, ignoring his last remark.

'No. Turning to Animals is an Eighth Level spell. I never even completed my training. I only know one spell.'

'Well, that'll do.'

'I doubt it,' said Rincewind hopelessly.

'What does it do, then?'

'Can't tell you. Don't really want to talk about it. But frankly,' he sighed, 'no spells are much good. It takes three months to commit even a simple one to memory, and then once you've used it, pouf! it's gone. That's what's so stupid about the whole magic thing, you know. You spend twenty years learning the spell that makes nude virgins appear in your bedroom, and then you're so poisoned by quicksilver fumes and half-blind from reading old grimoires that you can't remember what happens next.'

'I never thought of it like that,' said the imp.

'Hey, look – this is all wrong. When Twoflower said they'd got a better kind of magic in the Empire I thought – I thought . . .'

The imp looked at him expectantly. Rincewind cursed to himself.

'Well, if you must know, I thought he didn't *mean* magic. Not as such.'

'What else is there, then?'

Rincewind began to feel really wretched. 'I don't know,' he said. 'A better way of doing things, I suppose. Something with a bit of sense in it. Harnessing – harnessing the lightning, or something.'

The imp gave him a kind but pitying look.

'Lightning is the spears hurled by the thunder giants when they fight,' it said gently. 'Established meteorological fact. You can't *harness* it.'

'I know,' said Rincewind miserably. 'That's the flaw in the argument, of course.'

The imp nodded, and disappeared into the depths of the iconograph. A few moments later Rincewind smelled bacon frying. He waited until his stomach couldn't stand the strain any more, and rapped on the box. The imp reappeared.

'I've been thinking about what you said,' it said before Rincewind could open his mouth. 'And even if you could get a harness on it, how could you get it to pull a cart?'

'What the hell are you talking about?'

'Lightning. It just goes up and down. You'd want it to go along, not up and down. Anyway, it'd probably burn through the harness.'

'I don't care about the lightning! How can I think on an empty stomach?'

'Eat something, then. That's logic.'

'How? Every time I move that damn box flexes its hinges at me!'

The Luggage, on cue, gaped widely.

'See?'

'It's not trying to bite you,' said the imp. 'There's food in there. You're no use to it starved.'

Rincewind peered into the dark recesses of the Luggage. There were indeed, among the chaos of boxes and bags of gold, several bottles and packages in oiled paper. He gave a cynical laugh, mooched around the abandoned jetty until he found a piece of wood about the right length, wedged it as politely as possible in the gap between the lid and the box, and pulled out one of the flat packages.

It held biscuits that turned out to be as hard as diamond-wood.

' 'loody 'ell,' he muttered, nursing his teeth.

'Captain Eightpanther's Travellers' Digestives, them,' said the imp from the doorway to his box. 'Saved many a life at sea, they have.'

'Oh, sure. Do you use them as a raft, or just throw them to the sharks and sort of watch them sink? What's in the bottles? Poison?'

'Water.'

'But there's water everywhere! Why'd he want to bring water?'

'Trust.'

'Trust?'

'Yes. That's what he didn't, the water here. See?'

Rincewind opened a bottle. The liquid inside might have been water. It had a flat, empty flavour, with no trace of life. 'Neither taste nor smell,' he grumbled.

The Luggage gave a little creak, attracting his attention. With a lazy air of calculated menace it shut its lid slowly, grinding Rincewind's impromptu wedge like a dry loaf.

'All right, all right,' he said. 'I'm thinking.'

Ymor's headquarters were in the Leaning Tower at the junction of Rime Street and Frost Alley. At midnight the solitary guard leaning in the shadows looked up at the conjoining planets and wondered idly what change in his fortunes they might herald.

There was the faintest of sounds, as of a gnat yawning.

The guard glanced down the deserted street, and now caught the glimmer of moonlight on something lying in the mud a few yards away. He picked it up. The lunar light gleamed on gold, and his intake of breath was almost loud enough to echo down the alleyway.

There was a slight sound again, and another coin rolled into the gutter on the other side of the street.

By the time he had picked it up there was another one, a little way off and still spinning. Gold was, he remembered, said to be formed from the crystallized light of stars. Until now he had never believed it to be true, that something as heavy as gold could fall naturally from the sky.

As he drew level with the opposite alley mouth some more fell. It was still in its bag, there was an awful lot of it, and Rincewind brought it down heavily onto his head.

When the guard came to he found himself looking up into the wild-eyed face of a wizard, who was menacing his throat with a sword. In the darkness, too, something was gripping his leg.

It was the disconcerting sort of grip that suggested that the gripper could grip a whole lot harder, if he wanted to.

'Where is he, the rich foreigner?' hissed the wizard. 'Quickly!'

'What's holding my leg?' said the man, with a note of terror in his voice. He tried to wriggle free. The pressure increased.

'You wouldn't want to know,' said Rincewind. 'Pay attention, please. Where's the foreigner?'

'Not here! They've got him at Broadman's place! Everyone's looking for him! You're Rincewind, aren't you? The box – the box that bites people – ononono . . . pleasssse . . .'

Rincewind had gone. The guard felt the unseen leg-gripper release his – or, as he was beginning to fear, *its* – hold. Then, as he tried to pull himself to his feet, *something* big and heavy and square cannoned into him out of the dark and plunged off after the wizard. Something with hundreds of tiny feet.

With only his home-made phrase book to help him, Twoflower was trying to explain the mysteries of *inn-sewer-ants* to Broadman. The fat innkeeper was listening intently, his little black eyes glittering.

From the other end of the table Ymor watched with mild amusement, occasionally feeding one of his ravens with scraps from his plate. Beside him Withel paced up and down.

'You fret too much,' said Ymor, without taking his eyes from the two men opposite him. 'I can feel it, Stren. Who would dare attack us here? And the gutter wizard will come. He's too much of a coward not to. And he'll try to bargain. And we shall have him. And the gold. And the chest.'

Withel's one eye glared, and he smacked a fist into the palm of a black-gloved hand.

'Who would have thought there was so much sapient pearwood in the whole of the disc?' he said. 'How could we have known?'

'You fret too much, Stren. I'm sure you can do better this time,' said Ymor pleasantly.

The lieutenant snorted in disgust, and strode off around the room to bully his men. Ymor carried on watching the tourist.

It was strange, but the little man didn't seem to realize the seriousness of his position. Ymor had on several occasions seen him look around the room with an expression of deep satisfaction. He had also been talking for ages to Broadman and Ymor had seen a piece of paper change hands. And Broadman had given the foreigner some coins. It was strange.

When Broadman got up and waddled past Ymor's chair the thiefmaster's arm shot out like a steel spring and grabbed the fat man by his apron.

'What was that all about, friend?' asked Ymor quietly.

'N-nothing, Ymor. Just private business, like.'

'There are no secrets between friends, Broadman.'

'Yar. Well, I'm not sure about it myself, really. It's a sort of bet, see?' said the innkeeper nervously. '*Inn-sewer-ants*, it's called. It's like a bet that the Broken Drum won't get burned down.'

Ymor held the man's gaze until Broadman twitched

in fear and embarrassment. Then the thiefmaster laughed.

'This worm-eaten old tinder pile?' he said. 'The man must be mad!'

'Yes, but mad with money. He says now he's got the – can't remember the word, begins with a P, it's what you might call the stake money – the people he works for in the Agatean Empire will pay up. If the Broken Drum burns down. Not that I hope it does. Burn down. The Broken Drum, I mean. I mean, it's like a home to me, is the Drum . . .'

'Not entirely stupid, are you?' said Ymor, and pushed the innkeeper away.

The door slammed back on its hinges and thudded into the wall.

'Hey, that's my door!' screamed Broadman. Then he realized who was standing at the top of the steps, and ducked behind the table a mere shaving of time before a short black dart sped across the room and thunked into the woodwork.

Ymor moved his hand carefully, and poured out another flagon of beer.

'Won't you join me, Zlorf?' he said levelly. 'And put that sword away, Stren. Zlorf Flannelfoot is our friend.'

The president of the Assassins' Guild spun his short blowgun dexterously and slotted it into its holster in one smooth movement.

'Stren!' said Ymor.

The black-clad thief hissed, and sheathed his sword. But he kept his hand on the hilt, and his eyes on the assassin.

That wasn't easy. Promotion in the Assassins' Guild was by competitive examination, the Practical being the most important – indeed, the only – part. Thus Zlorf's broad, honest face was a welter of scar tissue, the result of many a close encounter. It probably hadn't been all that good-looking in any case – it was said that Zlorf had chosen a profession in which dark hoods, cloaks and nocturnal prowlings figured largely because there was a day-fearing trollish streak in his parentage. People who said this in earshot of Zlorf tended to carry their ears home in their hats.

He strolled down the stairs, followed by a number of assassins. When he was directly in front of Ymor he said: 'I've come for the tourist.'

'Is it any of your business, Zlorf?'

'Yes. Grinjo, Urmond – take him.'

Two of the assassins stepped forward. Then Stren was in front of them, his sword appearing to materialize an inch from their throats without having to pass through the intervening air.

'Possibly I could only kill one of you,' he murmured, 'but I suggest you ask yourselves – which one?'

'Look up, Zlorf,' said Ymor.

A row of yellow, baleful eyes looked down from the darkness among the rafters.

'One step more and you'll leave here with fewer eyeballs than you came with,' said the thiefmaster. 'So sit down and have a drink, Zlorf, and let's talk about this sensibly. *I* thought we had an agreement. You don't rob – I don't kill. Not for payment, that is,' he added after a pause.

Zlorf took the proffered beer.

'So?' he said. 'I'll kill him. Then you rob him. Is he that funny looking one over there?'

'Yes.'

Zlorf stared at Twoflower, who grinned at him. He shrugged. He seldom wasted time wondering why people wanted other people dead. It was just a living.

'Who is your client, may I ask?' said Ymor.

Zlorf held up a hand. 'Please!' he protested. 'Professional etiquette.'

'Of course. By the way—'

'Yes?'

'I believe I have a couple of guards outside—'

'Had.'

'And some others in the doorway across the street—'

'Formerly.'

'And two bowmen on the roof.'

A flicker of doubt passed across Zlorf's face, like the last shaft of sunlight over a badly ploughed field.

The door flew open, badly damaging the assassin who was standing beside it.

'Stop doing that!' shrieked Broadman, from under his table.

Zlorf and Ymor stared up at the figure on the threshold. It was short, fat and richly dressed. Very richly dressed. There were a number of tall, big shapes looming behind it. Very big, *threatening* shapes.

'Who's that?' said Zlorf.

'I know him,' said Ymor. 'His name's Rerpf. He runs the Groaning Platter tavern down by Brass Bridge. Stren – remove him.'

Rerpf held up a beringed hand. Stren Withel

hesitated halfway to the door as several very large trolls ducked under the doorway and stood on either side of the fat man, blinking in the light. Muscles the size of melons bulged in forearms like floursacks. Each troll held a double-headed axe. Between thumb and forefinger.

Broadman erupted from cover, his face suffused with rage.

'Out!' he screamed. 'Get those trolls out of here!'

No-one moved. The room was suddenly quiet. Broadman looked around quickly. It began to dawn on him just what he had said, and to whom. A whimper escaped from his lips, glad to be free.

He reached the doorway to his cellars just as one of the trolls, with a lazy flick of one ham-sized hand, sent his axe whirling across the room. The slam of the door and its subsequent splitting as the axe hit it merged into one sound.

'Bloody hell!' exclaimed Zlorf Flannelfoot.

'What do you want?' said Ymor.

'I am here on behalf of the Guild of Merchants and Traders,' said Rerpf evenly. 'To protect our interests, you might say. Meaning the little man.'

Ymor wrinkled his brows.

'I'm sorry,' he said. 'I thought I heard you say the Guild of Merchants?'

'And traders,' agreed Rerpf. Behind him now, in addition to more trolls, were several humans that Ymor vaguely recognized. He had seen them, maybe, behind counters and bars. Shadowy figures, usually – easily ignored, easily forgotten. At the back of his mind a bad feeling began to grow. He thought about how it might be to be, say, a fox confronted with an angry sheep. A sheep, moreover, that could afford to employ wolves.

'How long has this – Guild – been in existence, may I ask?' he said.

'Since this afternoon,' said Rerpf. 'I'm vice-guildmaster in charge of tourism, you know.'

'What is this tourism of which you speak?'

'Uh – we are not quite sure . . .' said Rerpf. An old bearded man poked his head over the guildmaster's shoulder and cackled, 'Speaking on behalf of the wine-sellers of Morpork, Tourism means Business. See?'

'Well?' said Ymor coldly.

'Well,' said Rerpf, 'we're protecting our interests, like I said.'

'Thieves OUT, Thieves OUT!' cackled his elderly companion. Several others took up the chant. Zlorf grinned. 'And assassins,' chanted the old man. Zlorf growled.

'Stands to reason,' said Rerpf. 'People robbing and murdering all over the place, what sort of impression are visitors going to take away? You come all the way to see our fine city with its many points of historical and civic interest, also many quaint customs, and you wake up dead in some back alley or as it might be floating down the Ankh, how are you going to tell all your friends what a great time you're having? Let's face it, you've got to move with the times.'

Zlorf and Ymor met each other's gaze.

'We have, have we?' said Ymor.

'Then let us move, brother,' agreed Zlorf. In one movement he brought his blowgun to his mouth and sent a dart hissing towards the nearest troll. It spun around, hurling its axe, which whirred over the assassin's head and buried itself in a luckless thief behind him.

Rerpf ducked, allowing a troll behind him to raise its huge iron crossbow and fire a spear-length quarrel into the nearest assassin. That was the start . . .

It has been remarked before that those who are sensitive to radiations in the far octarine – the eighth colour, the pigment of the Imagination – can see things that others cannot.

Thus it was that Rincewind, hurrying through the crowded, flare-lit evening bazaars of Morpork with the Luggage trundling behind him, jostled a tall dark figure, turned to deliver a few suitable curses, and beheld Death.

It had to be Death. No-one else went around with empty eye sockets and, of course, the scythe over one shoulder was another clue. As Rincewind stared in horror a courting couple, laughing at some private joke, walked straight through the apparition without appearing to notice it.

Death, insofar as it was possible in a face with no movable features, looked surprised.

RINCEWIND? Death said, in tones as deep and heavy as the slamming of leaden doors, far underground.

'Um,' said Rincewind, trying to back away from that eyeless stare.

BUT WHY ARE YOU HERE? (Boom, boom went crypt lids, in the worm-haunted fastnesses under old mountains . . .)

'Um, why not?' said Rincewind. 'Anyway, I'm sure you've got lots to do, so if you'll just—'

I was surprised that you jostled me, Rincewind, for I have an appointment with thee this very night.

'Oh no, not—'

Of course, what's so bloody vexing about the whole business is that I was expecting to meet thee in Psephopololis.

'But that's five hundred miles away!'

You don't have to tell me, the whole system's got screwed up again, I can see that. Look, there's no chance of you—?

Rincewind backed away, hands spread protectively in front of him. The dried fish salesman on a nearby stall watched this madman with interest.

'Not a chance!'

I could lend you a very fast horse.

'No!'

It won't hurt a bit.

'No!' Rincewind turned and ran. Death watched him go, and shrugged bitterly.

Sod you, then, Death said. He turned, and noticed the fish salesman. With a snarl Death reached out a bony finger and stopped the man's heart, but He didn't take much pride in it.

Then Death remembered what was due to happen later that night. It would not be true to say that Death smiled, because in any case His features were perforce frozen in a calcareous grin. But He hummed a little tune, cheery as a plague pit, and – pausing only to extract the life from a passing mayfly, and one-ninth of the lives from a cat cowering under the fish stall (all cats can see into the octarine) – Death turned on His heel and set off towards the Broken Drum.

Short Street, Morpork, is in fact one of the longest in the city. Filigree Street crosses its turnwise end in the manner of the crosspiece of a T, and the Broken Drum is so placed that it looks down the full length of the street.

At the furthermost end of Short Street a dark oblong rose on hundreds of tiny legs, and started to run. At first it moved at no more than a lumbering trot, but by the time it was halfway up the street it was moving arrow-fast . . .

A darker shadow inched its way along one of the walls of the Drum, a few yards from the two trolls who were guarding the door. Rincewind was sweating. If they heard the faint clinking of the specially prepared bags at his belt . . .

One of the trolls tapped his colleague on the shoulder, producing a noise like two pebbles being knocked together. He pointed down the starlit street . . .

Rincewind darted from his hiding place, turned, and hurled his burden through the Drum's nearest window.

Withel saw it arrive. The bag arced across the room, turning slowly in the air, and burst on the edge of a table. A moment later gold coins were rolling across the floor, spinning, glittering.

The room was suddenly silent, save for the tiny

noises of gold and the whimpers of the wounded. With a curse Withel despatched the assassin he had been fighting. 'It's a trick!' he screamed. 'No-one move!'

Threescore men and a dozen trolls froze in mid-grope.

Then, for the third time, the door burst open. Two trolls hurried through it, slammed it behind them, dropped the heavy bar across it and fled down the stairs.

Outside there was a sudden crescendo of running feet. And, for the last time, the door opened. In fact it exploded, the great wooden bar being hurled far across the room and the frame itself giving way.

Door and frame landed on a table, which flew into splinters. It was then that the frozen fighters noticed that there was something else in the pile of wood. It was a box, shaking itself madly to free itself of the smashed timber around it.

Rincewind appeared in the ruined doorway, hurling another of his gold grenades. It smashed into a wall, showering coins.

Down in the cellar Broadman looked up, muttered to himself, and carried on with his work. His entire spindlewinter's supply of candles had already been strewn on the floor, mixed with his store of kindling wood. Now he was attacking a barrel of lamp oil.

'*Inn-sewer-ants*,' he muttered. Oil gushed out and swirled around his feet.

Withel stormed across the floor, his face a mask of rage. Rincewind took careful aim and caught the thief full in the chest with a bag of gold.

But now Ymor was shouting, and pointing an accusing finger. A raven swooped down from its perch in the rafters and dived at the wizard, talons open and gleaming.

It didn't make it. At about the halfway point the Luggage leapt from its bed of splinters, gaped briefly in mid-air, and snapped shut.

It landed lightly. Rincewind saw its lid open again, slightly. Just far enough for a tongue, large as a palm leaf, red as mahogany, to lick up a few errant feathers.

At the same moment the giant candlewheel fell from the ceiling, plunging the room into gloom. Rincewind, coiling himself like a spring, gave a standing jump and grasped a beam, swinging himself up into the relative safety of the roof with a strength that amazed him.

'Exciting, isn't it!' said a voice by his ear.

Down below, thieves, assassins, trolls and merchants all realized at about the same moment that they were in a room made treacherous of foothold by gold coins and containing something, among the suddenly menacing shapes in the semi-darkness, that was absolutely horrible. As one they made for the door, but had two dozen different recollections of its exact position.

High above the chaos Rincewind stared at Twoflower.

'Did you cut the lights down?' he hissed.

'Yes.'

'How come you're up here?'

'I thought I'd better not get in everyone's way.'

Rincewind considered this. There didn't seem to be much he could say. Twoflower added: 'A real brawl! Better than anything I'd imagined! Do you think I ought to thank them? Or did you arrange it?'

Rincewind looked at him blankly. 'I think we ought to be getting down now,' he said hollowly. 'Everyone's gone.'

He dragged Twoflower across the littered floor and up the steps. They burst out into the tail end of the night. There were still a few stars but the moon was down, and there was a faint grey glow to rimward. Most important, the street was empty.

Rincewind sniffed.

'Can you smell oil?' he said.

Then Withel stepped out of the shadows and tripped him up.

At the top of the cellar steps Broadman knelt down and fumbled in his tinderbox. It turned out to be damp.

'I'll kill that bloody cat,' he muttered, and groped for the spare box that was normally on the ledge by the door. It was missing. Broadman said a bad word.

A lighted taper appeared in mid-air, right beside him.

HERE, TAKE THIS.

'Thanks,' said Broadman.

DON'T MENTION IT.

Broadman went to throw the taper down the steps. His hand paused in mid-air. He looked at the taper, his brow furrowing. Then he turned around and held the taper up to illuminate the scene. It didn't shed much light, but it did give the darkness a shape . . .

'Oh, no—' he breathed.

BUT YES, said Death.

Rincewind rolled.

For a moment he thought Withel was going to spit him where he lay. But it was worse than that. He was waiting for him to get up.

'I see you have a sword, wizard,' he said quietly. 'I suggest you rise, and we shall see how well you use it.'

Rincewind stood up as slowly as he dared, and drew from his belt the short sword he had taken from the guard a few hours and a hundred years ago. It was a short blunt affair compared to Withel's hair-thin rapier.

'But I don't know how to use a sword,' he wailed.

'Good.'

'You know that wizards can't be killed by edged weapons?' said Rincewind desperately.

Withel smiled coldly. 'So I have heard,' he said. 'I look forward to putting it to the test.' He lunged.

Rincewind caught the thrust by sheer luck, jerked his hand away in shock, deflected the second stroke by coincidence, and took the third one through his robe at heart-height.

There was a clink.

Withel's snarl of triumph died in his throat. He drew the sword out and prodded again at the wizard, who was rigid with terror and guilt. There was another clink, and gold coins began to drop out of the hem of the wizard's robe.

'So you bleed gold, do you?' hissed Withel. 'But

have you got gold concealed in that raggedy beard, you little—'

As his sword went back for his final sweep the sullen glow that had been growing in the doorway of the Broken Drum flickered, dimmed, and erupted into a roaring fireball that sent the walls billowing outward and carried the roof a hundred feet into the air before bursting through it, in a gout of red-hot tiles.

Withel stared at the boiling flames, unnerved. And Rincewind leapt. He ducked under the thief's sword arm and brought his own blade around in an arc so incompetently misjudged that it hit the man flat-first and jolted out of the wizard's hand. Sparks and droplets of flaming oil rained down as Withel reached out with both gauntleted hands and grabbed Rincewind's neck, forcing him down.

'You did this!' he screamed. 'You and your box of trickery!'

His thumb found Rincewind's windpipe. This is it, the wizard thought. Wherever I'm going, it can't be worse than here . . .

'Excuse me,' said Twoflower.

Rincewind felt the grip lessen. And now Withel was slowly getting up, a look of absolute hatred on his face.

A glowing ember landed on the wizard. He brushed it off hurriedly, and scrambled to his feet.

Twoflower was behind Withel, holding the man's own needle-sharp sword with the point resting in the small of the thief's back. Rincewind's eyes narrowed. He reached into his robe, then withdrew his hand bunched into a fist.

'Don't move,' he said.

'Am I doing this right?' asked Twoflower anxiously.

'He says he'll skewer your liver if you move,' Rincewind translated freely.

'I doubt it,' said Withel.

'Bet?'

'No.'

As Withel tensed himself to turn on the tourist Rincewind lashed out and caught the thief on the jaw. Withel stared at him in amazement for a moment, and then quietly toppled into the mud.

The wizard uncurled his stinging fist and the roll of gold coins slipped between his throbbing fingers. He looked down at the recumbent thief.

'Good grief,' he gasped.

He looked up and yelled as another ember landed on his neck. Flames were racing along the rooftops on either side of the street. All around him people were hurling possessions from windows and dragging horses from smoking stables. Another explosion in the white-hot volcano that was the Drum sent a whole marble mantelpiece scything overhead.

'The Widdershins Gate's the nearest!' Rincewind shouted above the crackle of collapsing rafters. 'Come on!'

He grabbed Twoflower's reluctant arm and dragged him down the street.

'My Luggage—'

'Blast your luggage! Stay here much longer and you'll go where you don't need luggage! Come on!' screamed Rincewind.

They jogged on through the crowd of frightened people leaving the area, while the wizard took great mouthfuls of cool dawn air. Something was puzzling him.

'I'm sure all the candles went out,' he said. 'So how did the Drum catch fire?'

'I don't know,' moaned Twoflower. 'It's terrible, Rincewind. We were getting along so well, too.'

Rincewind stopped in astonishment, so that another refugee cannoned into him and spun away with an oath.

'*Getting on?*'

'Yes, a great bunch of fellows, I thought – language was a bit of a problem, but they were so keen for me to join their party, they just wouldn't take no for an answer – really friendly people, I thought . . .'

Rincewind started to correct him, then realized he didn't know how to begin.

'It'll be a blow for old Broadman,' Twoflower continued. 'Still, he was wise. I've still got the *rhinu* he paid as his first premium.'

Rincewind didn't know the meaning of the word premium, but his mind was working fast.

'You *inn-sewered* the Drum?' he said. 'You bet Broadman it wouldn't catch fire?'

'Oh yes. Standard valuation. Two hundred *rhinu*. Why do you ask?'

Rincewind turned and stared at the flames racing towards them, and wondered how much of Ankh-Morpork could be bought for two hundred *rhinu*. Quite a large piece, he decided. Only not now, not the way those flames were moving . . .

He glanced down at the tourist.

'You—' he began, and searched his memory for the

worst word in the Trob tongue; the happy little beTrobi didn't really know how to swear properly.

'You,' he repeated. Another hurrying figure bumped into him, narrowly missing him with the blade over its shoulder. Rincewind's tortured temper exploded.

'You little (such a one who, while wearing a copper nose ring, stands in a footbath atop Mount Raruaruaha during a heavy thunderstorm and shouts that Alohura, Goddess of Lightning, has the facial features of a diseased uloruaha root)!'

JUST DOING MY JOB, said the figure, stalking away.

Every word fell as heavily as slabs of marble; moreover, Rincewind was certain that he was the only one who heard them.

He grabbed Twoflower again.

'Let's get out of here!' he suggested.

One interesting side-effect of the fire in Ankh-Morpork concerns the *inn-sewer-ants* policy, which left the city through the ravaged roof of the Broken Drum, was wafted high into the discworld's atmosphere on the ensuing thermal, and came to earth several days and a few thousand miles away on an uloruaha bush in the beTrobi islands. The simple, laughing islanders subsequently worshipped it as a god, much to the amusement of their more sophisticated neighbours. Strangely enough the rainfall and harvests in the next few years were almost supernaturally abundant, and this led to a research team being despatched to the islands by the Minor Religions faculty of Unseen University. Their verdict was that it only went to show.

* * *

The fire, driven by the wind, spread out from the Drum faster than a man could walk. The timbers of the Widdershins Gate were already on fire when Rincewind, his face blistered and reddened from the flames, reached them. By now he and Twoflower were on horseback – mounts hadn't been that hard to obtain. A wily merchant had asked fifty times their worth, and had been left gaping when one thousand times their worth had been pressed into his hands.

They rode through just before the first of the big gate timbers descended in an explosion of sparks. Morpork was already a cauldron of flame.

As they galloped up the red-lit road Rincewind glanced sideways at his travelling companion, currently trying hard to learn to ride a horse.

'Bloody hell,' he thought. 'He's alive! Me too. Who'd have thought it? Perhaps there is something in this *reflected-sound-of-underground-spirits*?' It was a cumbersome phrase. Rincewind tried to get his tongue round the thick syllables that were the word in Twoflower's own language.

'Ecolirix?' he tried. 'Ecro-gnothics? Echo-gnomics?' That would do. That sounded about right.

Several hundred yards downriver from the last smouldering suburb of the city a strangely rectangular and apparently heavily waterlogged object touched the mud on the widdershins bank. Immediately it sprouted numerous legs and scrabbled for a purchase.

Hauling itself to the top of the bank the Luggage – streaked with soot, stained with water and very, very angry – shook itself and took its bearings. Then it moved away at a brisk trot, the small and incredibly ugly imp that was perching on its lid watching the scenery with interest.

Bravd looked at the Weasel and raised his eyebrows.

'And that's it,' said Rincewind. 'The Luggage caught up with us, don't ask me how. Is there any more wine?'

The Weasel picked up the empty wineskin.

'I think you have had just about enough wine this night,' he said.

Bravd's forehead wrinkled.

'Gold is gold,' he said finally. 'How can a man with plenty of gold consider himself poor? You're either poor or rich. It stands to reason.'

Rincewind hiccupped. He was finding Reason rather difficult to hold on to. 'Well,' he said, 'what I think is, the point is, well, you know octiron?'

The two adventurers nodded. The strange iridescent metal was almost as highly valued in the lands around the Circle Sea as sapient pearwood, and was about as rare. A man who owned a needle made of octiron would never lose his way, since it always pointed to the Hub of the discworld, being acutely sensitive to the disc's magical field; it would also miraculously darn his socks.

'Well, my point is, you see, that gold also has its sort of magical field. Sort of financial wizardry. Echo-gnomics.' Rincewind giggled.

The Weasel stood up and stretched. The sun was well up now, and the city below them was wreathed in mists and full of foul vapours. Also gold, he decided. Even a citizen of Morpork would, at the very point of death, desert his treasure to save his skin. Time to move.

The little man called Twoflower appeared to be asleep. The Weasel looked down at him and shook his head.

'The city awaits, such as it is,' he said. 'Thank you for a pleasant tale, Wizard. What will you do now?' He eyed the Luggage, which immediately backed away and snapped its lid at him.

'Well, there are no ships leaving the city now,' giggled Rincewind. 'I suppose we'll take the coast road to Chirm. I've got to look after him, you see. But look, I didn't make it—'

'Sure, sure,' said the Weasel soothingly. He turned away and swung himself into the saddle of the horse that Bravd was holding. A few moments later the two heroes were just specks under a cloud of dust, heading down towards the charcoal city.

Rincewind stared muzzily at the recumbent tourist. At two recumbent tourists. In his somewhat defenceless state a stray thought, wandering through the dimensions in search of a mind to harbour it, slid into his brain.

'Here's another fine mess you've got me into,' he moaned, and slumped backwards.

'Mad,' said the Weasel. Bravd, galloping along a few feet away, nodded.

'All wizards get like that,' he said. 'It's the quicksilver fumes. Rots their brains. Mushrooms, too.'

'However—' said the brown-clad one. He reached into his tunic and took out a golden disc on a short chain. Bravd raised his eyebrows.

'The wizard said that the little man had some sort of golden disc that told him the time,' said the Weasel.

'Arousing your cupidity, little friend? You always were an expert thief, Weasel.'

'Aye,' agreed the Weasel modestly. He touched the knob at the disc's rim, and it flipped open.

The very small demon imprisoned within looked up from its tiny abacus and scowled. 'It lacks but ten minutes to eight of the clock,' it snarled. The lid slammed shut, almost trapping the Weasel's fingers.

With an oath the Weasel hurled the time-teller far out into the heather, where it possibly hit a stone. Something, in any event, caused the case to split; there was a vivid octarine flash and a whiff of brimstone as the time being vanished into whatever demonic dimension it called home.

'What did you do that for?' said Bravd, who hadn't been close enough to hear the words.

'Do what?' said the Weasel. 'I didn't do anything. Nothing happened at all. Come on – we're wasting opportunities!'

Bravd nodded. Together they turned their steeds and galloped towards ancient Ankh, and honest enchantments.

THE SENDING OF EIGHT

OF EIGHT

· Prologue ·

THE DISCWORLD OFFERS SIGHTS FAR more impressive than those found in universes built by Creators with less imagination but more mechanical aptitude.

Although the disc's sun is but an orbiting moonlet, its prominences hardly bigger than croquet hoops, this slight drawback must be set against the tremendous sight of Great A'Tuin the Turtle, upon Whose ancient and meteor-riddled shell the disc ultimately rests. Sometimes, in His slow journey across the shores of Infinity, He moves His country-sized head to snap at a passing comet.

But perhaps the most impressive sight of all – if only because most brains, when faced with the sheer galactic enormity of A'Tuin, refuse to believe it – is the endless Rimfall, where the seas of the disc boil ceaselessly over the Edge into space. Or perhaps it is the Rimbow, the eight-coloured, world-girdling rainbow that hovers in the mist-laden air over the Fall. The eighth colour is octarine, caused by the scatter-effect of strong sunlight on an intense magical field.

Or perhaps, again, the most magnificent sight is the Hub. There, a spire of green ice ten miles high rises through the clouds and supports at its peak the realm of Dunmanifestin, the abode of the disc gods. The disc gods themselves, despite the splendour of the world below them, are seldom satisfied. It is embarrassing to know that one is a god of a world that only exists because every improbability curve must have its far end; especially when one can peer into other dimensions at worlds whose Creators had more mechanical aptitude than imagination. No wonder, then, that the disc gods spend more time in bickering than in omnicognizance.

On this particular day Blind Io, by dint of constant vigilance the chief of the gods, sat with his chin on his hand and looked at the gaming board on the red marble table in front of him. Blind Io had got his name because, where his eye sockets should have been, there were nothing but two areas of blank skin. His eyes, of which he had an impressively large number, led a semi-independent life of their own. Several were currently hovering above the table.

The gaming board was a carefully carved map of the discworld, overprinted with squares. A number of beautifully modelled playing pieces were now occupying some of the squares. A human onlooker would, for example, have recognized in two of them the likenesses of Bravd and the Weasel. Others represented yet more heroes and champions, of which the disc had a more than adequate supply.

Still in the game were Io, Offler the Crocodile God, Zephyrus the god of slight breezes, Fate, and the Lady. There was an air of concentration around the board now that the lesser players had been removed from the Game. Chance had been an early casualty, running her hero into a full house of armed gnolls (the result of a lucky throw by Offler) and shortly afterwards Night had cashed his chips, pleading an appointment with Destiny. Several minor deities had drifted up and were kibitzing over the shoulders of the players.

Side bets were made that the Lady would be the next to leave the board. Her last champion of any standing was now a pinch of potash in the ruins of still-smoking Ankh-Morpork, and there were hardly any pieces that she could promote to first rank.

Blind Io took up the dice-box, which was a skull whose various orifices had been stoppered with rubies, and with several of his eyes on the Lady he rolled three fives.

She smiled. This was the nature of the Lady's eyes: they were bright green, lacking iris or pupil, and they glowed from within.

The room was silent as she scrabbled in her box of pieces and, from the very bottom, produced a couple that she set down on the board with two decisive clicks. The rest of the players, as one God, craned forward to peer at them.

'A wenegade wiffard and fome fort of clerk,' said Offler the Crocodile God, hindered as usual by his tusks. 'Well, weally!' With one claw he pushed a pile of bone-white tokens into the centre of the table.

The Lady nodded slightly. She picked up the dice-cup and held it as steady as a rock, yet all the Gods could hear the three cubes rattling about inside. And then she sent them bouncing across the table.

A six. A three. A five.

Something was happening to the five, however. Battered by the chance collision of several billion molecules, the die flipped onto a point, spun gently and came down a seven.

Blind Io picked up the cube and counted the sides. 'Come *on*,' he said wearily. 'Play fair.'

THE SENDING
OF EIGHT

THE ROAD FROM ANKH-MORPORK to Quirm is high, white and winding, a thirty-league stretch of pot-holes and half-buried rocks that spirals around mountains and dips into cool green valleys of citrus trees, crosses liana-webbed gorges on creaking rope bridges and is generally more picturesque than useful.

Picturesque. That was a new word to Rincewind the wizard (BMgc, Unseen University [failed]). It was one of a number he had picked up since leaving the charred ruins of Ankh-Morpork. Quaint was another one. Picturesque meant – he decided after careful observation of the scenery that inspired Twoflower to use the word – that the landscape was horribly pre-cipitous. Quaint, when used to describe the occasional village through which they passed, meant fever-ridden and tumbledown.

Twoflower was a tourist, the first ever seen on the discworld. Tourist, Rincewind had decided, meant 'idiot'.

As they rode leisurely through the thyme-scented, bee-humming air, Rincewind pondered on the experiences of the last few days. While the little foreigner was obviously insane, he was also generous and considerably less lethal than half the people the wizard had mixed with in the city. Rincewind rather liked him. Disliking him would be like kicking a puppy.

Currently Twoflower was showing a great interest

in the theory and practice of magic.

'It all seems, well, rather useless to me,' he said. 'I always thought that, you know, a wizard just said the magic words and that was that. Not all this tedious memorizing.'

Rincewind agreed moodily. He tried to explain that magic had indeed once been wild and lawless, but had been tamed back in the mists of time by the Olden Ones, who had bound it to obey among other things the Law of Conservation of Reality; this demanded that the effort needed to achieve a goal should be the same regardless of the means used. In practical terms this meant that, say, creating the illusion of a glass of wine was relatively easy, since it involved merely the subtle shifting of light patterns. On the other hand, lifting a genuine wineglass a few feet in the air by sheer mental energy required several hours of systematic preparation if the wizard wished to prevent the simple principle of leverage flicking his brain out through his ears.

He went on to add that some of the ancient magic could still be found in its raw state, recognizable – to the initiated – by the eightfold shape it made in the crystalline structure of space-time. There was the metal octiron, for example, and the gas octogen. Both radiated dangerous amounts of raw enchantment.

'It's all very depressing,' he finished.

'Depressing?'

Rincewind turned in his saddle and glanced at Twoflower's Luggage, which was currently ambling along on its little legs, occasionally snapping its lid at butterflies. He sighed.

'Rincewind thinks he ought to be able to harness the lightning,' said the picture-imp, who was observing the passing scene from the tiny doorway of the box slung around Twoflower's neck. He had spent the morning painting picturesque views and quaint scenes for his master, and had been allowed to knock off for a smoke.

'When I said *harness* I didn't mean harness,' snapped Rincewind. 'I meant, well I just meant that – I dunno, I just can't think of the right words. I just think the world ought to be more sort of organized.'

'That's just fantasy,' said Twoflower.

'I know. That's the trouble.' Rincewind sighed again. It was all very well going on about pure logic and how the universe was ruled by logic and the harmony of numbers, but the plain fact of the matter was that the disc was manifestly traversing space on the back of a giant turtle and the gods had a habit of going round to atheists' houses and smashing their windows.

There was a faint sound, hardly louder than the noise of the bees in the rosemary by the road. It had a curiously bony quality, as of rolling skulls or a whirling dice-box. Rincewind peered around. There was no-one nearby.

For some reason that worried him.

Then came a slight breeze, that grew and went in the space of a few heartbeats. It left the world unchanged save in a few interesting particulars.

There was now, for example, a five-metre-tall mountain troll standing in the road. It was exceptionally angry. This was partly because trolls generally are, in any case, but it was exacerbated by the fact that the sudden and instantaneous teleportation from its lair in the Rammerorck Mountains three thousand miles away and a thousand yards closer to the Rim had raised its internal temperature to a dangerous level, in accordance with the laws of conservation of energy. So it bared its fangs and charged.

'What a strange creature,' Twoflower remarked. 'Is it dangerous?'

'Only to people!' shouted Rincewind. He drew his sword and, with a smooth overarm throw, completely failed to hit the troll. The blade plunged on into the heather at the side of the track.

There was the faintest of sounds, like the rattle of old teeth.

The sword struck a boulder concealed in the heather – concealed, a watcher might have considered, so artfully that a moment before it had not appeared to be there at all. It sprang up like a leaping salmon and in mid-ricochet plunged deeply into the back of the troll's grey neck.

The creature grunted, and with one swipe of a claw gouged a wound in the flank of Twoflower's horse, which screamed and bolted into the trees at the roadside. The troll spun around and made a grab for Rincewind.

Then its sluggish nervous system brought it the message that it was dead. It looked surprised for a moment, and then toppled over and shattered into gravel (trolls being silicaceous lifeforms, their bodies reverted instantly to stone at the moment of death).

'Aaargh,' thought Rincewind as his horse reared in

terror. He hung on desperately as it staggered two-legged across the road and then, screaming, turned and galloped into the woods.

The sound of hoofbeats died away, leaving the air to the hum of bees and the occasional rustle of butterfly wings. There was another sound, too, a strange noise for the bright time of noonday.

It sounded like dice.

'Rincewind?'

The long aisles of trees threw Twoflower's voice from side to side and eventually tossed it back to him, unheeded. He sat down on a rock and tried to think.

Firstly, he was lost. That was vexing, but it did not worry him unduly. The forest looked quite interesting and probably held elves or gnomes, perhaps both. In fact on a couple of occasions he had thought he had seen strange green faces peering down at him from the branches. Twoflower had always wanted to meet an elf. In fact what he really wanted to meet was a dragon, but an elf would do. Or a real goblin.

His Luggage was missing, and that was annoying. It was also starting to rain. He squirmed uncomfortably on the damp stone, and tried to look on the bright side. For example, during its mad dash his plunging horse had burst through some bushes and disturbed a she-bear with her cubs, but had gone on before the bear could react. Then it had suddenly been galloping over the sleeping bodies of a large wolf pack and, again, its mad speed had been such that the furious yelping had been left far behind. Nevertheless, the day was wearing on and perhaps it would be a good idea

– Twoflower thought – not to hang about in the open. Perhaps there was a . . . he racked his brains trying to remember what sort of accommodation forests traditionally offered . . . perhaps there was a ginger-bread house or something?

The stone really *was* uncomfortable. Twoflower looked down and, for the first time, noticed the strange carving.

It looked like a spider. Or was it a squid? Moss and lichens rather blurred the precise details. But they didn't blur the runes carved below it. Twoflower could read them clearly, and they said: Traveller, the hospitable temple of Bel-Shamharoth lies one thousand paces Hubwards. Now this was strange, Twoflower realized, because although he could read the message the actual letters were completely unknown to him. Somehow the message was arriving in his brain without the tedious necessity of passing through his eyes.

He stood up and untied his now-biddable horse from a sapling. He wasn't sure which way the Hub lay, but there seemed to be an old track of sorts leading away between the trees. This Bel-Shamharoth seemed prepared to go out of his way to help stranded travellers. In any case, it was that or the wolves. Twoflower nodded decisively.

It is interesting to note that, several hours later, a couple of wolves who were following Twoflower's scent arrived in the glade. Their green eyes fell on the strange eight-legged carving – which may indeed have been a spider, or an octopus, or may yet again have been something altogether more strange – and they immediately decided that they weren't so hungry, at that.

About three miles away a failed wizard was hanging by his hands from a high branch in a beech tree.

This was the end result of five minutes of crowded activity. First, an enraged she-bear had barged through the undergrowth and taken the throat out of his horse with one swipe of her paw. Then, as Rincewind had fled the carnage, he had run into a glade in which a number of irate wolves were milling about. His instructors at Unseen University, who had despaired of Rincewind's inability to master levitation, would have then been amazed at the speed with which he reached and climbed the nearest tree, without apparently touching it.

Now there was just the matter of the snake.

It was large and green, and wound itself along the branch with reptilian patience. Rincewind wondered if it was poisonous, then chided himself for asking such a silly question. Of course it would be poisonous.

'What are you grinning for?' he asked the figure on the next branch.

I CAN'T HELP IT, said Death. NOW WOULD YOU BE SO KIND AS TO LET GO? I CAN'T HANG AROUND ALL DAY.

'I can,' said Rincewind defiantly.

The wolves clustered around the base of the tree looked up with interest at their next meal talking to himself.

IT WON'T HURT, said Death. If words had weight, a single sentence from Death would have anchored a ship.

Rincewind's arms screamed their agony at him. He scowled at the vulture-like, slightly transparent figure.

'Won't hurt?' he said. 'Being torn apart by wolves won't hurt?'

He noticed another branch crossing his dangerously narrowing one a few feet away. If he could just reach it . . .

He swung himself forward, one hand outstretched.

The branch, already bending, did not break. It simply made a wet little sound and twisted.

Rincewind found that he was now hanging on to the end of a tongue of bark and fibre, lengthening as it peeled away from the tree. He looked down, and with a sort of fatal satisfaction realized that he would land right on the biggest wolf.

Now he was moving slowly as the bark peeled back in a longer and longer strip. The snake watched him thoughtfully.

But the growing length of bark held. Rincewind began to congratulate himself until, looking up, he saw what he had hitherto not noticed. There was the largest hornets' nest he had ever seen, hanging right in his path.

He shut his eyes tightly.

Why the troll? he asked himself. Everything else is just my usual luck, but why the troll? What the hell is going on?

Click. It might have been a twig snapping, except that the sound appeared to be inside Rincewind's head. Click, click. And a breeze that failed to set a single leaf atremble.

The hornets' nest was ripped from the branch as

the strip passed by. It shot past the wizard's head and he watched it grow smaller as it plummeted towards the circle of upturned muzzles.

The circle suddenly closed.

The circle suddenly expanded.

The concerted yelp of pain as the pack fought to escape the furious cloud echoed among the trees. Rincewind grinned inanely.

Rincewind's elbow nudged something. It was the tree trunk. The strip had carried him right to the end of the branch. But there were no other branches. The smooth bark beside him offered no handholds.

It offered hands, though. Two were even now thrusting through the mossy bark beside him; slim hands, green as young leaves. Then a shapely arm followed, and then the hamadryad leaned right out and grasped the astonished wizard firmly and, with that vegetable strength that can send roots questing into rock, drew him into the tree. The solid bark parted like a mist, closed like a clam.

Death watched impassively.

He glanced at the cloud of mayflies that were dancing their joyful zigzags near His skull. He snapped His fingers. The insects fell out of the air. But, somehow, it wasn't quite the same.

Blind Io pushed his stack of chips across the table, glowered through such of his eyes as were currently in the room, and strode out. A few demigods tittered. At least Offler had taken the loss of a perfectly good troll with precise, if somewhat reptilian, grace.

The Lady's last opponent shifted his seat until he faced her across the board.

'Lord,' she said, politely.

'Lady,' he acknowledged. Their eyes met.

He was a taciturn god. It was said that he had arrived in the discworld after some terrible and mysterious incident in another Eventuality. It is of course the privilege of gods to control their apparent outward form, even to other gods; the Fate of the discworld was currently a kindly man in late middle age, greying hair brushed neatly around features that a maiden would confidently proffer a glass of small beer to, should they appear at her back door. It was a face a kindly youth would gladly help over a stile. Except for his eyes, of course.

No deity can disguise the manner and nature of his eyes. The nature of the two eyes of the Fate of the discworld was this: that while at a mere glance they were simply dark, a closer look would reveal – too late! – that they were but holes opening on to a blackness so remote, so deep that the watcher would feel himself inexorably drawn into the twin pools of infinite night and their terrible, wheeling stars . . .

The Lady coughed politely, and laid twenty-one white chips on the table. Then from her robe she took another chip, silvery and translucent and twice the size of the others. The soul of a true Hero always finds a better rate of exchange, and is valued highly by the gods.

Fate raised an eyebrow.

'And no cheating, Lady,' he said.

'But who could cheat Fate?' she asked. He shrugged.

'No-one. Yet everyone tries.'

'And yet, again, I believe I felt you giving me a little assistance against the others?'

'But of course. So that the endgame could be the sweeter, Lady. And now . . .'

He reached into his gaming box and brought forth a piece, setting it down on the board with a satisfied air. The watching deities gave a collective sigh. Even the Lady was momentarily taken aback.

It was certainly ugly. The carving was uncertain, as if the craftsman's hands were shaking in horror of the thing taking shape under his reluctant fingers. It seemed to be all suckers and tentacles. And mandibles, the Lady observed. And one great eye.

'I thought such as He died out at the beginning of Time,' she said.

'Mayhap our necrotic friend was loath even to go near this one,' laughed Fate. He was enjoying himself.

'It should never have been spawned.'

'Nevertheless,' said Fate gnomically. He scooped the dice into their unusual box, and then glanced up at her.

'Unless,' he added, 'you wish to resign . . . ?'

She shook her head.

'Play,' she said.

'You can match my stake?'

'*Play.*'

Rincewind knew what was inside trees: wood, sap, possibly squirrels. Not a palace.

Still – the cushions underneath him were definitely softer than wood, the wine in the wooden cup beside him was much tastier than sap, and there could be absolutely no comparison between a squirrel and the girl sitting before him, clasping her knees and watching him thoughtfully, unless mention was made of certain hints of furriness.

The room was high, wide and lit with a soft yellow light which came from no particular source that Rincewind could identify. Through gnarled and knotted archways he could see other rooms, and what looked like a very large winding staircase. And it had looked a perfectly normal tree from the outside, too.

The girl was green – flesh green. Rincewind could be absolutely certain about that, because all she was wearing was a medallion around her neck. Her long hair had a faintly mossy look about it. Her eyes had no pupils and were a luminous green. Rincewind wished he had paid more attention to anthropology lectures at University.

She had said nothing. Apart from indicating the couch and offering him the wine she had done no more than sit watching him, occasionally rubbing a deep scratch on her arm.

Rincewind hurriedly recalled that a dryad was so linked to her tree that she suffered wounds in sympathy—

'Sorry about that,' he said quickly. 'It was just an accident. I mean, there were these wolves, and—'

'You had to climb my tree, and I rescued you,' said the dryad smoothly. 'How lucky for you. And for your friend, perhaps?'

'Friend?'

'The little man with the magic box,' said the dryad.

'Oh, sure, him,' said Rincewind vaguely. 'Yeah. I hope he's OK.'

'He needs your help.'

'He usually does. Did he make it to a tree too?'

'He made it to the Temple of Bel-Shamharoth.'

Rincewind choked on his wine. His ears tried to crawl into his head in terror of the syllables they had just heard. The Soul Eater! Before he could stop them the memories came galloping back. Once, while a student of practical magic at Unseen University, and for a bet, he'd slipped into the little room off the main library – the room with walls covered in protective lead pentagrams, the room no-one was allowed to occupy for more than four minutes and thirty-two seconds, which was a figure arrived at after two hundred years of cautious experimentation . . .

He had gingerly opened the Book, which was chained to the octiron pedestal in the middle of the rune-strewn floor not lest someone steal it, but lest it escape; for it was the Octavo, so full of magic that it had its own vague sentience. One spell had indeed leapt from the crackling pages and lodged itself in the dark recesses of his brain. And, apart from knowing that it was one of the Eight Great Spells, no-one would know which one until he said it. Even Rincewind did not. But he could feel it sometimes, sidling out of sight behind his Ego, biding its time . . .

On the front of the Octavo had been a representation of Bel-Shamharoth. He was not Evil, for even Evil has a certain vitality – Bel-Shamharoth was the flip side of the coin of which Good and Evil are but one side.

'The Soul Eater. His number lyeth between seven and nine; it is twice four,' Rincewind quoted, his mind frozen with fear. '*Oh no*. Where's the Temple?'

'Hubwards, towards the centre of the forest,' said the dryad. 'It is very old.'

'But who would be so stupid as to worship Bel—him? I mean, devils *yes*, but he's the Soul Eater—'

'There were – certain advantages. And the race that used to live in these parts had strange notions.'

'What happened to them, then?'

'I did say they *used* to live in these parts.' The dryad stood up and stretched out her hand. 'Come. I am Druellae. Come with me and watch your friend's fate. It should be interesting.'

'I'm not sure that—' began Rincewind.

The dryad turned her green eyes on him.

'Do you believe you have a choice?' she asked.

A staircase broad as a major highway wound up through the tree, with vast rooms leading off at every landing. The sourceless yellow light was everywhere. There was also a sound like – Rincewind concentrated, trying to identify it – like far off thunder, or a distant waterfall.

'It's the tree,' said the dryad shortly.

'What's it doing?' said Rincewind.

'Living.'

'I wondered about that. I mean, are we really in a tree? Have I been reduced in size? From outside it looked narrow enough for me to put my arms around.'

'It is.'

'Um, but here I am inside it?'

'You are.'

'Um,' said Rincewind.

Druellae laughed.

'I can see into your mind, false wizard! Am I not a dryad? Do you not know that what you belittle by the name *tree* is but the mere four-dimensional analogue of a whole multidimensional universe which – no, I can see you do not. I should have realized that you weren't a real wizard when I saw you didn't have a staff.'

'Lost it in a fire,' lied Rincewind automatically.

'No hat with magic sigils embroidered on it.'

'It blew off.'

'No familiar.'

'It died. Look, thanks for rescuing me, but if you don't mind I think I ought to be going. If you could show me the way out—'

Something in her expression made him turn around. There were three he-dryads behind him. They were as naked as the woman, and unarmed. That last fact was irrelevant, however. They didn't look as though they would need weapons to fight Rincewind. They looked as though they could shoulder their way through solid rock and beat up a regiment of trolls into the bargain. The three handsome giants looked down at him with wooden menace. Their skins were the colour of walnut husks, and under it muscles bulged like sacks of melons.

He turned around again and grinned weakly at Druellae. Life was beginning to take on a familiar shape again.

'I'm not rescued, am I?' he said. 'I'm captured, right?'

'Of course.'

'And you're not letting me go?' It was a statement.

Druellae shook her head. '*You hurt the Tree.* But you are lucky. Your friend is going to meet Bel-Shamharoth. *You* will only die.'

From behind two hands gripped his shoulders in much the same way that an old tree root coils relentlessly around a pebble.

'With a certain amount of ceremony, of course,' the dryad went on. 'After the Sender of Eight has finished with your friend.'

All Rincewind could manage to say was, 'You know, I never imagined there were he-dryads. Not even in an oak tree.'

One of the giants grinned at him.

Druellae snorted. 'Stupid! Where do you think acorns come from?'

There was a vast empty space like a hall, its roof lost in the golden haze. The endless stair ran right through it.

Several hundred dryads were clustered at the other end of the hall. They parted respectfully when Druellae approached, and stared through Rincewind as he was propelled firmly along behind.

Most of them were females, although there were a few of the giant males among them. They stood like god-shaped statues among the small, intelligent females. Insects, thought Rincewind. The Tree is like a hive.

But why were there dryads at all? As far as he could recall, the tree people had died out centuries before.

They had been out-evolved by humans, like most of the other Twilight Peoples. Only elves and trolls had survived the coming of Man to the discworld; the elves because they were altogether too clever by half, and the trollen folk because they were at least as good as humans at being nasty, spiteful and greedy. Dryads were supposed to have died out, along with gnomes and pixies.

The background roar was louder here. Sometimes a pulsing golden glow would race up the translucent walls until it was lost in the haze overhead. Some power in the air made it vibrate.

'O incompetent wizard,' said Druellae, 'see some magic. Not your weasel-faced tame magic, but root-and-branch magic, the old magic. Wild magic. Watch.'

Fifty or so of the females formed a tight cluster, joined hands and walked backwards until they formed the circumference of a large circle. The rest of the dryads began a low chant. Then, at a nod from Druellae, the circle began to spin widdershins.

As the pace began to quicken and the complicated threads of the chant began to rise Rincewind found himself watching fascinated. He had heard about the Old Magic at University, although it was forbidden to wizards. He knew that when the circle was spinning fast enough against the standing magical field of the discworld itself in its slow turning, the resulting astral friction would build up a vast potential difference which would earth itself by a vast discharge of the Elemental Magical Force.

The circle was a blur now, and the walls of the Tree rang with the echoes of the chant—

Rincewind felt the familiar sticky prickling in the scalp that indicated the build-up of a heavy charge of raw enchantment in the vicinity, and so he was not utterly amazed when, a few seconds later, a shaft of vivid octarine light speared down from the invisible ceiling and focused, crackling, in the centre of the circle.

There it formed an image of a storm-swept, tree-girt hill with a temple on its crest. Its shape did unpleasant things to the eye. Rincewind knew that if it was a temple to Bel-Shamharoth it would have eight sides. (Eight was also the Number of Bel-Shamharoth, which was why a sensible wizard would never mention the number if he could avoid it. Or you'll be eight alive, apprentices were jocularly warned. Bel-Shamharoth was especially attracted to dabblers in magic who, by being as it were beachcombers on the shores of the unnatural, were already half-enmeshed in his nets. Rincewind's room number in his hall of residence had been 7a. He hadn't been surprised.)

Rain streamed off the black walls of the temple. The only sign of life was the horse tethered outside, and it wasn't Twoflower's horse. For one thing, it was too big. It was a white charger with hooves the size of meat dishes and leather harness aglitter with ostentatious gold ornamentation. It was currently enjoying a nosebag.

There was something familiar about it. Rincewind tried to remember where he had seen it before.

It looked as though it was capable of a fair turn of speed, anyway. A speed which, once it had lumbered up to it, it could maintain for a long time. All Rincewind had to do was shake off his guards, fight his way out of the Tree, find the temple and steal the horse out from under whatever it was that Bel-Shamharoth used for a nose.

'The Sender of Eight has two for dinner, it seems,' said Druellae, looking hard at Rincewind. 'Who does that steed belong to, false wizard?'

'I've no idea.'

'No? Well, it does not matter. We shall see soon enough.'

She waved a hand. The focus of the image moved inwards, darted through a great octagonal archway and sped along the corridor within.

There was a figure there, sidling along stealthily with its back against one wall. Rincewind saw the gleam of gold and bronze.

There was no mistaking that shape. He'd seen it many times. The wide chest, the neck like a tree trunk, the surprisingly small head under its wild thatch of black hair looking like a tomato on a coffin ... he could put a name to the creeping figure, and that name was Hrun the Barbarian.

Hrun was one of the Circle Sea's more durable heroes: a fighter of dragons, a despoiler of temples, a hired sword, the kingpost of every street brawl. He could even – and unlike many heroes of Rincewind's acquaintance – speak words of more than two syllables, if given time and maybe a hint or two.

There was a sound on the edge of Rincewind's hearing. It sounded like several skulls bouncing down the steps of some distant dungeon. He looked sideways at his guards to see if they had heard it.

They had all their limited attention focused on Hrun, who was admittedly built on the same lines as themselves. Their hands were resting lightly on the wizard's shoulders.

Rincewind ducked, jerked backwards like a tumbler, and came up running. Behind him he heard Druellae shout, and he redoubled his speed.

Something caught the hood of his robe, which tore off. A he-dryad waiting at the stairs spread his arms wide and grinned woodenly at the figure hurtling towards him. Without breaking his stride Rincewind ducked again, so low that his chin was on a level with his knees, while a fist like a log sizzled through the air by his ear.

Ahead of him a whole spinney of the tree men awaited. He spun around, dodged another blow from the puzzled guard, and sped back towards the circle, passing on the way the dryads who were pursuing him and leaving them as disorganized as a set of skittles.

But there were still more in front, pushing their way through the crowds of females and smacking their fists into the horny palms of their hands with anticipatory concentration.

'Stand still, false wizard,' said Druellae, stepping forward. Behind her the enchanted dancers spun on; the focus of the circle was now drifting along a violet-lit corridor.

Rincewind cracked.

'Will you knock that off!' he snarled. 'Let's just get this straight, right? I *am* a real wizard!' He stamped a foot petulantly.

'Indeed?' said the dryad. 'Then let us see you pass a spell.'

'Uh—' began Rincewind. The fact was that, since the ancient and mysterious spell had squatted in his mind, he had been unable to remember even the simplest cantrap for, say, killing cockroaches or scratching the small of his back without using his hands. The mages at Unseen University had tried to explain this by suggesting that the involuntary memorizing of the spell had, as it were, tied up all his spell-retention cells. In his darker moments Rincewind had come up with his own explanation as to why even minor spells refused to stay in his head for more than a few seconds.

They were scared, he decided.

'Um—' he repeated.

'A small one would do,' said Druellae, watching him curl his lips in a frenzy of anger and embarrassment. She signalled, and a couple of he-dryads closed in.

The Spell chose that moment to vault into the temporarily abandoned saddle of Rincewind's consciousness. He felt it sitting there, leering defiantly at him.

'I do know a spell,' he said wearily.

'Yes? Pray tell,' said Druellae.

Rincewind wasn't sure that he dared, although the spell was trying to take control of his tongue. He fought it.

'You thed you could read by bind,' he said indistinctly. 'Read it.'

She stepped forward, looking mockingly into his eyes.

Her smile froze. Her hands raised protectively, she crouched back. From her throat came a sound of pure terror.

Rincewind looked around. The rest of the dryads were also backing away. What had he done? Something terrible, apparently.

But in his experience it was only a matter of time before the normal balance of the universe restored itself and started doing the usual terrible things to him. He backed away, ducked between the still-spinning dryads who were creating the magic circle, and watched to see what Druellae would do next.

'Grab him,' she screamed. 'Take him a long way from the Tree and kill him!'

Rincewind turned and bolted.

Across the focus of the circle.

There was a brilliant flash.

There was a sudden darkness.

There was a vaguely Rincewind-shaped violet shadow, dwindling to a point and winking out.

There was nothing at all.

Hrun the Barbarian crept soundlessly along the corridors, which were lit with a light so violet that it was almost black. His earlier confusion was gone. This was obviously a magical temple, and that explained everything.

It explained why, earlier in the afternoon, he had espied a chest by the side of the track while riding through this benighted forest. Its top was invitingly open, displaying much gold. But when he had leapt off his horse to approach it the chest had sprouted legs and had gone trotting off into the forest, stopping again a few hundred yards away.

Now, after several hours of teasing pursuit, he had lost it in these hell-lit tunnels. On the whole, the unpleasant carvings and occasional disjointed skeletons he passed held no fears for Hrun. This was partly because he was not exceptionally bright while being at the same time exceptionally unimaginative, but it was also because odd carvings and perilous tunnels were all in a day's work. He spent a great deal of time in similar situations, seeking gold or demons or distressed virgins and relieving them respectively of their owners, their lives and at least one cause of their distress.

Observe Hrun, as he leaps cat-footed across a suspicious tunnel mouth. Even in this violet light his skin gleams coppery. There is much gold about his person, in the form of anklets and wristlets, but otherwise he is naked except for a leopardskin loincloth. He took that in the steaming forests of Howondaland, after killing its owner with his teeth.

In his right hand he carried the magical black sword Kring, which was forged from a thunderbolt and has a soul but suffers no scabbard. Hrun had stolen it only three days before from the impregnable palace of the Archmandrite of B'Ituni, and he was already regretting it. It was beginning to get on his nerves.

'I tell you it went down that last passage on the right,' hissed Kring in a voice like the scrape of a blade over stone.

'Be silent!'

'All I said was—'

'Shut up!'

* * *

And Twoflower . . .

He was lost, he knew that. Either the building was much bigger than it looked, or he was now on some wide underground level without having gone down any steps, or – as he was beginning to suspect – the inner dimensions of the place disobeyed a fairly basic rule of architecture by being bigger than the outside. And why all these strange lights? They were eight-sided crystals set at regular intervals in the walls and ceiling, and they shed a rather unpleasant glow that didn't so much illuminate as outline the darkness.

And whoever had done those carvings on the wall, Twoflower thought charitably, had probably been drinking too much. For years.

On the other hand, it was certainly a fascinating building. Its builders had been obsessed with the number eight. The floor was a continuous mosaic of eight-sided tiles, the corridor walls and ceilings were angled to give the corridors eight sides if the walls and ceilings were counted and, in those places where part of the masonry had fallen in, Twoflower noticed that even the stones themselves had eight sides.

'I don't like it,' said the picture imp, from his box around Twoflower's neck.

'Why not?' enquired Twoflower.

'It's weird.'

'But you're a demon. Demons can't call things weird. I mean, what's weird to a demon?'

'Oh, you know,' said the demon cautiously, glancing around nervously and shifting from claw to claw. 'Things. Stuff.'

Twoflower looked at him sternly. 'What things?'

The demon coughed nervously (demons do not breathe; however, every intelligent being, whether it breathes or not, coughs nervously at some time in its life. And this was it as far as the demon was concerned).

'Oh, things,' it said wretchedly. 'Evil things. Things we don't talk about is the point I'm broadly trying to get across, master.'

Twoflower shook his head wearily. 'I wish Rincewind was here,' he said. 'He'd know what to do.'

'*Him?*' sneered the demon. 'Can't see a wizard coming here. They can't have anything to do with the number eight.' The demon slapped a hand across his mouth guiltily.

Twoflower looked up at the ceiling.

'What was that?' he asked. 'Didn't you hear something?'

'Me? Hear? No! Not a thing!' the demon insisted. It jerked back into its box and slammed the door. Twoflower tapped on it. The door opened a crack.

'It sounded like a stone moving,' he explained. The door banged shut. Twoflower shrugged.

'The place is probably falling to bits,' he said to himself. He stood up.

'I say!' he shouted. 'Is anyone there?'

AIR, Air, air, replied the dark tunnels.

'Hallo?' he tried.

LO, Lo, lo.

'I know there's someone here, I just heard you playing dice!'

ICE, Ice, ice.

'Look, I had just—'

Twoflower stopped. The reason for this was the bright point of light that had popped into existence a few feet from his eyes. It grew rapidly, and after a few seconds was the tiny bright shape of a man. At this stage it began to make a noise, or, rather, Twoflower started to hear the noise it had been making all along. It sounded like a sliver of a scream, caught in one long instant of time.

The iridescent man was doll-sized now, a tortured shape tumbling in slow motion while hanging in mid-air. Twoflower wondered why he had thought of the phrase 'a sliver of a scream' . . . and began to wish he hadn't.

It was beginning to look like Rincewind. The wizard's mouth was open, and his face was brilliantly lit by the light of – what? Strange suns, Twoflower found himself thinking. Suns men don't usually see. He shivered.

Now the turning wizard was half man-size. At that point the growth was faster, there was a sudden crowded moment, a rush of air, and an explosion of sound. Rincewind tumbled out of the air, screaming. He hit the floor hard, choked, then rolled over with his head cradled in his arms and his body curled up tightly.

When the dust had settled Twoflower reached out gingerly and tapped the wizard on the shoulder. The human ball rolled up tighter.

'It's me,' explained Twoflower helpfully. The wizard unrolled a fraction.

'What?' he said.

'Me.'

In one movement Rincewind unrolled and bounced up in front of the little man, his hands gripping his shoulders desperately. His eyes were wild and wide.

'Don't say it!' he hissed. 'Don't say it and we might get out!'

'Get out? How did you get in? Don't you know—'

'Don't say it!'

Twoflower backed away from this madman.

'Don't say it!'

'Don't say what?'

'The number!'

'Number?' said Twoflower. 'Hey, Rincewind—'

'Yes, number! Between seven and nine. Four plus four!'

'What, ei—'

Rincewind's hands clapped over the man's mouth. 'Say it and we're doomed. Just don't think about it, right. Trust me!'

'I don't understand!' wailed Twoflower. Rincewind relaxed slightly, which was to say that he still made a violin string look like a bowl of jelly.

'Come on,' he said. 'Let's try and get out. And I'll try and tell you.'

After the first Age of Magic the disposal of grimoires began to become a severe problem on the discworld. A spell is still a spell even when imprisoned temporarily in parchment and ink. It has potency. This is not a problem while the book's owner still lives, but on his death the spell book becomes a source of uncontrolled power that cannot easily be defused.

In short, spell books leak magic. Various solutions have been tried. Countries near the Rim simply loaded down the books of dead mages with leaden pentalphas and threw them over the Edge. Near the Hub less satisfactory alternatives were available. Inserting the offending books in canisters of negatively polarized octiron and sinking them in the fathomless depths of the sea was one (burial in deep caves on land was earlier ruled out after some districts complained of walking trees and five-headed cats) but before long the magic seeped out and eventually fishermen complained of shoals of invisible fish or psychic clams.

A temporary solution was the construction, in various centres of magical lore, of large rooms made of denatured octiron, which is impervious to most forms of magic. Here the more critical grimoires could be stored until their potency had attenuated.

That was how there came to be at Unseen University the Octavo, greatest of all grimoires, formerly owned by the Creator of the Universe. It was this book that Rincewind had once opened for a bet. He had only a second to stare at a page before setting off various alarm spells, but that was time enough for one spell to leap from it and settle in his memory like a toad in a stone.

'Then what?' said Twoflower.

'Oh, they dragged me out. Thrashed me, of course.'

'And no-one knows what the spell *does*?'

Rincewind shook his head.

'It'd vanished from the page,' he said. 'No-one will know until I say it. Or until I die, of course. Then it will sort of say itself. For all I know it stops the universe, or ends Time, or anything.'

Twoflower patted him on the shoulder.

'No sense in brooding,' he said cheerfully. 'Let's have another look for a way out.'

Rincewind shook his head. All the terror had been spent now. He had broken through the terror barrier, perhaps, and was in the dead calm state of mind that lies on the other side. Anyway, he had ceased to gibber.

'We're doomed,' he stated. 'We've been walking around all night. I tell you, this place is a spiderweb. It doesn't matter which way we go, we'll end up in the centre.'

'It was kind of you to come looking for me, anyway,' said Twoflower. 'How did you manage it exactly? It was very impressive.'

'Oh, well,' began the wizard awkwardly. 'I just thought "I can't leave old Twoflower there" and—'

'So what we've got to do now is find this Bel-Shamharoth person and explain things to him and perhaps he'll let us out,' said Twoflower.

Rincewind ran a finger around his ear.

'It must be the funny echoes in here,' he said. 'I thought I heard you use words like *find* and *explain*.'

'That's right.'

Rincewind glared at him in the hellish purple glow.

'*Find* Bel-Shamharoth?' he said.

'Yes. We don't have to get involved.'

'Find the Soul Render and not get involved? Just give him a nod, I suppose, and ask the way to the exit?

Explain things to the Sender of Eignnnngh,' Rincewind bit off the end of the word just in time and finished, 'You're *insane*! Hey! *Come back!*'

He darted down the passage after Twoflower, and after a few moments came to a halt with a groan.

The violet light was intense here, giving everything new and unpleasant colours. This wasn't a passage, it was a wide room with walls to a number that Rincewind didn't dare to contemplate, and ei— and 7a passages radiating from it.

Rincewind saw, a little way off, a low altar with the same number of sides as four times two. It didn't occupy the centre of the room, however. The centre was occupied by a huge stone slab with twice as many sides as a square. It looked massive. In the strange light it appeared to be slightly tilted, with one edge standing proud of the slabs around it.

Twoflower was standing on it.

'Hey. Rincewind! Look what's here!'

The Luggage came ambling down one of the other passages that radiated from the room.

'That's great,' said Rincewind. 'Fine. It can lead us out of here. Now.'

Twoflower was already rummaging in the chest.

'Yes,' he said. 'After I've taken a few pictures. Just let me fit the attachment—'

'I said *now*—'

Rincewind stopped. Hrun the Barbarian was standing in the passage mouth directly opposite him, a great black sword held in one ham-sized fist.

'You?' said Hrun uncertainly.

'Ahaha. Yes,' said Rincewind. 'Hrun, isn't it?

Long time no see. What brings you here?'

Hrun pointed to the Luggage.

'That,' he said. This much conversation seemed to exhaust Hrun. Then he added, in a tone that combined statement, claim, threat and ultimatum: 'Mine.'

'It belongs to Twoflower here,' said Rincewind. 'Here's a tip. Don't touch it.'

It dawned on him that this was precisely the wrong thing to say, but Hrun had already pushed Twoflower away and was reaching for the Luggage . . .

. . . which sprouted legs, backed away, and raised its lid threateningly. In the uncertain light Rincewind thought he could see rows of enormous teeth, white as bleached beechwood.

'Hrun,' he said quickly, 'there's something I ought to tell you.'

Hrun turned a puzzled face to him.

'What?' he said.

'It's about numbers. Look, you know if you add seven and one, or three and five, or take two from ten, you get a number. While you're here don't say it, and we might all stand a chance of getting out of here alive. Or merely just dead.'

'Who is he?' asked Twoflower. He was holding a cage in his hands, dredged from the bottom-most depths of the Luggage. It appeared to be full of sulking pink lizards.

'I am Hrun,' said Hrun proudly. Then he looked at Rincewind.

'What?' he said.

'Just don't say it, OK?' said Rincewind.

He looked at the sword in Hrun's hand. It was

black, the sort of black that is less a colour than a graveyard of colours, and there was a highly ornate runic inscription up the blade. More noticeable still was the faint octarine glow that surrounded it. The sword must have noticed him, too, because it suddenly spoke in a voice like a claw being scraped across glass.

'Strange,' it said. 'Why can't he say eight?'

EIGHT, Hate, ate, said the echoes. There was the faintest of grinding noises, deep under the earth.

And the echoes, although they became softer, refused to die away. They bounced from wall to wall, crossing and recrossing, and the violet light flickered in time with the sound.

'You did it!' screamed Rincewind. 'I said you shouldn't say eight!'

He stopped, appalled at himself. But the word was out now, and joined its colleagues in the general susurration.

Rincewind turned to run, but the air suddenly seemed to be thicker than treacle. A charge of magic bigger than he had ever seen was building up; when he moved, in painful slow motion, his limbs left trails of golden sparks that traced their shape in the air.

Behind him there was a rumble as the great octagonal slab rose into the air, hung for a moment on one edge, and crashed down on the floor.

Something thin and black snaked out of the pit and wrapped itself around his ankle. He screamed as he landed heavily on the vibrating flagstones. The tentacle started to pull him across the floor.

Then Twoflower was in front of him, reaching out

for his hands. He grasped the little man's arms desperately and they lay looking into each other's faces. Rincewind slid on, even so.

'What's holding you?' he gasped.

'N-nothing!' said Twoflower. 'What's happening?'

'I'm being dragged into this pit, what do you think?'

'Oh Rincewind, I'm sorry—'

'*You're* sorry—'

There was a noise like a singing saw and the pressure on Rincewind's legs abruptly ceased. He turned his head and saw Hrun crouched by the pit, his sword a blur as it hacked at the tentacles racing out towards him.

Twoflower helped the wizard to his feet and they crouched by the altar stone, watching the manic figure as it battled the questing arms.

'It won't work,' said Rincewind. 'The Sender can materialize tentacles. *What are you doing?*'

Twoflower was feverishly attaching the cage of subdued lizards to the picturebox, which he had mounted on a tripod.

'I've just got to get a picture of this,' he muttered. 'It's stupendous! Can you hear me, imp?'

The picture imp opened his tiny hatch, glanced momentarily at the scene around the pit, and vanished into the box. Rincewind jumped as something touched his leg, and brought his heel down on a questing tentacle.

'Come on,' he said. 'Time to go zoom.' He grabbed Twoflower's arm, but the tourist resisted.

'Run away and leave Hrun with that thing?' he said.

Rincewind looked blank. 'Why not?' he said. 'It's his job.'

'But it'll kill him!'

'It could be worse,' said Rincewind.

'What?'

'It could be *us*,' Rincewind pointed out logically. 'Come on!'

Twoflower pointed. 'Hey!' he said. 'It's got my Luggage!'

Before Rincewind could restrain him Twoflower ran around the edge of the pit to the box, which was being dragged across the floor while its lid snapped ineffectually at the tentacle that held it. The little man began to kick at the tentacle in fury.

Another one snapped out of the mêlée around Hrun and caught him around the waist. Hrun himself was already an indistinct shape amid the tightening coils. Even as Rincewind stared in horror the Hero's sword was wrenched from his grasp and hurled against a wall.

'Your spell!' shouted Twoflower.

Rincewind did not move. He was looking at the Thing rising out of the pit. It was an enormous eye, and it was staring directly at him. He whimpered as a tentacle fastened itself around his waist.

The words of the spell rose unbidden in his throat. He opened his mouth as in a dream, shaping it around the first barbaric syllable.

Another tentacle shot out like a whip and coiled around his throat, choking him. Staggering and gasping, Rincewind was dragged across the floor.

One flailing arm caught Twoflower's picturebox as

it skittered past on its tripod. He snatched it up instinctively, as his ancestors might have snatched up a
stone when faced with a marauding tiger. If only he
could get enough room to swing it against the Eye . . .

. . . the Eye filled the whole universe in front of him.
Rincewind felt his will draining away like water from
a sieve.

In front of him the torpid lizards stirred in their
cage on the picturebox. Irrationally, as a man about
to be beheaded notices every scratch and stain on the
executioner's block, Rincewind saw that they had
overlarge tails that were bluish-white and, he realized,
throbbing alarmingly.

As he was drawn towards the Eye the terror-struck
Rincewind raised the box protectively, and at the
same time heard the picture imp say, 'They're about
ripe now, can't hold them any longer. Everyone smile,
please.'

There was a—

—flash of light so white and so bright—

—it didn't seem like light at all.

Bel-Shamharoth screamed, a sound that started in
the far ultrasonic and finished somewhere in
Rincewind's bowels. The tentacles went momentarily
as stiff as rods, hurling their various cargoes around
the room, before bunching up protectively in front
of the abused Eye. The whole mass dropped into the
pit and a moment later the big slab was snatched up
by several dozen tentacles and slammed into place,
leaving a number of thrashing limbs trapped around
the edge.

Hrun landed rolling, bounced off a wall and came

up on his feet. He found his sword and started to chop methodically at the doomed arms. Rincewind lay on the floor, concentrating on not going mad. A hollow wooden noise made him turn his head.

The Luggage had landed on its curved lid. Now it was rocking angrily and kicking its little legs in the air.

Warily, Rincewind looked around for Twoflower. The little man was in a crumpled heap against the wall, but at least he was groaning.

The wizard pulled himself across the floor, painfully, and whispered, 'What the hell was that?'

'Why were they so bright?' muttered Twoflower. 'Gods, my head . . .'

'So bright?' said Rincewind. He looked across the floor to the cage on the picturebox. The lizards inside, now noticeably thinner, were watching him with interest.

'The salamanders,' moaned Twoflower. 'The picture'll be over-exposed, I know it . . .'

'They're salamanders?' asked Rincewind incredulously.

'Of course. Standard attachment.'

Rincewind staggered across to the box and picked it up. He'd seen salamanders before, of course, but they had been small specimens. They had also been floating in a jar of pickle in the curiobiological museum down in the cellars of Unseen University, since live salamanders were extinct around the Circle Sea.

He tried to remember the little he knew about them. They were magical creatures. They also had no mouths, since they subsisted entirely on the nourishing quality of the octarine wavelength in the discworld's sunlight, which they absorbed through their skins. Of course, they also absorbed the rest of the sunlight as well, storing it in a special sac until it was excreted in the normal way. A desert inhabited by discworld salamanders was a veritable lighthouse at night.

Rincewind put them down and nodded grimly. With all the octarine light in this magical place the creatures had been gorging themselves, and then nature had taken its course.

The picturebox sidled away on its tripod. Rincewind aimed a kick at it, and missed. He was beginning to dislike sapient pearwood.

Something small stung his cheek. He brushed it away irritably.

He looked around at a sudden grinding noise, and a voice like a carving knife cutting through silk said, 'This is very undignified.'

'Shuddup,' said Hrun. He was using Kring to lever the top off the altar. He looked up at Rincewind and grinned. Rincewind hoped that rictus-strung grimace was a grin.

'Mighty magic,' commented the barbarian, pushing down heavily on the complaining blade with a hand the size of a ham. 'Now we share the treasure, eh?'

Rincewind grunted as something small and hard struck his ear. There was a gust of wind, hardly felt.

'How do you know there's treasure in there?' he said.

Hrun heaved, and managed to hook his fingers under the stone. 'You find chokeapples under a chokeapple tree,' he said. 'You find treasure under altars. Logic.'

He gritted his teeth. The stone swung up and landed heavily on the floor.

This time something struck Rincewind's hand, heavily. He clawed at the air and looked at the thing he had caught. It was a piece of stone with five-plus-three sides. He looked up at the ceiling. Should it be sagging like that? Hrun hummed a little tune as he began to pull crumbling leather from the desecrated altar.

The air crackled, fluoresced, hummed. Intangible winds gripped the wizard's robe, flapping it out in eddies of blue and green sparks. Around Rincewind's head mad, half-formed spirits howled and gibbered as they were sucked past.

He tried raising a hand. It was immediately surrounded by a glowing octarine corona as the rising magical wind roared past. The gale raced through the room without stirring one iota of dust, yet it was blowing Rincewind's eyelids inside out. It screamed along the tunnels, its banshee-wail bouncing madly from stone to stone.

Twoflower staggered up, bent double in the teeth of the astral gale.

'What the hell is *this*?' he shouted.

Rincewind half-turned. Immediately the howling wind caught him, nearly pitching him over. Poltergeist eddies, spinning in the rushing air, snatched at his feet.

Hrun's arm shot out and caught him. A moment later he and Twoflower had been dragged into the lee of the ravaged altar, and lay panting on the floor. Beside them the talking sword Kring sparkled, its magical field boosted a hundredfold by the storm.

'Hold on!' screamed Rincewind.

'The wind!' shouted Twoflower. 'Where's it coming from? Where's it blowing *to*?' He looked into Rincewind's mask of sheer terror, which made him redouble his own grip on the stones.

'We're doomed,' murmured Rincewind, while overhead the roof cracked and shifted. 'Where do shadows come from? *That's* where the wind is blowing!'

What was in fact happening, as the wizard knew, was that as the abused spirit of Bel-Shamharoth sank through the deeper chthonic planes his brooding spirit was being sucked out of the very stones into the region which, according to the discworld's most reliable priests, was both under the ground and Somewhere Else. In consequence his temple was being abandoned to the ravages of Time, who for thousands of shamefaced years had been reluctant to go near the place. Now the suddenly released, accumulated weight of all those pent-up seconds was bearing down heavily on the unbraced stones.

Hrun glanced up at the widening cracks and sighed. Then he put two fingers into his mouth and whistled.

Strangely the real sound rang out loudly over the pseudosound of the widening astral whirlpool that was forming in the middle of the great octagonal slab. It was followed by a hollow echo which sounded, Rincewind fancied, strangely like the bouncing of strange bones. Then came a noise with no hint of strangeness. It was hollow hoofbeats.

Hrun's warhorse cantered through a creaking

archway and reared up by its master, its mane streaming in the gale. The barbarian pulled himself to his feet and slung his treasure bags into a sack that hung from the saddle, then hauled himself onto the beast's back. He reached down and grabbed Twoflower by the scruff of his neck, dragging him across the saddle tree. As the horse turned around Rincewind took a desperate leap and landed behind Hrun, who raised no objection.

The horse pounded surefooted along the tunnels, leaping sudden slides of rubble and adroitly side-stepping huge stones as they thundered down from the straining roof. Rincewind, clinging on grimly, looked behind them.

No wonder the horse was moving so swiftly. Close behind, speeding through the flickering violet light, were a large ominous-looking chest and a picturebox that skittered along dangerously on its three legs. So great was the ability of sapient pearwood to follow its master anywhere, the grave-goods of dead emperors had traditionally been made of it . . .

They reached the outer air a moment before the octagonal arch finally broke and smashed into the flags.

The sun was rising. Behind them a column of dust rose as the temple collapsed in on itself, but they did not look back. That was a shame, because Twoflower might have been able to obtain pictures unusual even by discworld standards.

There was movement in the smoking ruins. They seemed to be growing a green carpet. Then an oak tree spiralled up, branching out like an exploding green rocket, and was in the middle of a venerable copse even before the tips of its aged branches had stopped quivering. A beech burst out like a fungus, matured, rotted, and fell in a cloud of tinder dust amid its struggling offspring. Already the temple was a half-buried heap of mossy stones.

But Time, having initially gone for the throat, was now setting out to complete the job. The boiling interface between decaying magic and ascendant entropy roared down the hill and overtook the galloping horse, whose riders, being themselves creatures of Time, completely failed to notice it. But it lashed into the enchanted forest with the whip of centuries.

'Impressive, isn't it?' observed a voice by Rincewind's knee as the horse cantered through the haze of decaying timber and falling leaves.

The voice had an eerie metallic ring to it. Rincewind looked down at Kring the sword. It had a couple of rubies set in the pommel. He got the impression they were watching him.

From the moorland rimwards of the wood they watched the battle between the trees and Time, which could only have one ending. It was a sort of cabaret to the main business of the halt, which was the consumption of quite a lot of a bear which had incautiously come within bowshot of Hrun.

Rincewind watched Hrun over the top of his slab of greasy meat. Hrun going about the business of being a hero, he realized, was quite different to the wine-bibbing, carousing Hrun who occasionally came to Ankh-Morpork. He was cat-cautious, lithe as a panther, and thoroughly at home.

And I've survived Bel-Shamharoth, Rincewind reminded himself. Fantastic.

Twoflower was helping the hero sort through the treasure stolen from the temple. It was mostly silver set with unpleasant purple stones. Representations of spiders, octopi and the tree-dwelling octarsier of the hubland wastes figured largely in the heap.

Rincewind tried to shut his ears to the grating voice beside him. It was no use.

'—and then I belonged to the Pasha of Re'durat and played a prominent part in the battle of the Great Nef, which is where I received the slight nick you may have noticed some two-thirds of the way up my blade,' Kring was saying from its temporary home in a tussock. 'Some infidel was wearing an octiron collar, most unsporting, and of course I was a lot sharper in those days and my master used to use me to cut silk handkerchiefs in mid-air and – am I boring you?'

'Huh? Oh, no, no, not at all. It's all very interesting,' said Rincewind, with his eyes still on Hrun. How trustworthy would he be? Here they were, out in the wilds, there were trolls about . . .

'I could see you were a cultured person,' Kring went on. 'So seldom do I get to meet really interesting people, for any length of time, anyway. What I'd really like is a nice mantelpiece to hang over, somewhere nice and quiet. I spent a couple of hundred years on the bottom of a lake once.'

'That must have been fun,' said Rincewind absently.

'Not really,' said Kring.

'No, I suppose not.'

'What I'd *really* like is to be a ploughshare. I don't

know what that is, but it sounds like an existence with some point to it.'

Twoflower hurried over to the wizard.

'I had a great idea,' he burbled.

'Yah,' said Rincewind, wearily. 'Why don't we get Hrun to accompany us to Quirm?'

Twoflower looked amazed. 'How did you know?' he said.

'I just thought you'd think it,' said Rincewind.

Hrun ceased stuffing silverware into his saddlebags and grinned encouragingly at them. Then his eyes strayed back to the Luggage.

'If we had him with us, who'd attack us?' said Twoflower.

Rincewind scratched his chin. 'Hrun?' he suggested.

'But we saved his life in the Temple!'

'Well, if by *attack* you mean *kill*,' said Rincewind, 'I don't think he'd do that. He's not that sort. He'd just rob us and tie us up and leave us for the wolves, I expect.'

'Oh, come *on*.'

'Look, this is real life,' snapped Rincewind. 'I mean, here you are, carrying around a box full of gold, don't you think anyone in their right minds would jump at the chance of pinching it?' I would, he added mentally – if I hadn't seen what the Luggage does to prying fingers.

Then the answer hit him. He looked from Hrun to the picturebox. The picture imp was doing its laundry in a tiny tub, while the salamanders dozed in their cage.

'I've got an idea,' he said. 'I mean, what is it heroes

really want?'

'Gold?' said Twoflower.

'No. I mean *really* want.'

Twoflower frowned. 'I don't quite understand,' he said. Rincewind picked up the picturebox.

'Hrun,' he said. 'Come over here, will you?'

The days passed peacefully. True, a small band of bridge trolls tried to ambush them on one occasion, and a party of brigands nearly caught them unawares one night (but unwisely tried to investigate the Luggage before slaughtering the sleepers). Hrun demanded, and got, double pay for both occasions.

'If any harm comes to us,' said Rincewind, 'then there will be no-one to operate the magic box. No more pictures of Hrun, you understand?'

Hrun nodded, his eyes fixed on the latest picture. It showed Hrun striking a heroic pose, with one foot on a heap of slain trolls.

'Me and you and little friend Two Flowers, we all get on hokay,' he said. 'Also tomorrow, may we get a better profile, hokay?'

He carefully wrapped the picture in trollskin and stowed it in his saddlebag, along with the others.

'It seems to be working,' said Twoflower admiringly, as Hrun rode ahead to scout the road.

'Sure,' said Rincewind. 'What heroes like best is themselves.'

'You're getting quite good at using the picturebox, you know that?'

'Yar.'

'So you might like to have this.' Twoflower held out

a picture.

'What is it?' asked Rincewind.

'Oh, just the picture you took in the temple.'

Rincewind looked in horror. There, bordered by a few glimpses of tentacle, was a huge, whorled, calloused, potion-stained and unfocused thumb.

'That's the story of my life,' he said wearily.

'You win,' said Fate, pushing the heap of souls across the gaming table. The assembled gods relaxed. 'There will be other games,' he added.

The Lady smiled into two eyes that were like holes in the universe.

And then there was nothing but the ruin of the forests and a cloud of dust on the horizon, which drifted away on the breeze. And, sitting on a pitted and moss-grown milestone, a black and raggedy figure. His was the air of one who is unjustly put upon, who is dreaded and feared, yet who is the only friend of the poor and the best doctor for the mortally wounded.

Death, although of course completely eyeless, watched Rincewind disappearing with what would, had His face possessed any mobility at all, have been a frown. Death, although exceptionally busy at all times, decided that He now had a hobby. There was something about the wizard that irked Him beyond measure. He didn't keep appointments for one thing.

I'LL GET YOU YET, CULLY, said Death, in the voice like the slamming of leaden coffin lids, SEE IF I DON'T.

THE LURE OF
THE WYRM

IT WAS CALLED THE WYRMBERG and it rose almost one half of a mile above the green valley; a mountain huge, grey and upside down.

At its base it was a mere score of yards across. Then it rose through clinging cloud, curving gracefully outward like an upturned trumpet until it was truncated by a plateau fully a quarter of a mile across. There was a tiny forest up there, its greenery cascading over the lip. There were buildings. There was even a small river, tumbling over the edge in a waterfall so wind-whipped that it reached the ground as rain.

There were also a number of cave mouths, a few yards below the plateau. They had a crudely carved, regular look about them, so that on this crisp autumn morning the Wyrmberg hung over the clouds like a giant's dovecote.

This would mean that the 'doves' had a wingspan slightly in excess of forty yards.

'I knew it,' said Rincewind. 'We're in a strong magical field.'

Twoflower and Hrun looked around the little hollow where they had made their noonday halt. Then they looked at each other.

The horses were quietly cropping the rich grass by the stream. Yellow butterflies skittered among the bushes. There was a smell of thyme and a buzzing of bees. The wild pig on the spit sizzled gently.

Hrun shrugged and went back to oiling his biceps. They gleamed.

'Looks alright to me,' he said.

'Try tossing a coin,' said Rincewind.

'What?'

'Go on. Toss a coin.'

'Hokay,' said Hrun. 'If it gives you any pleasure.' He reached into his pouch and withdrew a handful of loose change plundered from a dozen realms. With some care he selected a Zchloty leaden quarter-iotum and balanced it on a purple thumbnail.

'You call,' he said. 'Heads or—' he inspected the reverse with an air of intense concentration, 'some sort of a fish with legs.'

'When it's in the air,' said Rincewind. Hrun grinned and flicked his thumb.

The iotum rose, spinning.

'Edge,' said Rincewind, without looking at it.

Magic never dies. It merely fades away.

Nowhere was this more evident on the wide blue expanse of the discworld than in those areas that had been the scene of the great battles of the Mage Wars, which had happened very shortly after Creation. In those days magic in its raw state had been widely available, and had been eagerly utilized by the First Men in their war against the Gods.

The precise origins of the Mage Wars have been lost in the fogs of Time, but disc philosophers agree that the First Men, shortly after their creation, understandably lost their temper. And great and pyrotechnic were the battles that followed – the sun wheeled across the sky, the seas boiled, weird storms ravaged the land, small white pigeons mysteriously appeared in people's clothing, and the very stability of the disc (carried as it was through space on the backs of four giant turtle-riding elephants) was threatened. This resulted in stern action by the Old High Ones, to whom even the Gods themselves are answerable. The Gods were banished to high places, men were re-created a good deal smaller, and much of the old wild magic was sucked out of the earth.

That did not solve the problem of those places on the disc which, during the wars, had suffered a direct hit by a spell. The magic faded away – slowly, over the millennia, releasing as it decayed myriads of sub-astral particles that severely distorted the reality around it . . .

Rincewind, Twoflower and Hrun stared at the coin.

'Edge it is,' said Hrun. 'Well, you're a wizard. So what?'

'I don't do – that sort of spell.'

'You mean you can't.'

Rincewind ignored this, because it was true. 'Try it again,' he suggested.

Hrun pulled out a fistful of coins.

The first two landed in the usual manner. So did the fourth. The third landed on its edge and balanced there. The fifth turned into a small yellow caterpillar and crawled away. The sixth, upon reaching its zenith, vanished with a sharp 'spang!' A moment later there was a small thunder clap.

'Hey, that one was silver!' exclaimed Hrun, rising to his feet and staring upwards. 'Bring it back!'

'I don't know where it's gone,' said Rincewind wearily. 'It's probably still accelerating. The ones I tried this morning didn't come down, anyway.'

Hrun was still staring into the sky.

'What?' said Twoflower.

Rincewind sighed. He had been dreading this.

'We've strayed into a zone with a high magical index,' he said. 'Don't ask me how. Once upon a time a really powerful magic field must have been generated here, and we're feeling the after-effects.'

'Precisely,' said a passing bush.

Hrun's head jerked down.

'You mean this is one of *those* places?' he asked. 'Let's get out of here!'

'Right,' agreed Rincewind. 'If we retrace our steps we might make it. We can stop every mile or so and toss a coin.'

He stood up urgently and started stuffing things into his saddlebags.

'What?' said Twoflower.

Rincewind stopped. 'Look,' he snapped. 'Just don't argue. Come *on.*'

'It looks alright,' said Twoflower. 'Just a bit under-populated that's all . . .'

'Yes,' said Rincewind. 'Odd, isn't it? Come *on!*'

There was a noise high above them, like a strip of leather being slapped on a wet rock. Something glassy and indistinct passed over Rincewind's head, throwing up a cloud of ashes from the fire, and the pig carcass took off from the spit and rocketed into the sky.

It banked to avoid a clump of trees, righted itself, roared around in a tight circle, and headed hubwards leaving a trail of hot pork-fat droplets.

'What are they doing now?' asked the old man.

The young woman glanced at the scrying glass.

'Heading rimwards at speed,' she reported. 'By the way – they've still got that box on legs.'

The old man chuckled, an oddly disturbing sound in the dark and dusty crypt. 'Sapient pearwood,' he said. 'Remarkable. Yes, I think we will have that. Please see to it, my dear – before they go beyond your power, perhaps?'

'Silence! Or—'

'Or what, Liessa?' said the old man (in this dim light there was something odd about the way he was slumped in the stone chair). 'You killed me once already, remember?'

She snorted and stood up, tossing back her hair scornfully. It was red, flecked with gold. Erect, Liessa Wyrmbidder was entirely a magnificent sight. She was also almost naked, except for a couple of mere scraps of the lightest chain mail and riding boots of iridescent dragonhide. In one boot was thrust a riding crop, unusual in that it was as long as a spear and tipped with tiny steel barbs.

'My power will be quite sufficient,' she said coldly.

The indistinct figure appeared to nod, or at least to wobble. 'As you keep assuring me,' he said. Liessa snorted, and strode out of the hall.

Her father did not bother to watch her go. One reason for this was, of course, that since he had been dead for three months his eyes were in any case not in the best of condition. The other was that as a wizard – even a dead wizard of the fifteenth grade – his optic nerves had long since become attuned to seeing into levels and dimensions far removed from common reality, and were therefore somewhat inefficient at observing the merely mundane. (During his life they had appeared to others to be eight-faceted and eerily insectile.) Besides, since he was now suspended in the narrow space between the living world and the dark shadow-world of Death he could survey the whole of Causality itself. That was why, apart from a mild hope that this time his wretched daughter would get herself killed, he did not devote his considerable powers to learning more about the three travellers galloping desperately out of his realm.

Several hundred yards away, Liessa was in a strange humour as she strode down the worn steps that led into the hollow heart of the Wyrmberg, followed by half a dozen Riders. Would this be the opportunity? Perhaps here was the key to break the deadlock, the key to the throne of the Wyrmberg. It was rightfully hers, of course; but tradition said that only a man could rule the Wyrmberg. That irked Liessa, and when she was angry the Power flowed stronger and the dragons were especially big and ugly.

If she had a man, things would be different. Someone who, for preference, was a big strapping lad but short on brains. Someone who would do what he was told.

The biggest of the three now fleeing the dragon-lands might do. And if it turned out that he wouldn't, then dragons were always hungry and needed to be fed regularly. She could see to it that they got ugly.

Uglier than usual, anyway.

The stairway passed through a stone arch and ended in a narrow ledge near the roof of the great cavern where the Wyrms roosted.

Sunbeams from the myriad entrances around the walls criss-crossed the dusty gloom like amber rods in which a million golden insects had been preserved. Below, they revealed nothing but a thin haze. Above . . .

The walking rings started so close to Liessa's head that she could reach up and touch one. They stretched away in their thousands across the upturned acres of the cavern roof. It had taken a score of masons a score of years to hammer the pitons for all those, hanging from their work as they progressed. Yet they were as nothing compared to the eighty-eight major rings that clustered near the apex of the dome. A further fifty had been lost in the old days, as they were swung into place by teams of sweating slaves (and there had been slaves aplenty, in the first days of the Power) and the great rings had gone crashing into the depths, dragging their unfortunate manipulators with them.

But eighty-eight had been installed, huge as rainbows, rusty as blood. From them . . .

The dragons sense Liessa's presence. Air swishes around the cavern as eighty-eight pairs of wings unfold like a complicated puzzle. Great heads with green, multi-faceted eyes peer down at her.

The beasts are still faintly transparent. While the men around her take their hookboots from the rack, Liessa bends her mind to the task of full visualization; above her in the musty air the dragons become fully visible, bronze scales dully reflecting the sunbeam shafts. Her mind throbs, but now that the Power is flowing fully she can, with barely a waver of concentration, think of other things.

Now she too buckles on the hookboots and turns a graceful cartwheel to bring their hooks, with a faint clang, against a couple of the walking rings in the ceiling.

Only now it is the floor. The world has changed. Now she is standing on the edge of a deep bowl or crater, floored with the little rings across which the dragon-riders are already strolling with a pendulum gait. In the centre of the bowl their huge mounts wait among the herd. Far above are the distant rocks of the cavern floor, discoloured by centuries of dragon droppings.

Moving with the easy gliding movement that is second nature Liessa sets off towards her own dragon, Laolith, who turns his great horsey head towards her. His jowls are greasy with pork fat.

It was very enjoyable, he says in her mind.

'I thought I said there were to be no unaccompanied flights?' she snaps.

I was hungry, Liessa.

'Curb your hunger. Soon there will be horses to eat.'

The reins stick in our teeth. Are there any warriors? We like warriors.

Liessa swings down the mounting ladder and lands with her legs locked around Laolith's leathery neck.

'The warrior is mine. There are a couple of others you

can have. One appears to be a wizard of sorts,' she adds by way of encouragement.

Oh, you know how it is with wizards. Half an hour afterwards you could do with another one, the dragon grumbles.

He spreads his wings and drops.

'They're gaining!' screamed Rincewind. He bent even lower over his horse's neck and groaned. Twoflower was trying to keep up while at the same time craning round to look at the flying beasts.

'You don't understand!' screamed the tourist, above the terrible noise of the wingbeats. 'All my life I've wanted to see dragons!'

'From the inside?' shouted Rincewind. 'Shut up and ride!' He whipped at his horse with the reins and stared at the wood ahead, trying to drag it closer by sheer willpower. Under those trees they'd be safe. Under those trees no dragons could fly . . .

He heard the clap of wings before shadows folded around him. Instinctively he rolled in the saddle and felt the white-hot stab of pain as something sharp scored a line across his shoulders.

Behind him Hrun screamed, but it sounded more like a bellow of rage than a cry of pain. The barbarian had vaulted down into the heather and had drawn the black sword, Kring. He flourished it as one of the dragons curved in for another low pass.

'No bloody lizard does that to me!' he roared.

Rincewind leaned over and grabbed Twoflower's reins.

'Come *on*!' he hissed.

'But, the dragons—' said Twoflower, entranced.

'Blast the—' began the wizard, and froze. Another dragon had peeled off from the circling dots overhead and was gliding towards them. Rincewind let go of Twoflower's horse, swore bitterly, and spurred his own mount towards the trees, alone. He didn't look back at the sudden commotion behind him and, when a shadow passed over him, merely gibbered weakly and tried to burrow into the horse's mane.

Then, instead of the searing, piercing pain he had expected, there was a series of stinging blows as the terrified animal passed under the eaves of the wood. The wizard tried to hang on but another low branch, stouter than the others, knocked him out of the saddle. The last thing he heard before the flashing blue lights of unconsciousness closed in was a high reptilian scream of frustration, and the thrashing of talons in the treetops.

When he awoke a dragon was watching him; at least, it was staring in his general direction. Rincewind groaned and tried to dig his way into the moss with his shoulder-blades, then gasped as the pain hit him.

Through the mists of agony and fear he looked back at the dragon.

The creature was hanging from a branch of a large dead oak tree, several hundred feet away. Its bronze-gold wings were tightly wrapped around its body but the long equine head turned this way and that at the end of a remarkably prehensile neck. It was scanning the forest.

It was also semi-transparent. Although the sun

glinted off its scales, Rincewind could clearly make out the outlines of the branches behind it.

On one of them a man was sitting, dwarfed by the hanging reptile. He appeared to be naked except for a pair of high boots, a tiny leather holdall in the region of his groin, and a high-crested helmet. He was swinging a short sword back and forth idly, and stared out across the tree-tops with the air of one carrying out a tedious and unglamorous assignment.

A beetle began to crawl laboriously up Rincewind's leg.

The wizard wondered how much damage a half-solid dragon could do. Would it only half-kill him? He decided not to stay and find out.

Moving on heels, fingertips and shoulder muscles, Rincewind wriggled sideways until foliage masked the oak and its occupants. Then he scrambled to his feet and hared off between the trees.

He had no destination in mind, no provisions, and no horse. But while he still had legs he could run. Ferns and brambles whipped at him, but he didn't feel them at all.

When he had put about a mile between him and the dragon he stopped and collapsed against a tree, which then spoke to him.

'Psst,' it said.

Dreading what he might see, Rincewind let his gaze slide upwards. It tried to fasten on innocuous bits of bark and leaf, but the scourge of curiosity forced it to leave them behind. Finally it fixed on a black sword thrust straight through the branch above Rincewind's head.

'Don't just stand there,' said the sword (in a voice like the sound of a finger dragged around the rim of a large empty wineglass). 'Pull me out.'

'What?' said Rincewind, his chest still heaving.

'Pull me out,' repeated Kring. 'It's either that or I'll be spending the next million years in a coal measure. Did I ever tell you about the time I was thrown into a lake up in the—'

'What happened to the others?' said Rincewind, still clutching the tree desperately.

'Oh, the dragons got them. And the horses. And that box thing. Me too, except that Hrun dropped me. What a stroke of luck for you.'

'Well—' began Rincewind. Kring ignored him.

'I expect you'll be in a hurry to rescue them,' it added.

'Yes, well—'

'So if you'll just pull me out we can be off.'

Rincewind squinted up at the sword. A rescue attempt had hitherto been so far at the back of his mind that, if some advanced speculations on the nature and shape of the many-dimensioned multi-plexity of the universe were correct, it was right at the front; but a magic sword was a valuable item . . .

And it would be a long trek back home, wherever that was . . .

He scrambled up the tree and inched along the branch. Kring was buried very firmly in the wood. He gripped the pommel and heaved until lights flashed in front of his eyes.

'Try again,' said the sword encouragingly.

Rincewind groaned and gritted his teeth.

'Could be worse,' said Kring. 'This could have been an anvil.'

'Yaargh,' hissed the wizard, fearing for the future of his groin.

'I have had a multidimensional existence,' said the sword.

'Ungh?'

'I have had many names, you know.'

'Amazing,' said Rincewind. He swayed backwards as the blade slid free. It felt strangely light.

Back on the ground again he decided to break the news.

'I really don't think rescue is a good idea,' he said. 'I think we'd better head back to a city, you know. To raise a search party.'

'The dragons headed hubwards,' said Kring. 'However, I suggest we start with the one in the trees over there.'

'Sorry, but—'

'You can't leave them to their fate!'

Rincewind looked surprised. 'I can't?' he said.

'No. You can't. Look, I'll be frank. I've worked with better material than you, but it's either that or – have you ever spent a million years in a coal measure?'

'Look, I—'

'So if you don't stop arguing I'll chop your head off.'

Rincewind saw his own arm snap up until the shimmering blade was humming a mere inch from his throat. He tried to force his fingers to let go. They wouldn't.

'I don't know how to be a hero!' he shouted.

'I propose to teach you.'

* * *

Bronze Psepha rumbled deep in his throat.

K!sdra the dragonrider leaned forward and squinted across the clearing.

'I see him,' he said. He swung himself down easily from branch to branch and landed lightly on the tussocky grass, drawing his sword.

He took a long look at the approaching man, who was obviously not keen on leaving the shelter of the trees. He was armed, but the dragonrider observed with some interest the strange way in which the man held the sword in front of him at arm's length, as though embarrassed to be seen in its company.

K!sdra hefted his own sword and grinned expansively as the wizard shuffled towards him. Then he leapt.

Later, he remembered only two things about the fight. He recalled the uncanny way in which the wizard's sword curved up and caught his own blade with a shock that jerked it out of his grip. The other thing – and it was this, he averred, that led to his downfall – was that the wizard was covering his eyes with one hand.

K!sdra jumped back to avoid another thrust and fell full length on the turf. With a snarl Psepha unfolded his great wings and launched himself from his tree.

A moment later the wizard was standing over him, shouting, 'Tell it that if it singes me I'll let the sword go! I will! I'll let it go! So tell it!' The tip of the black sword was hovering over K!sdra's throat. What was odd was that the wizard was obviously struggling with it, and it appeared to be singing to itself.

'Psepha!' K!sdra shouted.

The dragon roared in defiance, but pulled out of the dive that would have removed Rincewind's head, and flapped ponderously back to the tree.

'Talk!' screamed Rincewind.

K!sdra squinted at him up the length of the sword.

'What would you like me to say?' he asked.

'What?'

'I said what would you like me to say?'

'Where are my friends? The barbarian and the little man is what I mean!'

'I expect they have been taken back to the Wyrmberg.'

Rincewind tugged desperately against the surge of the sword, trying to shut his mind to Kring's blood-thirsty humming.

'What's a Wyrmberg?' he said.

'*The* Wyrmberg. There is only one. It is Dragonhome.'

'And I suppose you were waiting to take me there, eh?'

K!sdra yelped involuntarily as the tip of the sword pricked a bead of blood from his Adam's apple.

'Don't want people to know you've got dragons here, eh?' snarled Rincewind. The dragonrider forgot himself enough to nod, and came within a quarter-inch of cutting his own throat.

Rincewind looked around desperately, and realized that this was something he was really going to have to go through with.

'Right then,' he said as diffidently as he could

manage. 'You'd better take me to this Wyrmberg of yours, hadn't you?'

'I was supposed to take you in dead,' muttered K!sdra sullenly.

Rincewind looked down at him and grinned slowly. It was a wide, manic and utterly humourless rictus. It was the sort of grin that is normally accompanied by small riverside birds wandering in and out, picking scraps out of the teeth.

'Alive will do,' said Rincewind. 'If we're talking about anyone being *dead*, remember whose sword is in which hand.'

'If you kill me nothing will prevent Psepha killing you!' shouted the prone dragonrider.

'So what I'll do is, I'll chop bits off,' agreed the wizard. He tried the effect of the grin again.

'Oh, all right,' said K!sdra sulkily. 'Do you think I've got no imagination?'

He wriggled out from under the sword and waved at the dragon, which took wing again and glided in towards them. Rincewind swallowed.

'You mean we've got to go on that?' he said. K!sdra looked at him scornfully, the point of Kring still aimed at his neck.

'How else would anyone get to the Wyrmberg?'

'I don't know,' said Rincewind. 'How else?'

'I mean, there is no other way. It's flying or nothing.'

Rincewind looked again at the dragon before him. He could quite clearly see through it to the crushed grass on which it lay but, when he gingerly touched a scale that was a mere golden sheen on thin air, it felt solid enough. Either dragons should exist completely or fail to exist at all, he felt. A dragon only half-existing was worse than the extremes.

'I didn't know dragons could be seen through,' he said.

K!sdra shrugged. 'Didn't you?' he said.

He swung himself astride the dragon awkwardly, because Rincewind was hanging on to his belt. Once uncomfortably aboard the wizard moved his white-knuckle grip to a convenient piece of harness and prodded K!sdra lightly with the sword.

'Have you ever flown before?' said the dragonrider, without looking round.

'Not as such, no.'

'Would you like something to suck?'

Rincewind stared at the back of the man's head, then dropped his gaze to the bag of red and yellow sweets that was being proffered.

'Is it necessary?' he asked.

'It is traditional,' said K!sdra. 'Please yourself.'

The dragon stood up, lumbered heavily across the meadow, and fluttered into the air.

Rincewind occasionally had nightmares about teetering on some intangible but enormously high place, and seeing a blue-distanced, cloud-punctuated landscape reeling away below him (this usually woke him up with his ankles sweating; he would have been even more worried had he known that the nightmare was not, as he thought, just the usual discworld vertigo. It was a backwards memory of an event in his future so terrifying that it had generated harmonics of fear all the way along his lifeline).

This was not that event, but it was good practice for it.

Psepha clawed its way into the air with a series of vertebrae-shattering bounds. At the top of its last leap the wide wings unfolded with a snap and spread out with a thump which shook the trees.

Then the ground was gone, dropping away in a series of gentle jerks. Psepha was suddenly rising gracefully, the afternoon sunlight gleaming off wings that were still no more than a golden film. Rincewind made the mistake of glancing downwards, and found himself looking through the dragon to the treetops below. Far below. His stomach shrank at the sight.

Closing his eyes wasn't much better, because it gave his imagination full rein. He compromised by gazing fixedly into the middle distance, where moorland and forest drifted by and could be contemplated almost casually.

Wind snatched at him. K!sdra half turned and shouted into his ear.

'Behold the Wyrmberg!'

Rincewind turned his head slowly, taking care to keep Kring resting lightly on the dragon's back. His streaming eyes saw the impossibly inverted mountain rearing out of the deep forested valley like a trumpet in a tub of moss. Even at this distance he could make out the faint octarine glow in the air that must be indicating a stable magic aura of at least – he gasped – several milliPrime? At least!

'Oh no,' he said.

Even looking at the ground was better than that. He averted his eyes quickly, and realized that he could now no longer see the ground *through* the dragon. As they glided around in a wide circle towards the Wyrmberg it was definitely taking on a more solid form, as if the creature's body was filling with a gold mist. By the time the Wyrmberg was in front of them, swinging wildly across the sky, the dragon was as real as a rock.

Rincewind thought he could see a faint streak in the air, as if something from the mountain had reached out and touched the beast. He got the strange feeling that the dragon was being made more *genuine*.

Ahead of it the Wyrmberg turned from a distant toy to several billion tons of rock poised between heaven and earth. He could see small fields, woods and a lake up there, and from the lake a river spilled out and over the edge . . .

He made the mistake of following the thread of foaming water with his eyes, and jerked himself back just in time.

The flared plateau of the upturned mountain drifted towards them. The dragon didn't even slow.

As the mountain loomed over Rincewind like the biggest fly-swatter in the universe he saw a cave mouth. Psepha skimmed towards it, shoulder muscles pumping.

The wizard screamed as the dark spread and enfolded him. There was a brief vision of rock flashing past, blurred by speed. Then the dragon was in the open again.

It was inside a cave, but bigger than any cave had a right to be. The dragon, gliding across its vast emptiness, was a mere gilded fly in a banqueting hall.

There were other dragons – gold, silver, black, white – flapping across the sun-shafted air on errands of their own or perched on outcrops of rock. High in the domed roof of the cavern scores of others hung from huge rings, their wings wrapped bat-like around their bodies. There were men up there, too. Rincewind swallowed hard when he saw them, because they were walking on that broad expanse of ceiling like flies.

Then he made out the thousands of tiny rings that studded the ceiling. A number of inverted men were watching Psepha's flight with interest. Rincewind swallowed again. For the life of him he couldn't think of what to do next.

'Well?' he asked, in a whisper. 'Any suggestions?'

'Obviously you attack,' said Kring scornfully.

'Why didn't I think of that?' said Rincewind. 'Could it be because they all have crossbows?'

'You're a defeatist.'

'Defeatist! That's because I'm going to be defeated!'

'You're your own worst enemy, Rincewind,' said the sword.

Rincewind looked up at grinning men.

'Bet?' he said wearily.

Before Kring could reply Psepha reared in mid-air and alighted on one of the large rings, which rocked alarmingly.

'Would you like to die now, or surrender first?' asked K!sdra calmly.

Men were converging on the ring from all directions, walking with a swaying motion as their hooked boots engaged the ceiling rings.

There were more boots on a rack that hung in a

small platform built on the side of the perch-ring. Before Rincewind could stop him the dragonrider had leapt from the creature's back to land on the platform, where he stood grinning at the wizard's discomfiture.

There was a small expressive sound made by a number of crossbows being cocked. Rincewind looked up at a number of impassive, upside down faces. The dragonfolk's taste in clothing didn't run to anything much more imaginative than a leather harness, studded with bronze ornaments. Knives and sword sheaths were worn inverted. Those who were not wearing helmets let their hair flow freely, so that it moved like seaweed in the ventilation breeze near the roof. There were several women among them. The inversion did strange things to their anatomy. Rincewind stared.

'Surrender,' said K!sdra again.

Rincewind opened his mouth to do so. Kring hummed a warning, and agonizing waves of pain shot up his arm. 'Never,' he squeaked. The pain stopped.

'Of course he won't!' boomed an expansive voice behind him. 'He's a hero, isn't he?'

Rincewind turned and looked into a pair of hairy nostrils. They belonged to a heavily built young man, hanging nonchalantly from the ceiling by his boots.

'What is your name, hero?' said the man. 'So that we know who you were.'

Agony shot up Rincewind's arm. 'I-I'm Rincewind of Ankh,' he managed to gasp.

'And I am Lio!rt Dragonlord,' said the hanging man, pronouncing the word with the harsh click in the back of the throat that Rincewind could only think of as a kind of integral punctuation. 'You have come to challenge me in mortal combat.'

'Well, no, I didn't—'

'You are mistaken. K!sdra, help our hero into a pair of hookboots. I am sure he is anxious to get started.'

'No, look, I just came here to find my friends. I'm sure there's no—' Rincewind began, as the dragonrider guided him firmly onto the platform, pushed him onto a seat, and proceeded to strap hookboots to his feet.

'Hurry up, K!sdra. We mustn't keep our hero from his destiny,' said Lio!rt.

'Look, I expect my friends are happy enough here, so if you could just, you know, set me down somewhere—'

'You will see your friends soon enough,' said the dragonlord airily. 'If you are religious, I mean. None who enter the Wyrmberg ever leave again. Except metaphorically, of course. Show him how to reach the rings, K!sdra.'

'Look what you've got me into!' Rincewind hissed.

Kring vibrated in his hand. 'Remember that I am a *magic* sword,' it hummed.

'How can I forget?'

'Climb the ladder and grab a ring,' said the dragonrider, 'then bring your feet up until the hooks catch.' He helped the protesting wizard climb until he was hanging upside down, robe tucked into his britches, Kring dangling from one hand. At this angle the dragonfolk looked reasonably bearable but the dragons themselves, hanging from their perches, loomed over the scene like immense gargoyles. Their eyes glowed with interest.

'Attention, please,' said Lio!rt. A dragonrider handed him a long shape, wrapped in red silk.

'We fight to the death,' he said. 'Yours.'

'And I suppose I earn my freedom if I win?' said Rincewind, without much hope.

Lio!rt indicated the assembled dragonriders with a tilt of his head.

'Don't be naïve,' he said.

Rincewind took a deep breath. 'I suppose I should warn you,' he said, his voice hardly quavering at all, 'that this is a *magic* sword.'

Lio!rt let the red silk wrapping drop away into the gloom and flourished a jet-black blade. Runes glowed on its surface.

'What a coincidence,' he said, and lunged.

Rincewind went rigid with fright, but his arm swung out as Kring shot forward. The swords met in an explosion of octarine light.

Lio!rt swung himself backwards, his eyes narrowing. Kring leapt past his guard and, although the dragonlord's sword jerked up to deflect most of the force, the result was a thin red line across its master's torso.

With a growl he launched himself at the wizard, boots clattering as he slid from ring to ring. The swords met again in another violent discharge of magic and, at the same time, Lio!rt brought his other hand down against Rincewind's head, jarring him so hard that one foot jerked out of its ring and flailed desperately.

* * *

Rincewind knew himself to be almost certainly the worst wizard on the discworld since he knew but one spell; yet for all that he was still a wizard, and thus by the inexorable laws of magic this meant that upon his demise it would be Death himself who appeared to claim him (instead of sending one of his numerous servants, as is usually the case).

Thus it was that, as a grinning Lio!rt swung back and brought his sword around in a lazy arc, time ran into treacle.

To Rincewind's eyes the world was suddenly lit by a flickering octarine light, tinged with violet as photons impacted on the sudden magical aura. Inside it the dragonlord was a ghastly-hued statue, his sword moving at a snail's pace in the glow.

Beside Lio!rt was another figure, visible only to those who can see into the extra four dimensions of magic. It was tall and dark and thin and, against a sudden night of frosty stars, it swung two-handed a scythe of proverbial sharpness . . .

Rincewind ducked. The blade hissed coldly through the air beside his head and entered the rock of the cavern roof without slowing. Death screamed a curse in his cold crypt voice. The scene vanished. What passed for reality on the discworld reasserted itself with a rush of sound. Lio!rt gasped at the sudden turn of speed with which the wizard had dodged his killing stroke and, with that desperation only available to the really terrified, Rincewind uncoiled like a snake and launched himself across the space between them. He locked both hands around the dragonlord's sword arm, and wrenched.

It was at that moment that Rincewind's one remaining ring, already overburdened, slid out of the rock with a nasty little metal sound.

He plunged down, swung wildly, and ended up dangling over a bone-splintering death with his hands gripping the dragonlord's arm so tightly that the man screamed.

Lio!rt looked up at his feet. Small flakes of rock were dropping out of the roof around the ring pitons.

'Let go, damn you!' he screamed. 'Or we'll both die!'

Rincewind said nothing. He was concentrating on maintaining his grip and keeping his mind closed to the pressing images of his fate on the rocks below.

'Shoot him!' bellowed Lio!rt.

Out of the corner of his eye Rincewind saw several crossbows levelled at him. Lio!rt chose that moment to flail down with his free hand, and a fistful of rings stabbed into the wizard's fingers.

He let go.

Twoflower grabbed the bars and pulled himself up.

'See anything?' said Hrun, from the region of his feet.

'Just clouds.'

Hrun lifted him down again, and sat on the edge of one of the wooden beds that were the only furnishings in the cell. 'Bloody hell,' he said.

'Don't despair,' said Twoflower.

'I'm not despairing.'

'I expect it's all some sort of misunderstanding. I expect they'll release us soon. They seem very civilized.'

Hrun stared at him from under bushy eyebrows. He started to say something, then appeared to think better of it. He sighed instead.

'And when we get back we can say we've seen dragons!' Twoflower continued. 'What about that, eh?'

'Dragons don't exist,' said Hrun flatly. 'Codice of Chimeria killed the last one two hundred years ago. I don't know what we're seeing, but they aren't dragons.'

'But they carried us up in the air! In that hall there must have been hundreds—'

'I expect it was just magic,' said Hrun, dismissively.

'Well, they looked like dragons,' said Twoflower, an air of defiance about him. 'I always wanted to see dragons, ever since I was a little lad. Dragons flying around in the sky, breathing flames . . .'

'They just used to crawl around in swamps and stuff, and all they breathed was stink,' said Hrun, lying down in the bunk. 'They weren't very big, either. They used to collect firewood.'

'*I* heard they used to collect treasure,' said Twoflower.

'*And* firewood. Hey,' Hrun added, brightening up, 'did you notice all those rooms they brought us through? Pretty impressive, I thought. Lot of good stuff about, plus some of those tapestries have got to be worth a fortune.' He scratched his chin thoughtfully, making a noise like a porcupine shouldering its way through gorse.

'What happens next?' asked Twoflower.

Hrun screwed a finger in his ear and inspected it absently.

'Oh,' he said, 'I expect in a minute the door will be flung back and I'll be dragged off to some sort of temple arena where I'll fight maybe a couple of giant spiders and an eight-foot slave from the jungles of Klatch and then I'll rescue some kind of a princess from the altar and then kill off a few guards or whatever and then this girl will show me the secret passage out of the place and we'll liberate a couple of horses and escape with the treasure.' Hrun leaned his head back on his hands and looked at the ceiling, whistling tunelessly.

'All that?' said Twoflower.

'Usually.'

Twoflower sat down on his bunk and tried to think. This proved difficult, because his mind was awash with dragons.

Dragons!

Ever since he was two years old he had been captivated by the pictures of the fiery beasts in *The Octarine Fairy Book*. His sister had told him they didn't really exist, and he recalled the bitter disappointment. If the world didn't contain those beautiful creatures, he'd decided, it wasn't half the world it ought to be. And then later he had been bound apprentice to Ninereeds the Masteraccount, who in his grey-mindedness was everything that dragons were not, and there was no time for dreaming.

But there was something wrong with these dragons. They were too small and sleek, compared to the ones in his mind's eye. Dragons ought to be big and green and clawed and exotic and fire-breathing – big and green with long sharp . . .

Something moved at the edge of his vision, in the furthest, darkest corner of the dungeon. When he turned his head it vanished, although he thought he heard the faintest of noises that might have been made by claws scrabbling on stone.

'Hrun?' he said.

There was a snore from the other bunk.

Twoflower padded over to the corner, poking gingerly at the stones in case there was a secret panel. At that moment the door was flung back, thumping against the wall. Half a dozen guards hurtled through it, spread out and flung themselves down on one knee. Their weapons were aimed exclusively at Hrun. When he thought about this later, Twoflower felt quite offended.

Hrun snored.

A woman strode into the room. Not many women can stride convincingly, but she managed it. She glanced briefly at Twoflower, as one might look at a piece of furniture, then glared down at the man on the bed.

She was wearing the same sort of leather harness that the dragonriders had been wearing, but in her case it was much briefer. That, and the magnificent mane of chestnut-red hair that fell to her waist, was her only concession to what even on the discworld passed for decency. She was also wearing a thoughtful expression.

Hrun made a glubbing noise, turned over, and slept on.

With a careful movement, as though handling some instrument of rare delicacy, the woman drew a slim black dagger from her belt and stabbed down-ward.

Before it was halfway through its arc Hrun's right hand moved so fast that it appeared to travel between two points in space without at any time occupying the intervening air. It closed around the woman's wrist with a dull smack. His other hand groped feverishly for a sword that wasn't there . . .

Hrun awoke.

'Gngh?' he said, looking up at the woman with a puzzled frown. Then he caught sight of the bowmen.

'Let go,' said the woman, in a voice that was calm and quiet and edged with diamonds. Hrun released his grip slowly.

She stepped back, massaging her wrist and looking at Hrun in much the same way that a cat watches a mousehole.

'So,' she said at last. 'You pass the first test. What is your name, barbarian?'

'Who are you calling a barbarian?' snarled Hrun.

'That is what I want to know.'

Hrun counted the bowmen slowly and made a brief calculation. His shoulders relaxed.

'I am Hrun of Chimeria. And you?'

'Liessa Dragonlady.'

'You are the lord of this place?'

'That remains to be seen. You have the look about you of a hired sword, Hrun of Chimeria. I could use you – if you pass the tests, of course. There are three of them. You have passed the first.'

'What are the other—' Hrun paused, his lips moved soundlessly and then he hazarded, 'two?'

'Perilous.'

'And the fee?'

'Valuable.'

'Excuse me,' said Twoflower.

'And if I fail these tests?' said Hrun, ignoring him. The air between Hrun and Liessa crackled with small explosions of charisma as their gazes sought for a hold.

'If you had failed the first test you would now be dead. This may be considered a typical penalty.'

'Um, look,' began Twoflower. Liessa spared him a brief glance, and appeared actually to notice him for the first time.

'Take that away,' she said calmly, and turned back to Hrun. Two of the guards shouldered their bows, grasped Twoflower by the elbows and lifted him off the ground. Then they trotted smartly through the doorway.

'Hey,' said Twoflower, as they hurried down the corridor outside, 'where' (as they stopped in front of another door) 'is my' (as they dragged the door open) 'Luggage?' He landed in a heap of what might once have been straw. The door banged shut, its echoes punctuated by the sound of bolts being slammed home.

In the other cell Hrun had barely blinked.

'OK,' he said, 'what is the second test?'

'You must kill my two brothers.' Hrun considered this.

'Both at the same time, or one after the other?' he said.

'Consecutively or concurrently,' she assured him.

'What?'

'Just kill them,' she said sharply.

'Good fighters, are they?'

'Renowned.'

'So in return for all this . . . ?'

'You will wed me and become Lord of the Wyrmberg.'

There was a long pause. Hrun's eyebrows twisted themselves in unaccustomed calculation.

'I get you and this mountain?' he said at last.

'Yes.' She looked him squarely in the eye, and her lips twitched. 'The fee is worthwhile, I assure you.'

Hrun dropped his gaze to the rings on her hand. The stones were large, being the incredibly rare blue milk diamonds from the clay basins of Mithos. When he managed to turn his eyes from them he saw Liessa glaring down at him in fury.

'So calculating?' she rasped. 'Hrun the Barbarian, who would boldly walk into the jaws of Death Himself?'

Hrun shrugged. 'Sure,' he said, 'the only reason for walking into the jaws of Death is so's you can steal His gold teeth.' He brought one arm around expansively, and the wooden bunk was at the end of it. It cannoned into the bowmen and Hrun followed it joyously, felling one man with a blow and snatching the weapon from another. A moment later it was all over.

Liessa had not moved.

'Well?' she said.

'Well what?' said Hrun, from the carnage.

'Do you intend to kill me?'

'What? Oh no. No, this is just, you know, kind of a habit. Just keeping in practice. So where are these brothers?' He grinned.

Twoflower sat on his straw and stared into the darkness. He wondered how long he had been there. Hours, at least. Days, probably. He speculated that perhaps it had been years, and he had simply forgotten.

No, that sort of thinking wouldn't do. He tried to think of something else – grass, trees, fresh air, dragons. Dragons . . .

There was the faintest of scrabblings in the darkness. Twoflower felt the sweat prickle on his forehead.

Something was in the cell with him. Something that made small noises, but even in the pitch blackness gave the impression of hugeness. He felt the air move.

When he lifted his arm there was the greasy feel and faint shower of sparks that betokened a localized magical field. Twoflower found himself fervently wishing for light.

A gout of flame rolled past his head and struck the far wall. As the rocks flashed into furnace heat he looked up at the dragon that now occupied more than half the cell.

I obey, lord, said a voice in his head.

By the glow of the crackling, spitting stone Twoflower looked into his own reflection in two enormous green eyes. Beyond them the dragon was as multi-hued, horned, spiked and lithe as the one in his memory – a *real* dragon. Its folded wings were nevertheless still wide enough to scrape the wall on both sides of the room. It lay with him between its talons.

'Obey?' he said, his voice vibrating with terror and delight.

Of course, lord.

The glow faded away. Twoflower pointed a trembling finger at where he remembered the door to be and said, 'Open it!'

The dragon raised its huge head. Again the ball of flame rolled out but this time, as the dragon's neck muscles contracted, its colour faded from orange to yellow, from yellow to white, and finally to the faintest of blues. By that time the flame was also very thin, and where it touched the wall the molten rock spat and ran. When it reached the door the metal exploded into a shower of hot droplets.

Black shadows arced and jiggered over the walls. The metal bubbled for an eye-aching moment, and then the door fell in two pieces in the passage beyond. The flame winked out with a suddenness that was almost as startling as its arrival.

Twoflower stepped gingerly over the cooling door and looked up and down the corridor. It was empty.

The dragon followed. The heavy door frame caused it some minor difficulty, which it overcame with a swing of its shoulders that tore the timber out and tossed it to one side. The creature looked expectantly at Twoflower, its skin rippling and twitching as it sought to open its wings in the confines of the passage.

'How did you get in there?' said Twoflower.

You summoned me, master.

'I don't remember doing that.'

In your mind. You called me up, in your mind, thought the dragon, patiently.

'You mean I just thought of you and there you were?'

Yes.

'It was magic?'

Yes.

'But I've thought about dragons all my life!'

In this place the frontier between thought and reality is probably a little confused. All I know is that once I was not, and then you thought me, and then I was. Therefore, of course, I am yours to command.

'Good grief!'

Half a dozen guards chose that moment to turn the bend in the corridor. They stopped, open-mouthed. Then one remembered himself sufficiently to raise his crossbow and fire.

The dragon's chest heaved. The quarrel exploded into flaming fragments in mid-air. The guards scurried out of sight. A fraction of a second later a wash of flame played over the stones where they had been standing.

Twoflower looked up in admiration.

'Can you fly too?' he said.

Of course.

Twoflower glanced up and down the corridor, and decided against following the guards. Since he knew himself to be totally lost already, any direction was probably an improvement. He edged past the dragon and hurried away, the huge beast turning with difficulty to follow him.

They padded down a series of passages that criss-crossed like a maze. At one point Twoflower thought he heard shouts, a long way behind them, but they soon faded away. Sometimes the dark arch of a crumbling doorway loomed past them in the gloom. Light filtered through dimly from various shafts and, here and there, bounced off big mirrors that had been mortared into angles of the passage. Sometimes there was a brighter glow from a distant light-well.

What was odd, thought Twoflower as he strolled down a wide flight of stairs and kicked up billowing clouds of silver dust motes, was that the tunnels here were much wider. And better constructed, too. There were statues in niches set in the walls, and here and there faded but interesting tapestries had been hung. They mainly showed dragons – dragons by the hundred, in flight or hanging from their perch rings, dragons with men on their backs hunting down deer and, sometimes, other men. Twoflower touched one tapestry gingerly. The fabric crumbled instantly in the hot dry air, leaving only a dangling mesh where some threads had been plaited with fine gold wire.

'I wonder why they left all this?' he said.

I don't know, said a polite voice in his head.

He turned and looked up into the scaly horse face above him.

'What is your name, dragon?' said Twoflower.

I don't know.

'I think I shall call you Ninereeds.'

That is my name, then.

183

They waded through the all-encroaching dust in a series of huge, dark-pillared halls which had been carved out of the solid rock. With some cunning too: from floor to ceiling the walls were a mass of statues, gargoyles, bas-reliefs and fluted columns that cast weirdly moving shadows when the dragon gave an obliging illumination at Twoflower's request. They crossed the lengthy galleries and vast carven amphitheatres, all awash with deep soft dust and completely uninhabited. No-one had come to these dead caverns in centuries.

Then he saw the path, leading away into yet another dark tunnel mouth. Someone had been using it regularly, and recently. It was a deep narrow trail in the grey blanket.

Twoflower followed it. It led through still more lofty halls and winding corridors quite big enough for a dragon (and dragons had come this way once, it seemed; there was a room full of rotting harness, dragon-sized, and another room containing plate armour and chain mail big enough for elephants). They ended in a pair of green bronze doors, each so high that they disappeared into the gloom. In front of Twoflower, at chest height, was a small handle shaped like a brass dragon.

When he touched it the doors swung open instantly and with a disconcerting noiselessness.

Instantly sparks crackled in Twoflower's hair and there was a sudden gust of hot dry wind that didn't disturb the dust in the way that ordinary wind should but, instead, whipped it up momentarily into unpleasantly half-living shapes before it settled again.

In Twoflower's ears came the strange shrill twittering of the Things locked in the distant dungeon Dimensions, out beyond the fragile lattice of time and space. Shadows appeared where there was nothing to cause them. The air buzzed like a hive.

In short, there was a vast discharge of magic going on around him.

The chamber beyond the door was lit by a pale green glow. Stacked around the walls, each on its own marble shelf, were tier upon tier of coffins. In the centre of the room was a stone chair on a raised dais, and it contained a slumped figure which did not move but said, in a brittle old voice, 'Come in, young man.'

Twoflower stepped forward. The figure in the seat was human, as far as he could make out in the murky light, but there was something about the awkward way it was sprawled in the chair that made him glad he couldn't see it any clearer.

'I'm dead, you know,' came a voice from what Twoflower fervently hoped was a head, in conversational tones. 'I expect you can tell.'

'Um,' said Twoflower. 'Yes.' He began to back away.

'Obvious, isn't it?' agreed the voice. 'You'd be Twoflower, wouldn't you? Or is that later?'

'Later?' said Twoflower. 'Later than what?' He stopped.

'Well,' said the voice. 'You see, one of the disadvantages of being dead is that one is released as it were from the bonds of time and therefore I can see everything that has happened or will happen, all at the same time except that of course I now know that Time does not, for all practical purposes, exist.'

'That doesn't sound like a disadvantage,' said Twoflower.

'You don't think so? Imagine every moment being at one and the same time a distant memory and a nasty surprise and you'll see what I mean. Anyway, I now recall what it was I am about to tell you. Or have I already done so? That's a fine looking dragon, by the way. Or don't I say that yet?'

'It is rather good. It just turned up,' said Twoflower.

'It turned up?' said the voice. 'You summoned it!'

'Yes, well, all I did—'

'You have the Power!'

'All I did was think of it.'

'That's what the Power is! Have I already told you that I am Greicha the First? Or is that next? I'm sorry, but I haven't had too much experience of trans-cendence. Anyway, yes – the Power. It summons dragons, you know.'

'I think you already told me that,' said Twoflower.

'Did I? I certainly intended to,' said the dead man.

'But *how* does it? I've been thinking about dragons all my life, but this is the first time one has turned up.'

'Oh well, you see, the truth of the matter is that dragons have never existed as you (and, until I was poisoned some three months ago, *I*) understand existence. I'm talking about the true dragon, *draconis nobilis*, you understand; the swamp dragon, *draconis vulgaris*, is a base creature and not worth our con-sideration. The *true* dragon, on the other hand, is a creature of such refinement of spirit that they can only take on form in this world if they are conceived by the most skilled imagination. And even then the

said imagination must be in some place heavily im-
pregnated with magic, which helps to weaken the
walls between the world of the seen and unseen. Then
the dragons pop through, as it were, and impress their
form on this world's possibility matrix. I was very
good at it when I was alive. I could imagine up to, oh,
five hundred dragons at a time. Now Liessa, the most
skilled of my children, can barely imagine fifty rather
nondescript creatures. So much for a progressive
education. She doesn't really *believe* in them. That's
why her dragons are rather boring – while yours,' said
the voice of Greicha, 'is almost as good as some of
mine used to be. A sight for sore eyes, not that I have
any to speak of now.'

Twoflower said hurriedly, 'You keep saying you're
dead . . .'

'Well?'

'Well, the dead, er, they, you know, don't talk much.
As a rule.'

'I used to be an exceptionally powerful wizard. My
daughter poisoned me, of course. It is the generally
accepted method of succession in our family, but,' the
corpse sighed, or at least a sigh came from the air a
few feet above it, 'it soon became obvious that none of
my three children is sufficiently powerful to wrest the
lordship of the Wyrmberg from the other two. A most
unsatisfactory arrangement. A kingdom like ours has
to have one ruler. So I resolved to remain alive in an
unofficial capacity, which of course annoys them all
immensely. I won't give my children the satisfaction
of burying me until there is only one of them left to
perform the ceremony.' There was a nasty wheezing

noise. Twoflower decided that it was meant to be a chuckle.

'So it was one of them that kidnapped us?' said Twoflower.

'Liessa,' said the dead wizard's voice. 'My daughter. Her power is strongest, you know. My sons' dragons are incapable of flying more than a few miles before they fade.'

'Fade? I did notice that we could see through the one that brought us here,' said Twoflower. 'I thought that was a bit odd.'

'Of course,' said Greicha. 'The Power only works near the Wyrmberg. It's the inverse square law, you know. At least, I think it is. As the dragons fly further away they begin to *dwindle*. Otherwise my little Liessa would be ruling the whole world by now, if I know anything about it. But I can see I mustn't keep you. I expect you'll be wanting to rescue your friend.'

Twoflower gaped. 'Hrun?' he said.

'Not him. The skinny wizard. My son Lio!rt is trying to hack him to pieces. I admired the way you rescued him. Will, I mean.'

Twoflower drew himself up to his full height, an easy task. 'Where is he?' he said, heading towards the door with what he hoped was an heroic stride.

'Just follow the pathway in the dust,' said the voice. 'Liessa comes to see me sometimes. She still comes to see her old dad, my little girl. She was the only one with the strength of character to murder me. A chip off the old block. Good luck, by the way. I seem to recall I said that. Will say it now, I mean.'

The rambling voice got lost in a maze of tenses as Twoflower ran along the dead tunnels, with the dragon loping along easily behind him. But soon he was leaning against a pillar, completely out of breath. It seemed ages since he'd had anything to eat.

Why don't you fly? said Ninereeds, inside his head. The dragon spread its wings and gave an experimental flap, which lifted it momentarily off the ground. Twoflower stared for a moment, then ran forward and clambered quickly on to the beast's neck. Soon they were airborne, the dragon skimming along easily a few feet from the floor and leaving a billowing cloud of dust in its wake.

Twoflower hung on as best he could as Ninereeds swooped through a succession of caverns and soared around a spiral staircase that could easily have accommodated a retreating army. At the top they emerged into the more inhabited regions, the mirrors at every corridor corner brightly polished and reflecting a pale light.

I smell other dragons.

The wings became a blur and Twoflower was jerked back as the dragon veered and sped off down a side corridor like a gnat-crazed swallow. Another sharp turn sent them soaring out of a tunnel mouth in the side of a vast cavern. There were rocks far below, and up above were broad shafts of light from great holes near the roof. A lot of activity on the ceiling, too . . . as Ninereeds hovered, thumping the air with his wings, Twoflower peered up at the shapes of roosting beasts and tiny man-shaped dots that were somehow walking upside down.

This is a roosting hall, said the dragon in a satisfied tone.

As Twoflower watched, one of the shapes far above detached itself from the roof and began to grow larger . . .

Rincewind watched as Lio!rt's pale face dropped away from him. This is funny, gibbered a small part of his mind, why am I rising?

Then he began to tumble in the air and reality took over. He was dropping to the distant, guano-speckled rocks.

His brain reeled with the thought. The words of the spell picked just that moment to surface from the depths of his mind, as they always did in time of crisis. Why not say us, they seemed to urge. What have you got to lose?

Rincewind waved a hand in the gathering slip-stream.

'Ashonai,' he called. The word formed in front of him in a cold blue flame that streamed in the wind.

He waved the other hand, drunk with terror and magic.

'Ebiris,' he intoned. The sound froze into a flickering orange word that hung beside its companion.

'Urshoring, Kvanti. Pythan. N'gurad. Feringomalee.' As the words blazed their rainbow colours around him he flung his hands back and prepared to say the eighth and final word that would appear in coruscating octarine and seal the spell. The imminent rocks were forgotten.

'—' he began.

The breath was knocked out of him, the spell scattered and snuffed out. A pair of arms locked around his waist and the whole world jerked sideways as the dragon rose out of its long dive, claws grazing just for a moment the topmost rock on the Wyrmberg's noisome floor. Twoflower laughed triumphantly.

'Got him!'

And the dragon, curving gracefully at the top of his flight, gave a lazy flip of his wings and soared through a cavemouth into the morning air.

At noon, in a wide green meadow on the lush table-land that was the top of the impossibly balanced Wyrmberg, the dragons and their riders formed a wide circle. There was room beyond them for a rabble of servants and slaves and others who scratched a living here on the roof of the world, and they were all watching the figures clustered in the centre of the grassy arena.

The group contained a number of senior dragonlords, and among them were Lio!rt and his brother Liartes. The former was still rubbing his legs, with small grimaces of pain. Slightly to one side stood Liessa and Hrun, with some of the woman's own followers. Between the two factions stood the Wyrmberg's hereditary Loremaster.

'As you know,' he said uncertainly, 'the not-fully-late Lord of the Wyrmberg, Greicha the First, has stipulated that there will be no succession until one of his children feels himself – or as it might be, herself – powerful enough to challenge and defeat his or her siblings in mortal combat.'

'Yes, yes, we know all that. Get on with it,' said a thin peevish voice from the air beside him.

The Loremaster swallowed. He had never come to terms with his former master's failure to expire properly. Is the old buzzard dead or isn't he? he wondered.

'It is not certain,' he quavered, 'whether it is allowable to issue a challenge by proxy—'

'It is, it is,' snapped Greicha's disembodied voice. 'It shows intelligence. Don't take all day about it.'

'I challenge you,' said Hrun, glaring at the brothers, 'both at once.'

Lio!rt and Liartes exchanged looks.

'You'll fight us both together?' said Liartes, a tall, wiry man with long black hair.

'Yah.'

'That's pretty uneven odds, isn't it?'

'Yah. I outnumber you one to two.'

Lio!rt scowled. 'You arrogant barbarian—'

'That just about does it!' growled Hrun. 'I'll—'

The Loremaster put out a blue-veined hand to restrain him.

'It is forbidden to fight on the Killing Ground,' he said, and paused while he considered the sense of this. 'You know what I mean, anyway,' he hazarded, giving up, and added: 'As the challenged parties my lords Lio!rt and Liartes have choice of weapons.'

'Dragons,' they said together. Liessa snorted.

'Dragons can be used offensively, therefore they are weapons,' said Lio!rt firmly. 'If you disagree we can fight over it.'

'Yah,' said his brother, nodding at Hrun.

The Loremaster felt a ghostly finger prod him in the chest.

'Don't stand there with your mouth open,' said Greicha's graveyard voice. 'Just hurry up, will you?'

Hrun stepped back, shaking his head.

'Oh no,' he said. 'Once was enough. I'd rather be dead than fight on one of those things.'

'Die, then,' said the Loremaster, as kindly as he could manage.

Lio!rt and Liartes were already striding back across the turf to where the servants stood waiting with their mounts. Hrun turned to Liessa. She shrugged.

'Don't I even get a sword?' he pleaded. 'A knife, even?'

'No,' she said. 'I didn't expect this.' She suddenly looked smaller, all defiance gone. 'I'm sorry.'

'*You're* sorry?'

'Yes. I'm sorry.'

'Yes, I thought you said you're sorry.'

'Don't glare at me like that! I can imagine you the finest dragon to ride—'

'No!'

The Loremaster wiped his nose on a handkerchief, held the little silken square aloft for a moment, then let it fall.

A boom of wings made Hrun spin around. Lio!rt's dragon was already airborne and circling around towards them. As it swooped low over the turf a billow of flame shot from its mouth, scoring a black streak across the grass that rushed towards Hrun.

At the last minute he pushed Liessa aside, and felt the wild pain of the flame on his arm as he dived for safety. He rolled as he hit the ground, and flipped on to his feet again while he looked around frantically for the other dragon. It came in from one side, and Hrun was forced to take a badly judged standing jump to escape the flame. The dragon's tail whipped around as it passed and caught him a stinging blow across the forehead. He pushed himself upright, shaking his head to make the wheeling stars go away. His blistered back screamed pain at him.

Lio!rt came in for a second run, but slower this time to allow for the big man's unexpected agility. As the ground drifted up he saw the barbarian standing stock still, chest heaving, arms hanging loosely by his sides. An easy target.

As his dragon swooped away Lio!rt turned his head, expecting to see a dreadfully big cinder.

There was nothing there. Puzzled, Lio!rt turned back.

Hrun, heaving himself over the dragon's shoulder scales with one hand and beating out his flaming hair with the other, presented himself to his view. Lio!rt's hand flew to his dagger, but pain had sharpened Hrun's normally excellent reflexes to needle point. A backhand blow hammered into the dragonlord's wrist, sending the dagger arcing away towards the ground, and another caught the man full on the chin.

The dragon, carrying the weight of two men, was only a few yards above the grass. This turned out to be fortunate, because at the moment Lio!rt lost consciousness the dragon winked out of existence.

Liessa hurried across the grass and helped Hrun stagger to his feet. He blinked at her.

'What happened? What happened?' he said thickly.

'That was really fantastic!' she said. 'The way you turned that somersault in mid-air and everything!'

'Yah, but what *happened*?'

'It's rather difficult to explain—'

Hrun peered up at the sky. Liartes, by far the more cautious of the two brothers, was circling high above them.

'Well, you've got about ten seconds to try,' he said.

'The dragons—'

'Yah?'

'They're imaginary.'

'Like all these imaginary burns on my arm, you mean?'

'Yes. No!' she shook her head violently. 'I'll have to tell you later!'

'Fine, if you can find a really good medium,' snapped Hrun. He glared up at Liartes, who was beginning to descend in wide sweeps.

'Just *listen*, will you? Unless my brother is conscious his dragon can't exist, it's got no pathway through to this—'

'Run!' shouted Hrun. He threw her away from him and flung himself flat on the ground as Liartes' dragon thundered by, leaving another smoking scar across the turf.

While the creature sought height for another sweep Hrun scrambled to his feet and set off at a dead run for the woods at the edge of the arena. They were sparse, little more than a wide and overgrown hedge, but at least no dragon would be able to fly through them.

It didn't try. Liartes brought his mount in to land on the turf a few yards away and dismounted casually. The dragon folded its wings and poked its head in among the greenery, while its master leaned against a tree and whistled tunelessly.

'I can burn you out,' said Liartes, after a while.

The bushes remained motionless.

'Perhaps you're in that holly bush over there?'

The holly bush became a waxy ball of flame.

'I'm sure I can see movement in those ferns.'

The ferns became mere skeletons of white ash.

'You're only prolonging it, barbarian. Why not give in now? I've burned lots of people; it doesn't hurt a bit,' said Liartes, looking sideways at the bushes.

The dragon continued through the spinney, incinerating every likely-looking bush and clump of ferns. Liartes drew his sword and waited.

Hrun dropped from a tree and landed running. Behind him the dragon roared and crashed through the bushes as it tried to turn around, but Hrun was running, running, with his gaze fixed on Liartes and a dead branch in his hands.

It is a little known but true fact that a two-legged creature can usually beat a four-legged creature over a short distance, simply because of the time it takes the quadruped to get its legs sorted out. Hrun heard the scrabble of claws behind him and then an ominous thump. The dragon had half-opened its wings and was trying to fly.

As Hrun bore down on the dragonlord Liartes' sword came up wickedly, to be caught on the branch.

Then Hrun cannoned into him and the two men sprawled on the ground.

The dragon roared.

Liartes screamed as Hrun brought a knee upwards with anatomical precision, but managed a wild blow that rebroke the barbarian's nose for him.

Hrun kicked away and scrambled to his feet, to find himself looking up into the wild horse-face of the dragon, its nostrils distended.

He lashed out with a foot and caught Liartes, who was trying to stand up, on the side of his head. The man slumped.

The dragon vanished. The ball of fire that was billowing towards Hrun faded until, when it reached him, it was no more than a puff of warm air. Then there was no sound but the crackle of burning bushes.

Hrun slung the unconscious dragonlord over his shoulder and set off at a trot back to the arena. Halfway there he found Lio!rt sprawled on the ground, one leg bent awkwardly. He stooped and, with a grunt, hoisted the man on to his vacant shoulder.

Liessa and the Loremaster were waiting on a raised dais at one end of the meadow. The dragonwoman had quite recovered her composure now, and looked levelly at Hrun as he threw the two men down on the steps before her. The people around her were standing in deferential poses, like a court.

'Kill them,' she said.

'I kill in my own time,' he said. 'In any case, killing unconscious people isn't right.'

'I can't think of a more opportune time,' said the Loremaster. Liessa snorted.

'Then I shall banish them,' she said. 'Once they are beyond the reach of the Wyrmberg's magic then they'll have no Power. They'll be simply brigands. Will that satisfy you?'

'Yes.'

'I am surprised that you are so merciful, ba— Hrun.'

Hrun shrugged. 'A man in my position, he can't afford to be anything else, he's got to consider his image.' He looked around. 'Where's the next test, then?'

'I warn you that it is perilous. If you wish, you may leave now. If you pass the test, however, you will become Lord of the Wyrmberg and, of course, my lawful husband.'

Hrun met her gaze. He thought about his life, to date. It suddenly seemed to him to have been full of long damp nights sleeping under the stars, desperate fights with trolls, city guards, countless bandits and evil priests and, on at least three occasions, actual demigods – and for what? Well, for quite a lot of treasure, he had to admit – but where had it all gone? Rescuing beleaguered maidens had a certain passing reward, but most of the time he'd finished up by setting them up in some city somewhere with a handsome dowry, because after a while even the most agreeable ex-maiden became possessive and had scant sympathy for his efforts to rescue her sister sufferers. In short, life had really left him with little more than a reputation and a network of scars. Being a lord might be fun. Hrun grinned. With a base like this, all these dragons and a good bunch of fighting men, a man could really be a contender.

Besides, the wench was not uncomely.

'The third test?' she said.

'Am I to be weaponless again?' said Hrun.

Liessa reached up and removed her helmet, letting the coils of red hair tumble out. Then she unfastened the brooch of her robe. Underneath, she was naked.

As Hrun's gaze swept over her his mind began to operate two notional counting machines. One assessed the gold in her bangles, the tiger-rubies that ornamented her toe-rings, the diamond spangle that adorned her navel, and two highly individual whirligigs of silver filigree. The other was plugged straight into his libido. Both produced tallies that pleased him mightily.

As she raised a hand and proffered a glass of wine she smiled, and said, 'I think not.'

'He didn't attempt to rescue you,' Rincewind pointed out as a last resort.

He clung desperately to Twoflower's waist as the dragon circled slowly, tilting the world at a dangerous angle. The new knowledge that the scaly back he was astride only existed as a sort of three-dimensional daydream did not, he had soon realized, do anything at all for his ankle-wrenching sensations of vertigo. His mind kept straying towards the possible results of Twoflower losing his concentration.

'Not even Hrun could have prevailed against those crossbows,' said Twoflower stoutly.

As the dragon rose higher above the patch of woodland, where the three of them had slept a damp and uneasy sleep, the sun rose over the edge of the disc.

Instantly the gloomy blues and greys of pre-dawn were transformed into a bright bronze river that flowed across the world, flaring into gold where it struck ice or water or a light-dam. (Owing to the density of the magical field surrounding the disc, light itself moved at sub-sonic speeds; this interesting property was well utilized by the Sorca people of the Great Nef, for example, who over the centuries had constructed intricate and delicate dams, and valleys walled with polished silica, to catch the slow sunlight and sort of *store* it. The scintillating reservoirs of the Nef, overflowing after several weeks of uninterrupted sunlight, were a truly magnificent sight from the air and it is therefore unfortunate that Twoflower and Rincewind did not happen to glance in that direction.)

In front of them the billion-ton impossibility that was the magic-wrought Wyrmberg hung against the sky and that was not too bad, until Rincewind turned his head and saw the mountain's shadow slowly unroll itself across the cloudscape of the world . . .

'What can you see?' said Twoflower to the dragon.

I see fighting on the top of the mountain came the gentle reply.

'See?' said Twoflower. 'Hrun's probably fighting for his life at this very moment.'

Rincewind was silent. After a moment Twoflower looked around. The wizard was staring intently at nothing at all, his lips moving soundlessly.

'Rincewind?'

The wizard made a small croaking noise.

'I'm sorry,' said Twoflower. 'What did you say?'

'. . . all the way . . . the great fall . . .' muttered Rincewind. His eyes focused, looked puzzled for a moment, then widened in terror. He made the mistake of looking down.

'Aargh,' he opined, and began to slide. Twoflower grabbed him.

'What's the matter?'

Rincewind tried shutting his eyes, but there were no eyelids to his imagination and it was staring widely.

'Don't you get scared of heights?' he managed to say.

Twoflower looked down at the tiny landscape, mottled with cloud shadows. The thought of fear hadn't actually occurred to him.

'No,' he said. 'Why should I? You're just as dead if you fall from forty feet as you are from four thousand fathoms, that's what I say.'

Rincewind tried to consider this dispassionately, but couldn't see the logic of it. It wasn't the actual falling, it was the *hitting* he . . .

Twoflower grabbed him quickly.

'Steady on,' he said cheerfully. 'We're nearly there.'

'I wish I was back in the city,' moaned Rincewind. 'I wish I was back on the ground!'

'I wonder if dragons can fly all the way to the stars?' mused Twoflower. 'Now *that* would be something . . .'

'You're mad,' said Rincewind flatly. There was no reply from the tourist, and when the wizard craned around he was horrified to see Twoflower looking up at the paling stars with an odd smile on his face.

'Don't you even think about it,' added Rincewind, menacingly.

The man you seek is talking to the dragonwoman said the dragon.

'Hmm?' said Twoflower, still looking at the paling stars.

'What?' said Rincewind urgently.

'Oh yes. Hrun,' said Twoflower. 'I hope we're in time. Dive now! Go low!'

Rincewind opened his eyes as the wind increased to a whistling gale. Perhaps they were blown open – the wind certainly made them impossible to shut.

The flat summit of the Wyrmberg rose up at them, lurched alarmingly, then somersaulted into a green blur that flashed by on either side. Tiny woods and fields blurred into a rushing patchwork. A brief silvery flash in the landscape may have been the little river that overflowed into the air at the plateau's rim. Rincewind tried to force the memory out of his mind, but it was rather enjoying itself there, terrorizing the other occupants and kicking over the furniture.

'I think not,' said Liessa.

Hrun took the wine cup, slowly. He grinned like a pumpkin.

Around the arena the dragons started to bay. Their riders looked up. And something like a green blur flashed across the arena, and Hrun had gone.

The wine cup hung momentarily in the air, then crashed down on the steps. Only then did a single drop spill.

This was because, in the instant of enfolding Hrun gently in his claws, Ninereeds the dragon had momentarily synchronized their bodily rhythms.

Since the dimension of the imagination is much more complex than those of time and space, which are very junior dimensions indeed, the effect of this was to instantly transform a stationary and priapic Hrun into a Hrun moving sideways at eighty miles an hour with no ill-effects whatsoever, except for a few wasted mouthfuls of wine. Another effect was to cause Liessa to scream with rage and summon her dragon. As the gold beast materialized in front of her she leapt astride it, still naked, and snatched a crossbow from one of the guards. Then she was airborne, while the other dragonriders swarmed towards their own beasts.

The Loremaster, watching from the pillar he had prudently slid behind in the mad scramble, happened at that moment to catch the cross-dimensional echoes of a theory being at the same instant hatched in the mind of an early psychiatrist in an adjacent universe, possibly because the dimension-leak was flowing both ways, and for a moment the psychiatrist saw the girl on the dragon. The Loremaster smiled.

'Want to bet that she won't catch him?' said Greicha, in a voice of worms and sepulchres, right by his ear.

The Loremaster shut his eyes and swallowed hard.

'I thought that my Lord would now be residing fully in the Dread Land,' he managed.

'I am a wizard,' said Greicha. 'Death Himself must claim a wizard. And, aha, He doesn't appear to be in the neighbourhood . . .'

SHALL WE GO? asked Death.

He was on a white horse, a horse of flesh and blood

but red of eye and fiery of nostril, and He stretched out a bony hand and took Greicha's soul out of the air and rolled it up until it was a point of painful light, and then He swallowed it.

Then He clapped spurs to his steed and it sprang into the air, sparks coruscating from its hooves.

'Lord Greicha!' whispered the old Loremaster, as the universe flickered around him.

'That was a mean trick,' came the wizard's voice, a mere speck of sound disappearing into the infinite black dimensions.

'My Lord . . . what is Death like?' called the old man tremulously.

'When I have investigated it fully, I will let you know,' came the faintest of modulations on the breeze.

'Yes,' murmured the Loremaster. A thought struck him. 'During daylight, please,' he added.

'You clowns,' screamed Hrun, from his perch on Ninereeds' foreclaws.

'What did he say?' roared Rincewind, as the dragon ripped its way through the air in the race for the heights.

'Didn't hear!' bellowed Twoflower, his voice torn away by the gale. As the dragon banked slightly he looked down at the little toy spinning top that was the mighty Wyrmberg and saw the swarm of creatures rising in pursuit. Ninereeds' wings pounded and flicked the air away contemptuously. Thinner air, too. Twoflower's ear popped for the third time.

Ahead of the swarm, he noticed, was a golden dragon. Someone on it, too.

'Hey, are you all right?' said Rincewind urgently. He had to drink in several lungfuls of the strangely distilled air in order to get the words out.

'I could have been a lord, and you clowns had to go and—' Hrun gasped, as the chill thin air drew the life even out of his mighty chest.

'Wass happnin to the air?' muttered Rincewind. Blue lights appeared in front of his eyes.

'Unk,' said Twoflower, and passed out.

The dragon vanished.

For a few seconds the three men continued upwards, Twoflower and the wizard presenting an odd picture as they sat one in front of the other with their legs astride something that wasn't there. Then what passed for gravity on the disc recovered from the surprise, and claimed them.

At that moment Liessa's dragon flashed by, and Hrun landed heavily across its neck. Liessa leaned over and kissed him.

This detail was lost to Rincewind as he dropped away, with his arms still clasped around Twoflower's waist. The disc was a little round map pinned against the sky. It didn't appear to be moving, but Rincewind knew that it was. The whole world was coming towards him like a giant custard pie.

'Wake up!' he shouted, above the roar of the wind. 'Dragons! Think of dragons!'

There was a flurry of wings as they plummeted through the host of pursuing creatures, which fell away and up. Dragons screamed and wheeled across the sky.

No answer came from Twoflower. Rincewind's robe whipped around him, but he did not wake.

Dragons, thought Rincewind in a panic. He tried to concentrate his mind, tried to envisage a really lifelike dragon. If he can do it, he thought, then so can I. But nothing happened.

The disc was bigger now, a cloud-swirled circle rising gently underneath them.

Rincewind tried again, screwing up his eyes and straining every nerve in his body. A dragon. His imagination, a somewhat battered and over-used organ, reached out for a dragon . . . any dragon.

IT WON'T WORK, laughed a voice like the dull tolling of a funereal bell, YOU DON'T BELIEVE IN THEM.

Rincewind looked at the terrible mounted apparition grinning at him, and his mind bolted in terror.

There was a brilliant flash.

There was utter darkness.

There was a soft floor under Rincewind's feet, a pink light around him, and the sudden shocked cries of many people.

He looked around wildly. He was standing in some kind of tunnel, which was mostly filled with seats in which outlandishly dressed people had been strapped. They were all shouting at him.

'Wake up!' he hissed. 'Help me!'

Dragging the still-unconscious tourist with him he backed away from the mob until his free hand found an oddly shaped door handle. He twisted it and ducked through, then slammed it hard.

He stared around the new room in which he found himself and met the terrified gaze of a young woman who dropped the tray she was holding and screamed.

It sounded like the sort of scream that brings muscular help. Rincewind, awash with fear distilled adrenalin, turned and barged past her. There were more seats here, and the people in them ducked as he dragged Twoflower urgently along the central gangway. Beyond the rows of seats were little windows. Beyond the windows, against a background of fleecy clouds, was a dragon's wing. It was silver.

I've been eaten by a dragon, he thought. That's ridiculous, he replied, you can't see out of dragons. Then his shoulder hit the door at the far end of the tunnel, and he followed it through into a cone-shaped room that was even stranger than the tunnel.

It was full of tiny glittering lights. Among the lights, in contoured chairs, were four men who were now staring at him open-mouthed. As he stared back he saw their gazes dart sideways.

Rincewind turned slowly. Beside him was a fifth man – youngish, bearded, as swarthy as the nomad folk of the Great Nef.

'Where am I?' said the wizard. 'In the belly of a dragon?'

The young man crouched back and shoved a small black box in the wizard's face. The men in the chairs ducked down.

'What is it?' said Rincewind. 'A picturebox?' He reached out and took it, a movement which appeared to surprise the swarthy man, who shouted and tried to snatch it back. There was another shout, this time from one of the men in the chairs. Only now he wasn't sitting. He was standing up, pointing something small and metallic at the young man.

It had an amazing effect. The man crouched back with his hands in the air.

'Please give me the bomb, sir,' said the man with the metallic thing. 'Carefully, please.'

'This thing?' said Rincewind. 'You have it! I don't want it!' The man took it very carefully and put it on the floor. The seated men relaxed, and one of them started speaking urgently to the wall. The wizard watched him in amazement.

'*Don't move!*' snapped the man with the metal – an amulet, Rincewind decided, it must be an amulet. The swarthy man backed into the corner.

'That was a very brave thing you did,' said Amulet-holder to Rincewind. 'You know that?'

'What?'

'What's the matter with your friend?'

'Friend?'

Rincewind looked down at Twoflower, who was still slumbering peacefully. That was no surprise. What was *really* surprising was that Twoflower was wearing new clothes. Strange clothes. His britches now ended just above his knees. Above that he wore some sort of vest of brightly striped material. On his head was a ridiculous little straw hat. With a feather in it.

An awkward feeling around the leg regions made Rincewind look down. *His* clothes had changed too. Instead of the comfortable old robe, so marvellously well adapted for speed into action in all possible contingencies, his legs were encased in cloth tubes. He was wearing a jacket of the same grey material . . .

Until now he'd never heard the language the man

with the amulet was using. It was uncouth and vaguely Hublandish – so why could he understand every word?

Let's see, they'd suddenly appeared in this dragon after, they'd materialized in this drag, they'd sudd, they'd, they'd – *they had struck up a conversation in the airport so naturally they had chosen to sit together on the plane, and he'd promised to show Jack Zweiblumen around when they got back to the States.* Yes, that was it. And then Jack had been taken ill and he'd panicked and come through here and surprised this hijacker. Of course. What on earth was 'Hublandish'?

Dr Rjinswand rubbed his forehead. What he could do with was a drink.

Ripples of paradox spread out across the sea of causality.

Possibly the most important point that would have to be borne in mind by anyone outside the sum totality of the multiverse was that although the wizard and the tourist had indeed only recently appeared in an aircraft in mid-air, they had also at one and the same time been riding on that aeroplane in the normal course of things. That is to say: while it was true that they had just appeared in this particular set of dimensions, it was also true that they had been living in them all along. It is at this point that normal language gives up, and goes and has a drink.

The point is that several quintillion atoms had just materialized (however, they had not. See below) in a universe where they should not strictly have been. The usual upshot of this sort of thing is a vast explosion but, since universes are fairly resilient things, this particular universe had saved itself by instantaneously unravelling its space-time continuum back to a point where the surplus atoms could safely be accommodated and then rapidly rewinding back to that circle of firelight which for want of a better term its inhabitants were wont to call The Present. This had of course changed history – there had been a few less wars, a few extra dinosaurs and so on – but on the whole the episode passed remarkably quietly.

Outside of this particular universe, however, the repercussions of the sudden double-take bounced to and fro across the face of The Sum of Things, bending whole dimensions and sinking galaxies without a trace.

All this was however totally lost on Dr Rjinswand, 33, a bachelor, born in Sweden, raised in New Jersey, and a specialist in the breakaway oxidation phenomena of certain nuclear reactors. Anyway, he probably would not have believed any of it.

Zweiblumen still seemed to be unconscious. The stewardess, who had helped Rjinswand to his seat to the applause of the rest of the passengers, was bending over him anxiously.

'We've radioed ahead,' she told Rjinswand. 'There'll be an ambulance waiting when we land. Uh, it says on the passenger list that you're a doctor—'

'I don't know what's wrong with him,' said Rjinswand hurriedly. 'It might be a different matter if he was a Magnox reactor of course. Is it shock of some kind?'

'I've never—'

Her sentence terminated in a tremendous crash from the rear of the plane. Several passengers screamed. A sudden gale of air swept every loose magazine and newspaper into a screaming whirlwind that twisted madly down the aisle.

Something else was coming *up* the aisle. Something big and oblong and wooden and brass-bound. It had hundreds of legs. If it was what it seemed – a walking chest of the kind that appeared in pirate stories brim full of ill-gotten gold and jewels – then what would have been its lid suddenly gaped open.

There were no jewels. But there *were* lots of big square teeth, white as sycamore, and a pulsating tongue, red as mahogany.

An ancient suitcase was coming to eat him.

Rjinswand clutched at the unconscious Zweiblumen for what little comfort there was there, and gibbered. He wished fervently that he was somewhere else . . .

There was a sudden darkness.

There was a brilliant flash.

The sudden departure of several quintillion atoms from a universe that they had no right to be in anyway caused a wild imbalance in the harmony of the Sum Totality which it tried frantically to retrieve, wiping out a number of sub-realities in the process. Huge surges of raw magic boiled uncontrolled around the very foundations of the multiverse itself, welling up through every crevice into hitherto peaceful dimensions and causing novas, supernovas, stellar collisions, wild flights of geese and drowning of imaginary continents. Worlds as far away as the other end of time experienced brilliant sunsets of coruscating octarine as highly charged magical particles roared through the atmosphere. In the cometary halo around the fabled Ice System of Zeret a noble comet died as a prince flamed across the sky.

All this was however lost on Rincewind as, clutching the inert Twoflower around the waist, he plunged towards the Disc's sea several hundred feet below. Not even the convulsions of all the dimensions could break the iron Law of the Conservation of Energy, and Rjinswand's brief journey in the plane had sufficed to carry him several hundred miles horizontally and seven thousand feet vertically.

The word 'plane' flamed and died in Rincewind's mind.

Was that a ship down there?

The cold waters of the Circle Sea roared up at him and sucked him down into their green, suffocating embrace. A moment later there was another splash as the Luggage, still bearing a label carrying the powerful travelling rune TWA, also hit the sea.

Later on, they used it as a raft.

CLOSE TO
THE EDGE

IT HAD BEEN A LONG time in the making. Now it was almost completed, and the slaves hacked away at the last clay remnants of the mantle.

Where other slaves were industriously rubbing its metal flanks with silver sand it was already beginning to gleam in the sun with the silken, organic sheen of young bronze. It was still warm, even after a week of cooling in the casting pit.

The Arch-astronomer of Krull motioned lightly with his hand and his bearers set the throne down in the shadow of the hull.

Like a fish, he thought. A great flying fish. And of what seas?

'It is indeed magnificent,' he whispered. 'A work of true art.'

'Craft,' said the thickset man by his side. The Arch-astronomer turned slowly and looked up at the man's impassive face. It isn't particularly hard for a face to look impassive when there are two golden spheres where the eyes should be. They glowed disconcertingly.

'Craft, indeed,' said the astronomer, and smiled. 'I would imagine that there is no greater craftsman on the entire disc than you, Goldeneyes. Would I be right?'

The craftsman paused, his naked body – naked, at

least, were it not for a toolbelt, a wrist abacus and a deep tan – tensing as he considered the implications of this last remark. The golden eyes appeared to be looking into some other world.

'The answer is both yes and no,' he said at last. Some of the lesser astronomers behind the throne gasped at this lack of etiquette, but the Arch-astronomer appeared not to have noticed it.

'Continue,' he said.

'There are some essential skills that I lack. Yet I am Goldeneyes Silverhand Dactylos,' said the craftsman. 'I made the Metal Warriors that guard the Tomb of Pitchiu, I designed the Light Dams of the Great Nef, I built the Palace of the Seven Deserts. And yet—' he reached up and tapped one of his eyes, which rang faintly, 'when I built the golem army for Pitchiu he loaded me down with gold and then, so that I would create no other work to rival my work for him, he had my eyes put out.'

'Wise but cruel,' said the Arch-astronomer sympathetically.

'Yah. So I learned to *hear* the temper of metals and to see with my fingers. I learned how to distinguish ores by taste and smell. I made these eyes, but I cannot make them see.

'Next I was summoned to build the Palace of the Seven Deserts, as a result of which the Emir showered me with silver and then, not entirely to my surprise, had my right hand cut off.'

'A grave hindrance in your line of business,' nodded the Arch-astronomer.

'I used some of the silver to make myself this new

hand, putting to use my unrivalled knowledge of levers and fulcrums. It suffices. After I created the first great Light Dam, which had a capacity of 50,000 daylight hours, the tribal councils of the Nef loaded me down with fine silks and then hamstrung me so that I could not escape. As a result I was put to some inconvenience to use the silk and some bamboo to build a flying machine from which I could launch myself from the top-most turret of my prison.'

'Bringing you, by various diversions, to Krull,' said the Arch-astronomer. 'And one cannot help feeling that some alternative occupation – lettuce farming, say – would offer somewhat less of a risk of being put to death by instalments. Why do you persist in it?'

Goldeneyes Dactylos shrugged.

'I'm good at it,' he said.

The Arch-astronomer looked up again at the bronze fish, shining now like a gong in the noontime sun.

'Such beauty,' he murmured. 'And unique. Come, Dactylos. Recall to me what it was that I promised should be your reward?'

'You asked me to design a fish that would swim through the seas of space that lie between the worlds,' intoned the master craftsman. 'In return for which – in return—'

'Yes? My memory is not what it used to be,' purred the Arch-astronomer, stroking the warm bronze.

'In return,' continued Dactylos, without much apparent hope, 'you would set me free, and refrain from chopping off any appendages. I require no treasure.'

'Ah, yes. I recall now.' The old man raised a blue-veined hand, and added, 'I lied.'

There was the merest whisper of sound, and the goldeneyed man rocked on his feet. Then he looked down at the arrowhead protruding from his chest, and nodded wearily. A speck of blood bloomed on his lips.

There was no sound in the entire square (save for the buzzing of a few expectant flies) as his silver hand came up, very slowly, and fingered the arrowhead.

Dactylos grunted.

'Sloppy workmanship,' he said, and toppled backwards.

The Arch-astronomer prodded the body with his toe, and sighed.

'There will be a short period of mourning, as befits a master craftsman,' he said. He watched a bluebottle alight on one golden eye and fly away puzzled . . . 'That would seem to be long enough,' said the Arch-astronomer, and beckoned a couple of slaves to carry the corpse away.

'Are the chelonauts ready?' he asked.

The Master Launchcontroller bustled forward.

'Indeed, your prominence,' he said.

'The correct prayers are being intoned?'

'Quite so, your prominence.'

'How long to the doorway?'

'The launch window,' corrected the Master Launch-controller carefully. 'Three days, your prominence. Great A'Tuin's tail will be in an unmatched position.'

'Then all that remains,' concluded the Arch-astronomer, 'is to find the appropriate sacrifices.'

The Master Launchcontroller bowed.

'The ocean shall provide,' he said.

The old man smiled. 'It always does,' he said.

'If only you could navigate—'

'If only you could steer—'

A wave washed over the deck. Rincewind and Twoflower looked at each other. 'Keep bailing!' they screamed in unison, and reached for the buckets.

After a while Twoflower's peevish voice filtered up from the waterlogged cabin.

'I don't see how it's my fault,' he said. He handed up another bucket, which the wizard tipped over the side.

'You were supposed to be on watch,' snapped Rincewind.

'I saved us from the slavers, remember,' said Twoflower.

'I'd rather be a slave than a corpse,' replied the wizard. He straightened up and looked out to sea. He appeared puzzled.

He was a somewhat different Rincewind from the one that had escaped the fire of Ankh-Morpork some six months before. More scarred, for one thing, and much more travelled. He had visited the Hublands, discovered the curious folkways of many colourful peoples – invariably obtaining more scars in the process – and had even, for a never-to-be-forgotten few days, sailed on the legendary Dehydrated Ocean at the heart of the incredibly dry desert known as the Great Nef. On a colder and wetter sea he had seen floating mountains of ice. He had ridden on an imaginary dragon. He had very nearly said the most powerful spell on the disc. He had—

There was *definitely* less horizon than there ought to be.

'Hmm?' said Rincewind.

'I said nothing's worse than slavery,' said Twoflower. His mouth opened as the wizard flung his bucket far out to sea and sat down heavily on the waterlogged deck, his face a grey mask.

'Look, I'm sorry I steered us into the reef, but this boat doesn't seem to want to sink and we're bound to strike land sooner or later,' said Twoflower comfortingly. 'This current must go somewhere.'

'Look at the horizon,' said Rincewind, in a monotone.

Twoflower squinted.

'It looks all right,' he said after a while. 'Admittedly, there seems to be *less* than there usually is, but—'

'That's because of the Rimfall,' said Rincewind. 'We're being carried over the edge of the world.'

There was a long silence, broken only by the lapping of the waves as the foundering ship spun slowly in the current. It was already quite strong.

'That's probably why we hit that reef,' Rincewind added. 'We got pulled off course during the night.'

'Would you like something to eat?' asked Twoflower. He began to rummage through the bundle that he had tied to the rail, out of the damp.

'Don't you understand?' snarled Rincewind. 'We are going over the *Edge*, godsdammit!'

'Can't we do anything about it?'

'No!'

'Then I can't see the sense in panicking,' said Twoflower calmly.

'I *knew* we shouldn't have come this far Edgewise,' complained Rincewind to the sky, 'I wish—'

'I wish I had my picturebox,' said Twoflower, 'but it's back on that slaver ship with the rest of the Luggage and—'

'You won't need luggage where we're going,' said Rincewind. He sagged, and stared moodily at a distant whale that had carelessly strayed into the rimward current and was now struggling against it.

There was a line of white on the foreshortened horizon, and the wizard fancied he could hear a distant roaring.

'What happens after a ship goes over the Rimfall?' said Twoflower.

'Who knows?'

'Well, in that case perhaps we'll just sail on through space and land on another world.' A faraway look came into the little man's eyes. 'I'd like that,' he said.

Rincewind snorted.

The sun rose in the sky, looking noticeably bigger this close to the Edge. They stood with their backs against the mast, busy with their own thoughts. Every so often one or other would pick up a bucket and do a bit of desultory bailing, for no very intelligent reason.

The sea around them seemed to be getting crowded. Rincewind noticed several tree trunks keeping station with them, and just below the surface the water was alive with fish of all sorts. Of course – the current must be teeming with food washed from the continents near the Hub. He wondered what kind of life it would be, having to keep swimming all the time to stay exactly in the same place. Pretty similar to his own, he decided. He spotted a small green frog which was paddling desperately in the grip of the inexorable current. To Twoflower's amazement he found a paddle and carefully extended it towards the little amphibian, which scrambled onto it gratefully. A moment later a pair of jaws broke the water and snapped impotently at the spot where it had been swimming.

The frog looked up at Rincewind from the cradle of his hands, and then bit him thoughtfully on the thumb. Twoflower giggled. Rincewind tucked the frog away in a pocket, and pretended he hadn't heard.

'All very humanitarian, but why?' said Twoflower. 'It'll all be the same in an hour.'

'Because,' said Rincewind vaguely, and did a bit of bailing. Spray was being thrown up now and the current was so strong that waves were forming and breaking all around them. It all seemed unnaturally warm. There was a hot golden haze on the sea.

The roaring was louder now. A squid bigger than anything Rincewind had seen before broke the surface a few hundred yards away and thrashed madly with its tentacles before sinking away. Something else that was large and fortunately unidentifiable howled in the mist. A whole squadron of flying fish tumbled up in a cloud of rainbow-edged droplets and managed to gain a few yards before dropping back and being swept in an eddy.

They were running out of world. Rincewind

dropped his bucket and snatched at the mast as the roaring, final end of everything raced towards them.

'I must see this—' said Twoflower, half falling and half diving towards the prow.

Something hard and unyielding smacked into the hull, which spun ninety degrees and came side-on to the invisible obstacle. Then it stopped suddenly and a wash of cold sea foam cascaded over the deck, so that for a few seconds Rincewind was under several feet of boiling green water. He began to scream and then the underwater world became the deep clanging purple colour of fading consciousness, because it was at about this point that Rincewind started to drown.

He awoke with his mouth full of burning liquid and, when he swallowed, the searing pain in his throat jerked him into full consciousness.

The boards of a boat pressed into his back and Twoflower was looking down at him with an expression of deep concern. Rincewind groaned, and sat up.

This turned out to be a mistake. The edge of the world was a few feet away.

Beyond it, at a level just below that of the lip of the endless Rimfall, was something altogether *magical*.

Some seventy miles away, and well beyond the tug of the rim current, a dhow with the red sails typical of a freelance slaver drifted aimlessly through the velvety twilight. The crew – such as remained – were clustered on the foredeck, surrounding the men working feverishly on the raft.

The captain, a thickset man who wore the elbow-turbans typical of a Great Nef tribesman, was much travelled and had seen many strange peoples and curious things, many of which he had subsequently enslaved or stolen. He had begun his career as a sailor on the Dehydrated Ocean in the heart of the disc's driest desert. (Water on the disc has an uncommon fourth state, caused by intense heat combined with the strange desiccating effects of octarine light: it dehydrates, leaving a silvery residue like free-flowing sand through which a well-designed hull can glide with ease. The Dehydrated Ocean is a strange place, but not so strange as its fish.) The captain had never before been really frightened. Now he was terrified.

'I can't hear anything,' he muttered to the first mate.

The mate peered into the gloom.

'Perhaps it fell overboard?' he suggested hopefully. As if in answer there came a furious pounding from the oar deck below their feet, and the sound of splintering wood. The crewmen drew together fearfully, brandishing axes and torches.

They probably wouldn't dare to use them, even if the Monster came rushing towards them. Before its terrible nature had been truly understood several men had attacked it with axes, whereupon it had turned aside from its single-minded searching of the ship and had either chased them overboard or had – *eaten* them? The captain was not quite certain. The Thing looked like an ordinary wooden sea chest. A bit larger than usual, maybe, but not suspiciously so. But while it sometimes seemed to contain things like old socks and miscellaneous luggage, at other times – and he shuddered – it seemed to be, seemed to *have* . . . He tried not to think about it. It was just that the men who had been drowned overboard had probably been more fortunate than those it had caught. He tried not to think about it. There had been *teeth*, teeth like white wooden gravestones, and a tongue red as mahogany . . .

He tried not to think about it. It didn't work.

But he thought bitterly about one thing. This was going to be the last time he rescued ungrateful drowning men in mysterious circumstances. Slavery was better than sharks, wasn't it? And then they had escaped and when his sailors had investigated their big chest – how had they appeared in the middle of an untroubled ocean sitting on a big chest, anyway? – it had bitt . . . He tried not to think about it again, but he found himself wondering what would happen when the damned thing realized that its owner wasn't on board any longer . . .

'Raft's ready, lord,' said the first mate.

'Into the water with it,' shouted the captain, and 'Get aboard!' and 'Fire the ship!'

After all, another ship wouldn't be too hard to come by, he philosophized, but a man might have to wait a long time in that Paradise the mullahs advertised before he was granted another life. Let the magical box eat lobsters.

Some pirates achieved immortality by great deeds of cruelty or derring-do. Some achieved immortality by amassing great wealth. But the captain had long ago decided that he would, on the whole, prefer to achieve immortality by not dying.

* * *

'What the hell is that?' demanded Rincewind.

'It's beautiful,' said Twoflower beatifically.

'I'll decide about that when I know what it is,' said the wizard.

'It is the Rimbow,' said a voice immediately behind his left ear, 'and you are fortunate indeed to be looking at it. From above, at any rate.'

The voice was accompanied by a gust of cold, fishy breath. Rincewind sat quite still.

'Twoflower?' he said.

'Yes?'

'If I turn around, what will I see?'

'His name is Tethis. He says he's a sea troll. This is his boat. He rescued us,' explained Twoflower. 'Will you look around now?'

'Not just at the moment, thank you. So why aren't we going over the Edge, then?' asked Rincewind with glassy calmness.

'Because your boat hit the Circumfence,' said the voice behind him (in tones that made Rincewind imagine submarine chasms and lurking Things in coral reefs).

'The Circumfence?' he repeated.

'Yes. It runs along the edge of the world,' said the unseen troll. Above the roar of the waterfall Rincewind thought he could make out the splash of oars. He *hoped* they were oars.

'Ah. You mean the *circumference*,' said Rincewind. 'The circumference makes the edge of things.'

'So does the Circumfence,' said the troll.

'He means this,' said Twoflower, pointing down.

Rincewind's eyes followed the finger, dreading what they might see . . .

Hubwards of the boat was a rope suspended a few feet above the surface of the white water. The boat was attached to it, moored yet mobile, by a complicated arrangement of pulleys and little wooden wheels. They ran along the rope as the unseen rower propelled the craft along the very lip of the Rimfall. That explained one mystery – but what supported the rope?

Rincewind peered along its length and saw a stout wooden post sticking up out of the water a few yards ahead. As he watched the boat neared it and then passed it, the little wheels clacking neatly around it in a groove obviously cut for the purpose.

Rincewind also noticed that smaller ropes hung down from the main rope at intervals of a yard or so.

He turned back to Twoflower.

'I can see what it *is*,' he said, 'but *what* is it?'

Twoflower shrugged. Behind Rincewind the sea troll said, 'Up ahead is my house. We will talk more when we are there. Now I must row.'

Rincewind found that looking ahead meant that he would have to turn and find out what a sea troll actually looked like, and he wasn't sure he wanted to do that yet. He looked at the Rimbow instead.

It hung in the mists a few lengths beyond the edge of the world, appearing only at morning and evening when the light of the disc's little orbiting sun shone past the massive bulk of Great A'Tuin the World Turtle and struck the disc's magical field at exactly the right angle.

A double rainbow coruscated into being. Close into the lip of the Rimfall were the seven lesser colours, sparkling and dancing in the spray of the dying seas.

But they were pale in comparison to the wider band that floated beyond them, not deigning to share the same spectrum.

It was the King Colour, of which all the lesser colours are merely partial and wishy-washy reflections. It was octarine, the colour of magic. It was alive and glowing and vibrant and it was the undisputed pigment of the imagination, because wherever it appeared it was a sign that mere matter was a servant of the powers of the magical mind. It was enchantment itself.

But Rincewind always thought it looked a sort of greenish-purple.

After a while a small speck on the rim of the world resolved itself into a eyot or crag, so perilously perched that the waters of the fall swirled around it at the start of their long drop. A driftwood shanty had been built on it, and Rincewind saw that the top rope of the Circumfence climbed over the rocky island on a number of iron stakes and actually passed through the shack by a small round window. He learned later that this was so that the troll could be alerted to the arrival of any salvage on his stretch of the Circumfence by means of a series of small bronze bells, balanced delicately on the rope.

A crude floating stockade had been built out of rough timber on the hubward side of the island. It contained one or two hulks and quite a large amount of floating wood in the form of planks, baulks and even whole natural tree trunks, some still sporting green leaves. This close to the Edge the disc's magical field was so intense that a hazy corona flickered across everything as raw illusion spontaneously discharged itself.

With a last few squeaky jerks the boat slid up against a small driftwood jetty. As it grounded itself and formed a circuit Rincewind felt all the familiar sensations of a huge occult aura – oily, bluish-tasting, and smelling of tin. All around them pure, unfocused magic was sleeting soundlessly into the world.

The wizard and Twoflower scrambled onto the planking and for the first time Rincewind saw the troll.

It wasn't half so dreadful as he had imagined.

Umm, said his imagination after a while.

It wasn't that the troll was *horrifying*. Instead of the rotting, betentacled monstrosity he had been expecting Rincewind found himself looking at a rather squat but not particularly ugly old man who would quite easily have passed for normal on any city street, always provided that other people on the street were *used* to seeing old men who were apparently composed of water and very little else. It was as if the ocean had decided to create life without going through all that tedious business of evolution, and had simply formed a part of itself into a biped and sent it walking squishily up the beach. The troll was a pleasant translucent blue colour. As Rincewind stared a small shoal of silver fish flashed across its chest.

'It's rude to stare,' said the troll. Its mouth opened

with a little crest of foam, and shut again in exactly the same way that water closes over a stone.

'Is it? Why?' said Rincewind. How does he hold himself together, his mind screamed at him. Why doesn't he spill?

'If you will follow me to my house I will find you food and a change of clothing,' said the troll solemnly. He set off over the rocks without turning to see if they would follow him. After all, where else could they go? It was getting dark, and a chilly damp breeze was blowing over the edge of the world. Already the transient Rimbow had faded and the mists above the waterfall were beginning to thin.

'Come on,' said Rincewind, grabbing Twoflower's elbow. But the tourist didn't appear to want to move.

'Come on,' the wizard repeated.

'When it gets really dark, do you think we'll be able to look down and see Great A'Tuin the World Turtle?' asked Twoflower, staring at the rolling clouds.

'I hope not,' said Rincewind, 'I really do. Now let's go, shall we?'

Twoflower followed him reluctantly into the shack. The troll had lit a couple of lamps and was sitting comfortably in a rocking chair. He got to his feet as they entered and poured two cups of a green liquid from a tall pitcher. In the dim light he appeared to phosphoresce, in the manner of warm seas on velvety summer nights. Just to add a baroque gloss to Rincewind's dull terror he seemed to be several inches taller, too.

Most of the furniture in the room appeared to be boxes.

'Uh. Really great place you've got here,' said Rincewind. 'Ethnic.'

He reached for a cup and looked at the green pool shimmering inside it. It'd better be drinkable, he thought. Because I'm going to drink it. He swallowed.

It was the same stuff Twoflower had given him in the rowing boat but, at the time, his mind had ignored it because there were more pressing matters. Now it had the leisure to savour the taste.

Rincewind's mouth twisted. He whimpered a little. One of his legs came up convulsively and caught him painfully in the chest.

Twoflower swirled his own drink thoughtfully while he considered the flavour.

'Ghlen Livid,' he said. 'The fermented *vul* nut drink they freeze-distil in my home country. A certain smokey quality ... Piquant. From the western plantations in, ah, Rehigreed Province, yes? Next year's harvest, I fancy, from the colour. May I ask how you came by it?'

(Plants on the disc, while including the categories known commonly as *annuals*, which were sown this year to come up later this year, *biennials*, sown this year to grow next year, and *perennials*, sown this year to grow until further notice, also included a few rare *re-annuals* which, because of an unusual four-dimensional twist in their genes, could be planted this year to come up *last year*. The *vul* nut vine was particularly exceptional in that it could flourish as many as eight years prior to its seed actually being sown. *Vul* nut wine was reputed to give certain drinkers an insight into the future which was, from the nut's point of view, the past. Strange but true.)

'All things drift into the Circumfence in time,' said the troll, gnomically, gently rocking in his chair. 'My job is to recover the flotsam. Timber, of course, and ships. Barrels of wine. Bales of cloth. You.'

Light dawned inside Rincewind's head.

'It's a net, isn't it? You've got a net right on the edge of the sea!'

'The Circumfence,' nodded the troll. Ripples ran across his chest.

Rincewind looked out into the phosphorescent darkness that surrounded the island, and grinned inanely.

'Of course,' he said. 'Amazing! You could sink piles and attach it to reefs and – good grief! The net would have to be *very* strong.'

'It is,' said Tethis.

'It could be extended for a couple of miles, if you found enough rocks and things,' said the wizard.

'Ten thousands of miles. I just patrol this league.'

'That's a third of the way around the disc!'

Tethis sloshed a little as he nodded again. While the two men helped themselves to some more of the green wine, he told them about the Circumfence, the great effort that had been made to build it, and the ancient and wise Kingdom of Krull which had constructed it several centuries before, and the seven navies that patrolled it constantly to keep it in repair and bring its salvage back to Krull, and the manner in which Krull had become a land of leisure ruled by the most learned seekers after knowledge, and the way in which they sought constantly to understand in every possible particular the wondrous complexity of the universe, and the way in which sailors marooned on the Circumfence were turned into slaves, and usually had their tongues cut out. After some interjections at this point he spoke, in a friendly way, on the futility of force, the impossibility of escaping from the island except by boat to one of the other three hundred and eighty isles that lay between the island and Krull itself, or by leaping over the Edge, and the high merit of muteness in comparison to, for example, death.

There was a pause. The muted night-roar of the Rimfall only served to give the silence a heavier texture.

Then the rocking chair started to creak again. Tethis seemed to have grown alarmingly during the monologue.

'There is nothing personal in all this,' he added. 'I too am a slave. If you try to overpower me I shall have to kill you, of course, but I won't take any particular pleasure in it.'

Rincewind looked at the shimmering fists that rested lightly in the troll's lap. He suspected they could strike with all the force of a tsunami.

'I don't think you understand,' explained Two-flower. 'I am a citizen of the Golden Empire. I'm sure Krull would not wish to incur the displeasure of the Emperor.'

'How will the Emperor know?' asked the troll. 'Do you think you're the first person from the Empire who has ended up on the Circumfence?'

'I won't be a slave!' shouted Rincewind. 'I'd – I'd jump over the Edge first!' He was amazed at the sound in his own voice.

'Would you, though?' asked the troll. The rocking chair flicked back against the wall and one blue arm caught the wizard around the waist. A moment later the troll was striding out of the shack with Rincewind gripped carelessly in one fist.

He did not stop until he came to the rimward edge of the island. Rincewind squealed.

'Stop that or I really will throw you over the edge,' snapped the troll. 'I'm holding you, aren't I? Look.'

Rincewind looked.

In front of him was a soft black night whose mist-muted stars glowed peacefully. But his eyes turned downwards, drawn by some irresistible fascination.

It was midnight on the disc and so, therefore, the sun was far, far below, swinging slowly under Great A'Tuin's vast and frosty plastron. Rincewind tried a last attempt to fix his gaze on the tips of his boots, which were protruding over the rim of the rock, but the sheer drop wrenched it away.

On either side of him two glittering curtains of water hurtled towards infinity as the sea swept around the island on its way to the long fall. A hundred yards below the wizard the largest sea salmon he had ever seen flicked itself out of the foam in a wild, jerky and ultimately hopeless leap. Then it fell back, over and over, in the golden underworld light.

Huge shadows grew out of that light like pillars supporting the roof of the universe. Hundreds of miles below him the wizard made out the shape of something, the edge of something—

Like those curious little pictures where the silhouette of an ornate glass suddenly becomes the outline of two faces, the scene beneath him flipped into a whole new, terrifying perspective. Because down there was the head of an elephant as big as a reasonably sized continent. One mighty tusk cut like a mountain against the golden light, trailing a widening shadow towards the stars. The head was slightly tilted, and a huge ruby eye might almost have been a red supergiant that had managed to shine at noonday.

Below the elephant—

Rincewind swallowed and tried not to think—

Below the elephant there was nothing but the distant, painful disc of the sun. And, sweeping slowly past it, was something that for all its city-sized scales, its crater-pocks, its lunar cragginess, was indubitably a flipper.

'Shall I let go?' suggested the troll.

'Gnah,' said Rincewind, straining backwards.

'I have lived *here on the Edge* for five years and I have not had the courage,' boomed Tethis. 'Nor have you, if I'm any judge.' He stepped back, allowing Rincewind to fling himself onto the ground.

Twoflower strolled up to the rim and peered over.

'Fantastic,' he said. 'If only I had my picturebox . . . What else is down there? I mean, if you jumped off, what would you see?'

Tethis sat down on an outcrop. High over the disc the moon came out from behind a cloud, giving him the appearance of ice.

'My home is down there, perhaps,' he said slowly. 'Beyond your silly elephants and that ridiculous turtle. A real world. Sometimes I come out here and look, but somehow I can never bring myself to take that extra step ... A real world, with real people. I have wives and little ones, somewhere down there ...' He stopped, and blew his nose. 'You soon learn what you're made of, *here on the Edge*.'

'Stop saying that. Please,' moaned Rincewind. He turned over and saw Twoflower standing unconcernedly at the very lip of the rock. 'Gnah,' he said, and tried to burrow into the stone.

'There's another world down there?' said Twoflower, peering over. 'Where, exactly?'

The troll waved an arm vaguely. 'Somewhere,' he said. 'That's all I know. It was quite a small world. Mostly blue.'

'So why are you here?' said Twoflower.

'Isn't it obvious?' snapped the troll. 'I fell off the edge!'

He told them of the world of Bathys, somewhere among the stars, where the seafolk had built a number of thriving civilizations in the three large oceans that sprawled across its disc. He had been a meatman, one of the caste which earned a perilous living in large, sail-powered land yachts that ventured far out to land and hunted the shoals of deer and buffalo that abounded in the storm-haunted continents. His particular yacht had been blown into uncharted lands by a freak gale. The rest of the crew had taken the yacht's little rowing trolley and had struck out for a distant lake, but Tethis, as master, had elected to remain with his vessel. The storm had carried it right over the rocky rim of the world, smashing it to matchwood in the process.

'At first I fell,' said Tethis, 'but falling isn't so bad, you know. It's only the landing that hurts, and there was nothing below me. As I fell I saw the world spin off into space until it was lost against the stars.'

'What happened next?' said Twoflower breathlessly, glancing towards the misty universe.

'I froze solid,' said Tethis simply. 'Fortunately it is something my race can survive. But I thawed out occasionally when I passed near other worlds. There was one, I think it was the one with what I thought was this strange ring of mountains around it that turned out to be the biggest dragon you could ever imagine, covered in snow and glaciers and holding its tail in its mouth – well, I came within a few leagues of that, I shot over the landscape like a comet, in fact, and then I was off again. Then there was a time I woke up and there was your world coming at me like a custard pie thrown by the Creator and, well, I landed in the sea not far from the Circumfence widdershins of Krull. All sorts of creatures get washed up against the Fence, and at the time they were looking for slaves to man the way stations, and I ended up here.' He stopped and stared intently at Rincewind. 'Every night I come out here and look down,' he finished, 'and I never jump. Courage is hard to come by, *here on the Edge*.'

Rincewind began to crawl determinedly towards the shack. He gave a little scream as the troll picked him up, not unkindly, and set him on his feet.

'Amazing,' said Twoflower, and leaned further out over the Edge. 'There are lots of other worlds out there?'

'Quite a number, I imagine,' said the troll.

'I suppose one could contrive some sort of, I don't know, some sort of a *thing* that could preserve one against the cold,' said the little man thoughtfully. 'Some sort of a ship that one could sail over the Edge and sail to far-off worlds, too. I wonder . . .'

'Don't even think about it!' moaned Rincewind. 'Stop talking like that, do you hear?'

'They all talk like that in Krull,' said Tethis. 'Those with tongues, of course,' he added.

'Are you awake?'

Twoflower snored on. Rincewind jabbed him viciously in the ribs.

'I said, are you awake?' he snarled.

'Scrdfngh . . .'

'We've got to get out of here before this salvage fleet comes!'

The dishwater light of dawn oozed through the shack's one window, slopping across the piles of salvaged boxes and bundles that were strewn around the interior. Twoflower grunted again and tried to burrow into the pile of furs and blankets that Tethis had given them.

'Look, there's all kinds of weapons and stuff in here,' said Rincewind. 'He's gone out somewhere. When he comes back we could overpower him and – and – well, then we can think of something. How about it?'

'That doesn't sound like a very good idea,' said Twoflower. 'Anyhow, it's a bit ungracious isn't it?'

'Tough buns,' snapped Rincewind. 'This is a rough universe.'

He rummaged through the piles around the walls and selected a heavy, wavy-bladed scimitar that had probably been some pirate's pride and joy. It looked the sort of weapon that relied as much on its weight as its edge to cause damage. He raised it awkwardly.

'Would he leave that sort of thing around if it could hurt him?' Twoflower wondered aloud.

Rincewind ignored him and took up a position beside the door. When it opened some ten minutes later he moved unhesitatingly, swinging it across the opening at what he judged was the troll's head height. It swished harmlessly through nothing at all and struck the doorpost, jerking him off his feet and on to the floor.

There was a sigh above him. He looked up into Tethis' face, which was shaking sadly from side to side.

'It wouldn't have harmed me,' said the troll, 'but nevertheless I am hurt. Deeply hurt.' He reached over the wizard and jerked the sword out of the wood. With no apparent effort he bent its blade into a circle and sent it bowling away over the rocks until it hit a stone and sprang, still spinning, in a silver arc that ended in the mists forming over the Rimfall.

'*Very* deeply hurt,' he concluded. He reached down beside the door and tossed a sack towards Twoflower.

'It's the carcass of a deer that is just about how you humans like it, and a few lobsters, and a sea salmon. The Circumfence provides,' he said casually.

He looked hard at the tourist, and then down again at Rincewind.

'What are you staring at?' he said.

'It's just that—' said Twoflower.

'—compared to last night—' said Rincewind.

'You're so *small*,' finished Twoflower.

'I *see*,' said the troll carefully. 'Personal remarks now.' He drew himself up to his full height, which was currently about four feet. 'Just because I'm made of water doesn't mean I'm made of wood, you know.'

'I'm sorry,' said Twoflower, climbing hastily out of the furs.

'You're made of *dirt*,' said the troll, 'but I didn't pass comments about things you can't help, did I? Oh, no. We can't help the way the Creator made us, that's my view. But if you must know, your moon here is rather more powerful than the ones around my own world.'

'The moon?' said Twoflower. 'I don't under—'

'If I've got to spell it out,' said the troll, testily, 'I'm suffering from chronic tides.'

A bell jangled in the darkness of the shack. Tethis strode across the creaking floor to the complicated device of levers, strings and bells that was mounted on the Circumfence's topmost strand where it passed through the hut.

The bell rang again, and then started to clang away in an odd jerky rhythm for several minutes. The troll stood with his ear pressed close to it.

When it stopped he turned slowly and looked at them with a worried frown.

'You're more important than I thought,' he said. 'You're not to wait for the salvage fleet. You're to be collected by a flyer. That's what they say in Krull.' He shrugged. 'And I hadn't even sent a message that you're here, yet. Someone's been drinking *vul* nut wine again.'

He picked up a large mallet that hung on a pillar beside the bell and used it to tap out a brief carillon.

'That'll be passed from lengthman to lengthman all the way back to Krull,' he said. 'Marvellous really, isn't it?'

It came speeding across the sea, floating a manlength above it, but still leaving a foaming wake as whatever power that held it up smacked brutally into the water. Rincewind *knew* what power held it up. He was, he would be the first to admit, a coward, an incompetent, and not even very good at being a failure; but he was still a wizard of sorts, he knew one of the Eight Great Spells, he would be claimed by Death himself when he died, and he recognized really finely honed magic when he saw it.

The lens skimming towards the island was perhaps twenty feet across, and totally transparent. Sitting around its circumference were a large number of black-robed men, each one strapped securely to the disc by a leather harness and each one staring down at the waves with an expression so tormented, so agonizing, that the transparent disc seemed to be ringed with gargoyles.

Rincewind sighed with relief. This was such an unusual sound that it made Twoflower take his eyes off the approaching disc and turn them on him.

'We're important, no lie,' explained Rincewind. 'They wouldn't be wasting all that magic on a couple of potential slaves.' He grinned.

'What is it?' said Twoflower.

'Well, the disc itself would have been created by

Fresnel's Wonderful Concentrator,' said Rincewind, authoritatively. 'That calls for many rare and unstable ingredients, such as demon's breath and so forth, and it takes at least eight fourth-grade wizards a week to envision. Then there's those wizards on it, who must all be gifted hydrophobes—'

'You mean they hate water?' said Twoflower.

'No, that wouldn't work,' said Rincewind. 'Hate is an attracting force, just like love. They really *loathe* it, the very idea of it revolts them. A really good hydrophobe has to be trained on dehydrated water from birth. I mean, that costs a fortune in magic alone. But they make great weather magicians. Rain clouds just give up and go away.'

'It sounds terrible,' said the water troll behind them.

'And they all die young,' said Rincewind, ignoring him. 'They just can't live with themselves.'

'Sometimes I think a man could wander across the disc all his life and not see everything there is to see,' said Twoflower. 'And now it seems there are lots of other worlds as well. When I think I might die without seeing a hundredth of all there is to see it makes me feel,' he paused, then added, 'well, humble, I suppose. And very angry, of course.'

The flyer halted a few yards hubward of the island, throwing up a sheet of spray. It hung there, spinning slowly. A hooded figure standing by the stubby pillar at the exact centre of the lens beckoned to them.

'You'd better wade out,' said the troll. 'It doesn't do to keep them waiting. It has been nice to make your acquaintance.' He shook them both, wetly, by the hand. As he waded out a little way with them the two nearest loathers on the lens shied away with expressions of extreme disgust.

The hooded figure reached down with one hand and released a rope ladder. In its other hand it held a silver rod, which had about it the unmistakable air of something designed for killing people. Rincewind's first impression was reinforced when the figure raised the stick and waved it carelessly towards the shore. A section of rock vanished, leaving a small grey haze of nothingness.

'That's so you don't think I'm afraid to use it,' said the figure.

'Don't think *you're* afraid?' said Rincewind. The hooded figure snorted.

'We know all about you, Rincewind the magician. You are a man of great cunning and artifice. You laugh in the face of Death. Your affected air of craven cowardice does not fool me.'

It fooled Rincewind. 'I—' he began, and paled as the nothingness-stick was turned towards him. 'I see you know all about me,' he finished weakly, and sat down heavily on the slippery surface. He and Twoflower, under instructions from the hooded commander, strapped themselves down to rings set in the transparent disc.

'If you make the merest suggestion of weaving a spell,' said the darkness under the hood, 'you die. Third quadrant *reconcile*, ninth quadrant *redouble*, *forward all!*'

A wall of water shot into the air behind Rincewind and the disc jerked suddenly. The dreadful presence of the sea troll had probably concentrated the hydrophobes' minds wonderfully, because it then rose at a very steep angle and didn't begin level flight until it was a dozen fathoms above the waves. Rincewind glanced down through the transparent surface and wished he hadn't.

'Well, off again then,' said Twoflower cheerfully. He turned and waved at the troll, now no more than a speck on the edge of the world.

Rincewind glared at him. 'Doesn't *anything* ever worry you?' he asked.

'We're still alive, aren't we?' asked Twoflower. 'And you yourself said they wouldn't be going to all this trouble if we were just going to be slaves. I expect Tethis was exaggerating. I expect it's all a misunderstanding. I expect we'll be sent home. After we've seen Krull, of course. And I must say it all sounds fascinating.'

'Oh yes,' said Rincewind, in a hollow voice. 'Fascinating.' He was thinking: I've seen excitement, and I've seen boredom. And boredom was best.

Had either of them happened to look down at that moment they would have noticed a strange v-shaped wave surging through the water far below them, its apex pointing directly at Tethis' island. But they weren't looking. The twenty-four hydrophobic magicians *were* looking, but to them it was just another piece of dreadfulness, not really any different from the liquid horror around it. They were probably right.

Sometime before all this the blazing pirate ship had hissed under the waves and started the long slow slide towards the distant ooze. It was more distant than average, because directly under the stricken keel was the Gorunna Trench – a chasm in the disc's surface that was so black, so deep and so reputedly evil that even the krakens went there fearfully, and in pairs. In less reputedly evil chasms the fish went about with natural lights on their heads and on the whole managed quite well. In Gorunna they left them unlit and, insofar as it is possible for something without legs to creep, they crept; they tended to bump into things, too. Horrible things.

The water around the ship turned from green to purple, from purple to black, from black to a darkness so complete that blackness itself seemed merely grey in comparison. Most of its timbers had already been crushed into splinters under the intense pressure.

It spiralled past groves of nightmare polyps and drifting forests of seaweed which glowed with faint, diseased colours. *Things* brushed it briefly with soft, cold tentacles as they darted away into the freezing silence.

Something rose up from the murk and ate it in one mouthful.

Some time later the islanders on a little rimward atoll were amazed to find, washed into their little local lagoon, the wave-rocked corpse of a hideous sea monster, all beaks, eyes and tentacles. They were further astonished at its size, since it was rather larger than their village. But their surprise was tiny compared to the huge, stricken expression on the face of the dead monster, which appeared to have been trampled to death.

Somewhat further rimward of the atoll a couple of little boats, trolling a net for the ferocious free-swimming oysters which abounded in those seas, caught something that dragged both vessels for several miles before one captain had the presence of mind to sever the lines.

But even his bewilderment was as nothing compared to that of the islanders on the last atoll in the archipelago. During the following night they were awakened by a terrific crashing and splintering noise coming from their minute jungle; when some of the bolder spirits went to investigate in the morning they found that the trees had been smashed in a broad swathe that started on the hubmost shore of the atoll and made a line of total destruction pointing precisely Edgewise, littered with broken lianas, crushed bushes and a few bewildered and angry oysters.

They were high enough now to see the wide curve of the Rim sweeping away from them, lapped by the fluffy clouds that mercifully hid the waterfall for most of the time. From up here the sea, a deep blue dappled with cloud-shadows, looked almost inviting. Rince-wind shuddered.

'Excuse me,' he said. The hooded figure turned from its contemplation of the distant haze and raised its wand threateningly.

'I don't want to use this,' it said.

'You don't?' said Rincewind.

'What is it, anyway?' said Twoflower.

'Ajandurah's Wand of Utter Negativity,' said Rincewind. 'And I wish you'd stop waving it about. It might go off,' he added, nodding at the wand's glittering point. 'I mean, it's all very flattering, all this magic being used just for our benefit, but there's no need to go quite that far. And—'

'*Shut up.*' The figure reached up and pulled back its hood, revealing itself to be a most unusually tinted young woman. Her skin was black. Not the dark brown of Urabewe, or the polished blue-black of monsoon-haunted Klatch, but the deep black of midnight at the bottom of a cave. Her hair and eyebrows were the colour of moonlight. There was the same pale sheen around her lips. She looked about fifteen, and very frightened.

Rincewind couldn't help noticing that the hand holding the wand was shaking; this was because a piece of sudden death, wobbling uncertainly a mere five feet from your nose, is very hard to miss. It dawned on him – very slowly, because it was a completely new sensation – that someone in the world was frightened of him. The complete reverse was so often the case that he had come to think of it as a kind of natural law.

'What is your name?' he said, as reassuringly as he could manage. She might be frightened, but she *did* have the wand. If I had a wand like that, he thought, I wouldn't be frightened of anything. So what in Creation can she imagine I could do?

'My name is immaterial,' she said.

'That's a pretty name,' said Rincewind. 'Where are you taking us, and why? I can't see any harm in your telling us.'

'You are being brought to Krull,' said the girl. 'And

don't mock me, hublander. Else I'll use the wand. I must bring you in alive, but no-one said anything about bringing you in whole. My name is Marchesa, and I am a wizard of the fifth level. Do you understand?'

'Well, since you know all about me then you know that I never even made it to Neophyte,' said Rincewind. 'I'm not even a wizard, really.' He caught Twoflower's astonished expression, and added hastily, 'Just a wizard of sorts.'

'You can't do magic because one of the Eight Great Spells is indelibly lodged in your mind,' said Marchesa, shifting her balance gracefully as the great lens described a wide arc over the sea. 'That's why you were thrown out of Unseen University. We know.'

'But you said just now that he was a magician of great cunning and artifice,' protested Twoflower.

'Yes, because anyone who survives all that he has survived – most of which he brought on himself by his tendency to think of himself as a wizard – well, he must be some kind of a magician,' said Marchesa. 'I warn you, Rincewind. If you give me the merest suspicion that you are intoning the Great Spell I really will kill you.' She scowled at him nervously.

'Seems to me your best course would be to just, you know, drop us off somewhere,' said Rincewind. 'I mean, thanks for rescuing us and everything, so if you'd just let us get on with leading our lives I'm sure we'd all—'

'I hope you're not proposing to enslave us,' said Twoflower.

Marchesa looked genuinely shocked. 'Certainly

not! Whatever could have given you that idea? Your lives in Krull will be rich, full and comfortable—'

'Oh, good,' said Rincewind.

'—just not very long.'

Krull turned out to be a large island, quite mountainous and heavily wooded, with pleasant white buildings visible here and there among the trees. The land sloped gradually up towards the rim, so that the highest point in Krull in fact slightly overhung the Edge. Here the Krullians had built their major city, also called Krull, and since so much of their building material had been salvaged from the Circumfence the houses of Krull had a decidedly nautical persuasion.

To put it bluntly, entire ships had been mortised artfully together and converted into buildings. Triremes, dhows and caravels protruded at strange angles from the general wooden chaos. Painted figureheads and hublandish dragonprows reminded the citizens of Krull that their good fortune stemmed from the sea; barquentines and carracks lent a distinctive shape to the larger buildings. And so the city rose tier on tier between the blue-green ocean of the disc and the soft cloud sea of the Edge, the eight colours of the Rimbow reflected in every window and in the many telescope lenses of the city's multitude of astronomers.

'It's absolutely awful,' said Rincewind gloomily.

The lens was approaching now along the very lip of the rimfall. The island not only got higher as it neared the Edge. It got narrower too, so that the lens was able to remain over water until it was very near the city.

The parapet along the edgewise cliff was dotted with gantries projecting into nothingness. The lens glided smoothly towards one of them and docked with it as smoothly as a boat might glide up to a quay. Four guards, with the same moonlight hair and nightblack faces as Marchesa, were waiting. They did not appear to be armed, but as Twoflower and Rincewind stumbled on to the parapet they were each grabbed by the arms and held quite firmly enough for any thought of escape to be instantly dismissed.

Then Marchesa and the watching hydrophobic wizards were quickly left behind and the guards and their prisoners set off briskly along a lane that wound between the ship-houses. Soon it led downwards, into what turned out to be a palace of some sort, half-hewn out of the rock of the cliff itself. Rincewind was vaguely aware of brightly lit tunnels, and courtyards open to the distant sky. A few elderly men, their robes covered in mysterious occult symbols, stood aside and watched with interest as the sextet passed. Several times Rincewind noticed hydrophobes – their ingrained expressions of self-revulsion at their own body-fluids were distinctive – and here and there trudging men who could only be slaves. He didn't have much time to reflect on all this before a door was opened ahead of them and they were pushed, gently but firmly, into a room. Then the door slammed behind them.

Rincewind and Twoflower regained their balance and stared around the room in which they now found themselves.

'Gosh,' said Twoflower ineffectually, after a pause

during which he had tried unsuccessfully to find a better word.

'This is a prison cell?' wondered Rincewind aloud.

'All that gold and silk and stuff,' Twoflower added. 'I've never seen anything like it!'

In the centre of the richly decorated room, on a carpet that was so deep and furry that Rincewind trod on it gingerly lest it be some kind of shaggy, floor-loving beast, was a long gleaming table laden with food. Most were fish dishes, including the biggest and most ornately prepared lobster Rincewind had ever seen, but there were also plenty of bowls and platters piled with strange creations that he had never seen before. He reached out cautiously and picked up some sort of purple fruit crusted with green crystals.

'Candied sea urchin,' said a cracked, cheerful voice behind him. 'A great delicacy.'

He dropped it quickly and turned around. An old man had stepped out from behind the heavy curtains. He was tall, thin and looked almost benign compared to some of the faces Rincewind had seen recently.

'The purée of sea cucumbers is very good too,' said the face, conversationally. 'Those little green bits are baby starfish.'

'Thank you for telling me,' said Rincewind weakly.

'Actually, they're rather good,' said Twoflower, his mouth full. 'I thought you liked seafood?'

'Yes, I thought I did,' said Rincewind. 'What's this wine – crushed octopus eyeballs?'

'Sea grape,' said the old man.

'Great,' said Rincewind, and swallowed a glassful. 'Not bad. A bit salty, maybe.'

'Sea grape is a kind of small jellyfish,' explained the stranger. 'And now I really think I should introduce myself. Why has your friend gone that strange colour?'

'Culture shock, I imagine,' said Twoflower. 'What did you say your name was?'

'I didn't. It's Garhartra. I'm the Guestmaster, you see. It is my pleasant task to make sure that your stay here is as delightful as possible.' He bowed. 'If there is anything you want you have only to say.'

Twoflower sat down on an ornate mother-of-pearl chair with a glass of oily wine in one hand and a crystallized squid in the other. He frowned.

'I think I've missed something along the way,' he said. 'First we were told we were going to be slaves—'

'A base canard!' interrupted Garhartra.

'What's a canard?' said Twoflower.

'I think it's a kind of duck,' said Rincewind from the far end of the long table. 'Are these biscuits made of something really nauseating, do you suppose?'

'—and then we were rescued at great magical expense—'

'They're made of pressed seaweed,' snapped the Guestmaster.

'—but then we're threatened, also at a vast expenditure of magic—'

'Yes, I thought it would be something like seaweed,' agreed Rincewind. 'They certainly taste like seaweed would taste if anyone was masochistic enough to eat seaweed.'

'—and then we're manhandled by guards and thrown in here—'

'Pushed gently,' corrected Garhartra.

'—which turned out to be this amazingly rich room and there's all this food and a man saying he's devoting his life to making us happy,' Twoflower concluded. 'What I'm getting at is this sort of lack of consistency.'

'Yar,' said Rincewind. 'What he means is, are you about to start being generally unpleasant again? Is this just a break for lunch?'

Garhartra held up his hands reassuringly.

'Please, please,' he protested. 'It was just necessary to get you here as soon as possible. We certainly do not want to enslave you. Please be reassured on that score.'

'Well, fine,' said Rincewind.

'Yes, you will in fact be sacrificed,' Garhartra continued placidly.

'*Sacrificed?* You're going to kill us?' shouted the wizard.

'Kill? Yes, of course. Certainly! It would hardly be a sacrifice if we didn't, would it? But don't worry – it'll be comparatively painless.'

'Comparatively? Compared to what?' said Rincewind. He picked up a tall green bottle that was full of sea grape jellyfish wine and hurled it hard at the Guestmaster, who flung up a hand as if to protect himself.

There was a crackle of octarine flame from his fingers and the air suddenly took on the thick, greasy feel that indicated a powerful magical discharge. The flung bottle slowed and then stopped in mid-air, rotating gently.

At the same time an invisible force picked Rincewind up and hurled him down the length of the room, pinning him awkwardly halfway up the far wall with no breath left in his body. He hung there with his mouth open in rage and astonishment.

Garhartra lowered his hand and brushed it slowly on his robe.

'I didn't enjoy doing that, you know,' he said.

'I could tell,' muttered Rincewind.

'But what do you want to sacrifice us for?' asked Twoflower. 'You hardly know us!'

'That's rather the point, isn't it? It's not very good manners to sacrifice a friend. Besides, you were, um, *specified*. I don't know a lot about the god in question, but He was quite clear on that point. Look, I must be running along now. So much to organize, you know how it is,' the Guestmaster opened the door, and then peered back around it. 'Please make yourselves comfortable, and don't worry.'

'But you haven't actually *told* us anything!' wailed Twoflower.

'It's not really worth it, is it? What with you being sacrificed in the morning,' said Garhartra, 'it's hardly worth the bother of knowing, really. Sleep well. Comparatively well, anyway.'

He shut the door. A brief octarine flicker of balefire around it suggested that it had now been sealed beyond the skills of any earthly locksmith.

Gling, clang, tang went the bells along the Circumfence in the moonlit, rimfall-roaring night.

Terton, lengthman of the 45th Length, hadn't heard

such a clashing since the night a giant kraken had been swept into the Fence five years ago. He leaned out of his hut, which for the lack of any convenient eyot on this Length had been built on wooden piles driven into the sea bed, and stared into the darkness. Once or twice he thought he could see movement, far off. Strictly speaking, he should row out to see what was causing the din. But here in the clammy darkness it didn't seem like an astoundingly good idea, so he slammed the door, wrapped some sacking around the madly jangling bells, and tried to get back to sleep.

That didn't work, because even the top strand of the Fence was thrumming now, as if something big and heavy was bouncing on it. After staring at the ceiling for a few minutes, and trying hard not to think of great long tentacles and pond-sized eyes, Terton blew out the lantern and opened the door a crack.

Something *was* coming along the Fence, in giant loping bounds that covered metres at a time. It loomed up at him and for a moment Terton saw something rectangular, multi-legged, shaggy with seaweed and – although it had absolutely no features from which he could have deduced this – it was also very angry indeed.

The hut was smashed to fragments as the monster charged through it, although Terton survived by clinging to the Circumfence; some weeks later he was picked up by a returning salvage fleet, subsequently escaped from Krull on a hijacked lens (having developed hydrophobia to an astonishing degree) and after a number of adventures eventually found his way to the Great Nef, an area of the disc so dry that it actually has negative rainfall, which he nevertheless considered uncomfortably damp.

'Have you tried the door?'

'Yes,' said Twoflower. 'And it isn't any less locked than it was last time you asked. There's the window, though.'

'A great way of escape,' muttered Rincewind, from his perch halfway up the wall. 'You said it looks out over the Edge. Just step out, eh, and plunge through space and maybe freeze solid or hit some other world at incredible speeds or plunge wildly into the burning heart of a sun?'

'Worth a try,' said Twoflower. 'Want a seaweed biscuit?'

'No!'

'When are you coming down?'

Rincewind snarled. This was partly in embarrassment. Garhartra's spell had been the little-used and hard-to-master Atavarr's Personal Gravitational Upset, the practical result of which was that until it wore off Rincewind's body was convinced that 'down' lay at ninety degrees to that direction normally accepted as of a downward persuasion by the majority of the disc's inhabitants. He was in fact standing on the wall.

Meanwhile the flung bottle hung supportless in the air a few yards away. In its case time had – well, not actually been stopped, but had been slowed by several orders of magnitude, and its trajectory had so far occupied several hours and a couple of inches as far as Twoflower and Rincewind were concerned. The glass gleamed in the moonlight. Rincewind sighed and tried to make himself comfortable on the wall.

'Why don't you ever *worry*?' he demanded petulantly. 'Here we are, going to be sacrificed to some god or other in the morning, and you just sit there eating barnacle canapés.'

'I expect something will turn up,' said Twoflower.

'I mean, it's not as if we know *why* we're going to be killed,' the wizard went on.

You'd like to, would you?

'Did you say that?' asked Rincewind.

'Say what?'

You're hearing things said the voice in Rincewind's head.

He sat bolt sideways. 'Who are you?' he demanded.

Twoflower gave him a worried look.

'I'm Twoflower,' he said. 'Surely you remember?'

Rincewind put his head in his hands.

'It's happened at last,' he moaned. 'I'm going out of my mind.'

Good idea said the voice. *It's getting pretty crowded in here*

The spell pinning Rincewind to the wall vanished with a faint 'pop'. He fell forward and landed in a heap on the floor.

Careful – you nearly squashed me

Rincewind struggled to his elbows and reached into the pocket of his robe. When he withdrew his hand the green frog was sitting on it, its eyes oddly luminous in the half-light.

'You?' said Rincewind.

Put me down on the floor and stand back The frog blinked.

The wizard did so, and dragged a bewildered Twoflower out of the way.

The room darkened. There was a windy, roaring sound. Streamers of green, purple and octarine cloud appeared out of nowhere and began to spiral rapidly towards the recumbent amphibian, shedding small bolts of lightning as they whirled. Soon the frog was lost in a golden haze which began to elongate upwards, filling the room with a warm yellow light. Within it was a darker, indistinct shape, which wavered and changed even as they watched. And all the time there was the high, brain-curdling whine of a huge magical field . . .

As suddenly as it had appeared, the magical tornado vanished. And there, occupying the space where the frog had been, was a frog.

'Fantastic,' said Rincewind.

The frog gazed at him reproachfully.

'Really amazing,' said Rincewind sourly. 'A frog magically transformed into a frog. Wondrous.'

'Turn around,' said a voice behind them. It was a soft, feminine voice, almost an inviting voice, the sort of voice you could have a few drinks with, but it was coming from a spot where there oughtn't to be a voice at all. They managed to turn without really moving, like a couple of statues revolving on plinths.

There was a woman standing in the pre-dawn light. She looked – she was – she had a – in point of actual fact she . . .

Later Rincewind and Twoflower couldn't quite agree on any single fact about her, except that she had appeared to be beautiful (precisely what physical

features made her beautiful they could not, defini-
tively, state) and that she had green eyes. Not the pale
green of ordinary eyes, either – these were the green
of fresh emeralds and as iridescent as a dragonfly. And
one of the few genuinely magical facts that Rincewind
knew was that no god or goddess, contrary and
volatile as they might be in all other respects, could
change the colour or nature of their eyes . . .

'L—' he began. She raised a hand.

'You know that if you say my name I must depart,'
she hissed. 'Surely you recall that I am the one goddess
who comes only when not invoked?'

'Uh. Yes, I suppose I do,' croaked the wizard, trying
not to look at the eyes. 'You're the one they call the
Lady?'

'Yes.'

'Are you a goddess then?' said Twoflower excitedly.
'I've always wanted to meet one.'

Rincewind tensed, waiting for the explosion of
rage. Instead, the Lady merely smiled.

'Your friend the wizard should introduce us,' she
said.

Rincewind coughed. 'Uh, yar,' he said. 'This is
Twoflower, Lady, he's a tourist—'

'—I have attended him on a number of occasions—'

'—and, Twoflower, this is the Lady. *Just* the Lady,
right? Nothing else. Don't try and give her any other
name, OK?' he went on desperately, his eyes darting
meaningful glances that were totally lost on the little
man.

Rincewind shivered. He was not, of course, an
atheist; on the disc the gods dealt severely with

atheists. On the few occasions when he had some spare change he had always made a point of dropping a few coppers into a temple coffer, somewhere, on the principle that a man needed all the friends he could get. But usually he didn't bother the Gods, and he hoped the Gods wouldn't bother him. Life was quite complicated enough.

There were two gods, however, who were really terrifying. The rest of the gods were usually only sort of large-scale humans, fond of wine and war and whoring. But Fate and the Lady were chilling.

In the Gods' Quarter, in Ankh-Morpork, Fate had a small, heavy, leaden temple, where hollow-eyed and gaunt worshippers met on dark nights for their pre-destined and fairly pointless rites. There were no temples at all to the Lady, although she was arguably the most powerful goddess in the entire history of Creation. A few of the more daring members of the Gamblers' Guild had once experimented with a form of worship, in the deepest cellars of Guild head-quarters, and had all died of penury, murder or just Death within the week. She was the Goddess Who Must Not Be Named; those who sought her never found her, yet she was known to come to the aid of those in greatest need. And, then again, sometimes she didn't. She was like that. She didn't like the click-ing of rosaries, but was attracted to the sound of dice. No man knew what She looked like, although there were many times when a man who was gambling his life on the turn of the cards would pick up the hand he had been dealt and stare Her full in the face. Of course, sometimes he didn't. Among all the gods she was at one and the same time the most courted and the most cursed.

'We don't have gods where I come from,' said Twoflower.

'You do, you know,' said the Lady. 'Everyone has gods. You just don't think they're gods.'

Rincewind shook himself mentally.

'Look,' he said. 'I don't want to sound impatient, but in a few minutes some people are going to come through that door and take us away and kill us.'

'Yes,' said the Lady.

'I suppose you wouldn't tell us *why*?' said Twoflower.

'Yes,' said the Lady. 'The Krullians intend to launch a bronze vessel over the edge of the disc. Their prime purpose is to learn the sex of A'Tuin the World Turtle.'

'Seems rather pointless,' said Rincewind.

'No. Consider. One day Great A'Tuin may encounter another member of the species *chelys galactica*, somewhere in the vast night in which we move. Will they fight? Will they mate? A little imagination will show you that the sex of Great A'Tuin could be very important to us. At least, so the Krullians say.'

Rincewind tried not to think of World Turtles mating. It wasn't completely easy.

'So,' continued the goddess, 'they intend to launch this ship of space, with two voyagers aboard. It will be the culmination of decades of research. It will also be very dangerous for the travellers. And so, in an attempt to reduce the risks, the Arch-astronomer of Krull has bargained with Fate to sacrifice two men at the moment of launch. Fate, in His turn, has agreed to smile on the space ship. A neat barter, is it not?'

'And we're the sacrifices,' said Rincewind.

'Yes.'

'I thought Fate didn't go in for that sort of bargaining. I thought Fate was implacable,' said Rincewind.

'Normally, yes. But you two have been thorns in his side for some time. He specified that the sacrifices should be you. He allowed you to escape from the pirates. He allowed you to drift into the Circumfence. Fate can be one mean god at times.'

There was a pause. The frog sighed and wandered off under the table.

'But you can help us?' prompted Twoflower.

'You amuse me,' said the Lady. 'I have a sentimental streak. You'd know that, if you were gamblers. So for a little while I rode in a frog's mind and you kindly rescued me, for, as we all know, no-one likes to see pathetic and helpless creatures swept to their death.'

'Thank you,' said Rincewind.

'The whole mind of Fate is bent against you,' said the Lady. 'But all I can do is give you one chance. Just one, small chance. The rest is up to you.'

She vanished.

'Gosh,' said Twoflower, after a while. 'That's the first time I've ever seen a goddess.'

The door swung open. Garhartra entered, holding a wand in front of him. Behind him were two guards, armed more conventionally with swords.

'Ah,' he said conversationally. 'You are ready, I see.'

Ready, said a voice inside Rincewind's head.

The bottle that the wizard had flung some eight hours earlier had been hanging in the air, imprisoned by magic in its own personal time-field. But during all those hours the original mana of the spell had been slowly leaking away until the total magical energy was no longer sufficient to hold it against the Universe's own powerful normality field, and when that happened Reality snapped back in a matter of microseconds. The visible sign of this was that the bottle suddenly completed the last part of its parabola and burst against the side of the Guestmaster's head, showering the guards with glass and jellyfish wine.

Rincewind grabbed Twoflower's arm, kicked the nearest guard in the groin, and dragged the startled tourist into the corridor. Before the stunned Garhartra had sunk to the floor his two guests were already pounding across distant flagstones.

Rincewind skidded around a corner and found himself on a balcony that ran around the four sides of a courtyard. Below them, most of the floor of the yard was taken up by an ornamental pond in which a few terrapins sunbathed among the lily leaves.

And ahead of Rincewind were a couple of very surprised wizards wearing the distinctive dark blue and black robes of trained hydrophobes. One of them, quicker on the uptake than his companion, raised a hand and began the first words of a spell.

There was a short sharp noise by Rincewind's side. Twoflower had spat. The hydrophobe screamed and dropped his hand as though it had been stung.

The other didn't have time to move before Rincewind was on him, fists swinging wildly. One stiff punch with the weight of terror behind it sent the man tumbling over the balcony rail and into the pond, which did a very strange thing: the water smacked aside as though a large invisible balloon had been dropped into it, and the hydrophobe hung screaming in his own revulsion field.

Twoflower watched him in amazement until Rincewind snatched at his shoulder and indicated a likely-looking passage. They hurried down it, leaving the remaining hydrophobe writhing on the floor and snatching at his damp hand.

For a while there was some shouting behind them, but they scuttled along a cross corridor and another courtyard and soon left the sounds of pursuit behind. Finally Rincewind picked a safe-looking door, peered around it, found the room beyond to be unoccupied, dragged Twoflower inside, and slammed it behind him. Then he leaned against it, wheezing horribly.

'We're totally lost in a palace on an island we haven't a hope of leaving,' he panted. 'And what's more we—hey!' he finished, as the sight of the contents of the room filtered up his deranged optic nerves.

Twoflower was already staring at the walls.

Because what was so odd about the room was, it contained the whole Universe.

Death sat in His garden, running a whetstone along the edge of His scythe. It was already so sharp that any passing breeze that blew across it was sliced smoothly into two puzzled zephyrs, although breezes were rare indeed in Death's silent garden. It lay on a sheltered plateau overlooking the discworld's complex dimensions, and behind it loomed the cold, still, immensely high and brooding mountains of Eternity.

Swish! went the stone. Death hummed a dirge, and tapped one bony foot on the frosty flagstones.

Someone approached through the dim orchard where the nightapples grew, and there came the sickly sweet smell of crushed lilies. Death looked up angrily, and found Himself staring into eyes that were black as the inside of a cat and full of distant stars that had no counterpart among the familiar constellations of the Realtime universe.

Death and Fate looked at each other. Death grinned – He had no alternative, of course, being made of implacable bone. The whetstone sang rhythmically along the blade as He continued His task.

'I have a task for you,' said Fate. His words drifted across Death's scythe and split tidily into two ribbons of consonants and vowels.

I HAVE TASKS ENOUGH THIS DAY, said Death in a voice as heavy as neutronium. THE WHITE PLAGUE ABIDES EVEN NOW IN PSEUDOPOLIS AND I AM BOUND THERE TO RESCUE MANY OF ITS CITIZENS FROM HIS GRASP. SUCH A ONE HAS NOT BEEN SEEN THESE HUNDRED YEARS. I AM EXPECTED TO STALK THE STREETS, AS IS MY DUTY.

'I refer to the matter of the little wanderer and the rogue wizard,' said Fate softly, seating himself beside Death's black-robed form and staring down at the distant, multifaceted jewel which was the disc universe as seen from this extra-dimensional vantage point.

The scythe ceased its song.

'They die in a few hours,' said Fate. 'It is fated.'

Death stirred, and the stone began to move again.

'I thought you would be pleased,' said Fate.

Death shrugged, a particularly expressive gesture for someone whose visible shape was that of a skeleton.

I DID INDEED CHASE THEM MIGHTILY, ONCE, he said, BUT AT LAST THE THOUGHT CAME TO ME THAT SOONER OR LATER ALL MEN MUST DIE. EVERYTHING DIES IN THE END. I CAN BE ROBBED BUT NEVER DENIED, I TOLD MYSELF. WHY WORRY?

'I too cannot be cheated,' snapped Fate.

SO I HAVE HEARD, said Death, still grinning.

'Enough!' shouted Fate, jumping to his feet. 'They will die!' He vanished in a sheet of blue fire.

Death nodded to Himself and continued at His work. After some minutes the edge of the blade seemed to be finished to His satisfaction. He stood up and levelled the scythe at the fat and noisome candle that burned on the edge of the bench and then, with two deft sweeps, cut the flame into three bright slivers. Death grinned.

A short while later he was saddling his white stallion, which lived in a stable at the back of Death's cottage. The beast snuffled at him in a friendly fashion; though it was crimson-eyed and had flanks like oiled silk, it was nevertheless a real flesh-and-blood horse and, indeed, was in all probability better treated than most beasts of burden on the disc. Death was not an unkind master. He weighed very little and, although He often rode back with His saddlebags bulging, they weighed nothing whatsoever.

'All those worlds!' said Twoflower. 'It's fantastic!'

Rincewind grunted, and continued to prowl warily

around the star-filled room. Twoflower turned to a complicated astrolabe, in the centre of which was the entire Great A'Tuin-Elephant-Disc system wrought in brass and picked out with tiny jewels. Around it stars and planets wheeled on fine silver wires.

'Fantastic!' he said again. On the walls around him constellations made of tiny phosphorescent seed pearls had been picked out on vast tapestries made of jet-black velvet, giving the room's occupants the impression of floating in the interstellar gulf. Various easels held huge sketches of Great A'Tuin as viewed from various parts of the Circumfence, with every mighty scale and cratered pock-mark meticulously marked in. Twoflower stared about him with a far-away look in his eyes.

Rincewind was deeply troubled. What troubled him most of all were the two suits that hung from supports in the centre of the room. He circled them uneasily.

They appeared to be made of fine white leather, hung about with straps and brass nozzles and other highly unfamiliar and suspicious contrivances. The leggings ended in high, thick-soled boots, and the arms were shoved into big supple gauntlets. Strangest of all were the big copper helmets that were obviously supposed to fit on heavy collars around the neck of the suits. The helmets were almost certainly useless for protection – a light sword would have no difficulty in splitting them, even if it didn't hit the ridiculous little glass windows in the front. Each helmet had a crest of white feathers on top, which went absolutely no way at all towards improving their overall appearance.

Rincewind was beginning to have the glimmerings of a suspicion about those suits.

In front of them was a table covered with celestial charts and scraps of parchment covered with figures. Whoever would be wearing those suits, Rincewind decided, was expecting to boldly go where no man – other than the occasional luckless sailor, who didn't really count – had boldly gone before, and he was now beginning to get not just a suspicion but a horrible premonition.

He turned round and found Twoflower looking at him with a speculative expression.

'No—' began Rincewind, urgently. Twoflower ignored him.

'The goddess said two men were going to be sent over the Edge,' he said, his eyes gleaming, 'and you remember Tethis the troll saying you'd need some kind of protection? The Krullians have got over that. These are suits of *space* armour.'

'They don't look very roomy to me,' said Rincewind hurriedly, and grabbed the tourist by the arm, 'so if you'd just come on, no sense in staying here—'

'Why must you always *panic*?' asked Twoflower petulantly.

'Because the whole of my future life just flashed in front of my eyes, and it didn't take very long, and if you don't move now I'm going to leave without you because any second now you're going to suggest that we put on—'

The door opened.

Two husky young men stepped into the room. All they were wearing was a pair of woollen pants apiece.

One of them was still towelling himself briskly. They both nodded at the two escapees with no apparent surprise.

The taller of the two men sat down on one of the benches in front of the seats. He beckoned to Rincewind, and said:

'? Tyø yur åtl hø sooten gåtrunen?'

And this was awkward, because although Rincewind considered himself an expert in most of the tongues of the hubwards segments of the disc it was the first time that he had ever been addressed in Krullian, and he did not understand one word of it. Neither did Twoflower, but that did not stop him stepping forward and taking a breath.

The speed of light through a magical aura such as the one that surrounded the disc was quite slow, being about the speed of sound in less highly tuned universes. But it was still the fastest thing around with the exception, in moments like this, of Rincewind's mind.

In an instant he became aware that the tourist was about to try his own peculiar brand of linguistics, which meant that he would speak loudly and slowly in his own language.

Rincewind's elbow shot back, knocking the breath from Twoflower's body. When the little man looked up in pain and astonishment Rincewind caught his eye and pulled an imaginary tongue out of his mouth and cut it with an imaginary pair of scissors.

The second chelonaut – for such was the profession of the men whose fate it would shortly be to voyage to Great A'Tuin – looked up from the chart table and watched this in puzzlement. His big heroic brow wrinkled with the effort of speech.

'? Hør yu latruin nør u?' he said.

Rincewind smiled and nodded and pushed Twoflower in his general direction. With an inward sigh of relief he saw the tourist pay sudden attention to a big brass telescope that lay on the table.

'! Sooten u!' commanded the seated chelonaut. Rincewind nodded and smiled and took one of the big copper helmets from the rack and brought it down on the man's head as hard as he possibly could. The chelonaut fell forward with a soft grunt.

The other man took one startled step before Twoflower hit him amateurishly but effectively with the telescope. He crumpled on top of his colleague.

Rincewind and Twoflower looked at each other over the carnage.

'All *right*!' snapped Rincewind, aware that he had lost some kind of contest but not entirely certain what it was. 'Don't bother to say it. Someone out there is expecting these two guys to come out in the suits in a minute. I suppose they thought we were slaves. Help me hide these behind the drapes and then, and then—'

'—we'd better suit up,' said Twoflower, picking up the second helmet.

'Yes,' said Rincewind. 'You know, as soon as I saw the suits I just *knew* I'd end up wearing one. Don't ask me how I knew – I suppose it was because it was just about the worst possible thing that was likely to happen.'

'Well, you said yourself we have no way of

escaping,' said Twoflower, his voice muffled as he pulled the top half of a suit over his head. 'Anything's better than being sacrificed.'

'As soon as we get a chance we run for it,' said Rincewind. 'Don't get any ideas.'

He thrust an arm savagely into his suit and banged his head on the helmet. He reflected briefly that someone up there was watching over him.

'Thanks a lot,' he said bitterly.

At the very edge of the city and country of Krull was a large semi-circular amphitheatre, with seating for several tens of thousands of people. The arena was only semi-circular for the very elegant reason that it overlooked the cloud sea that boiled up from the Rimfall, far below, and now every seat was occupied. And the crowd was growing restive. It had come to see a double sacrifice and also the launching of the great bronze space ship. Neither event had yet materialized.

The Arch-astronomer beckoned the Master Launchcontroller to him.

'Well?' he said, filling a mere four letters with a full lexicon of anger and menace. The Master Launchcontroller went pale.

'No news, lord,' said the Launchcontroller, and added with a brittle brightness, 'except that your prominence will be pleased to hear that Garhartra has recovered.'

'That is a fact he may come to regret,' said the Arch-astronomer.

'Yes, lord.'

'How much longer do we have?'

The Launchcontroller glanced at the rapidly climbing sun.

'Thirty minutes, your prominence. After that Krull will have revolved away from Great A'Tuin's tail and the *Potent Voyager* will be doomed to spin away into the interterrapene gulf. I have already set the automatic controls, so—'

'All right, all right,' the Arch-astronomer said, waving him away. 'The launch must go ahead. Maintain the watch on the harbour, of course. When the wretched pair are caught I will personally take a great deal of pleasure in executing them myself.'

'Yes, lord. Er—'

The Arch-astronomer frowned. 'What else have you got to say, man?'

The Launchcontroller swallowed. All this was very unfair on him, he was a practical magician rather than a diplomat, and that was why some wiser brains had seen to it that he would be the one to pass on the news.

'A monster has come out of the sea and it's attacking the ships in the harbour,' he said. 'A runner just arrived from there.'

'A big monster?' said the Arch-astronomer.

'Not particularly, although it is said to be exceptionally fierce, lord.'

The ruler of Krull and the Circumfence considered this for a moment, then shrugged.

'The sea is full of monsters,' he said. 'It is one of its prime attributes. Have it dealt with. And – Master Launchcontroller?'

'Lord?'

'If I am further vexed, you will recall that two people are due to be sacrificed. I may feel generous and increase the number.'

'Yes, lord.' The Master Launchcontroller scuttled away, relieved to be out of the autocrat's sight.

The *Potent Voyager*, no longer the blank bronze shell that had been smashed from the mould a few days earlier, rested in its cradle on top of a wooden tower in the centre of the arena. In front of it a railway ran down towards the Edge, where for the space of a few yards it turned suddenly upwards.

The late Dactylos Goldeneyes, who had designed the launching pad as well as the *Potent Voyager* itself, had claimed that this last touch was merely to ensure that the ship would not snag on any rocks as it began its long plunge. Maybe it was merely coincidental that it would also, because of that little twitch in the track, leap like a salmon and shine theatrically in the sunlight before disappearing into the cloud sea.

There was a fanfare of trumpets at the edge of the arena. The chelonauts' honour guard appeared, to much cheering from the crowd. Then the white-suited explorers themselves stepped out into the light.

It immediately dawned on the Arch-astronomer that something was wrong. Heroes always walked in a certain way, for example. They certainly didn't waddle, and one of the chelonauts was definitely waddling.

The roar of the assembled people of Krull was deafening. As the chelonauts and their guards crossed the great arena, passing between the many altars that had been set up for the various wizards and priests of

Krull's many sects to ensure the success of the launch, the Arch-astronomer frowned. By the time the party was halfway across the floor his mind had reached a conclusion. By the time the chelonauts were standing at the foot of the ladder that led to the ship – and was there more than a hint of reluctance about them? – the Arch-astronomer was on his feet, his words lost in the noise of the crowd. One of his arms shot out and back, fingers spread dramatically in the traditional spell-casting position, and any passing lip-reader who was also familiar with the standard texts on magic would have recognized the opening words of Vestcake's Floating Curse, and would then have prudently run away.

Its final words remained unsaid, however. The Arch-astronomer turned in astonishment as a commotion broke out around the big arched entrance to the arena. Guards were running out into the day-light, throwing down their weapons as they scuttled among the altars or vaulted the parapet into the stands.

Something emerged behind them, and the crowd around the entrance ceased its raucous cheering and began a silent, determined scramble to get out of the way.

The *something* was a low dome of seaweed, moving slowly but with a sinister sense of purpose. One guard overcame his horror sufficiently to stand in its path and hurl his spear, which landed squarely among the weeds. The crowd cheered – then went deathly silent as the dome surged forward and engulfed the man completely.

The Arch-astronomer dismissed the half-formed shape of Vestcake's famous Curse with a sharp wave of his hand, and quickly spoke the words of one of the most powerful spells in his repertoire: the Infernal Combustion Enigma.

Octarine fire spiralled around and between his fingers as he shaped the complex rune of the spell in mid-air and sent it, screaming and trailing blue smoke, towards the shape.

There was a satisfying explosion and a gout of flame shot up into the clear morning sky, shedding flakes of burning seaweed on the way. A cloud of smoke and steam concealed the monster for several minutes, and when it cleared the dome had completely disappeared.

There was a large charred circle on the flagstones, however, in which a few clumps of kelp and bladderwrack still smouldered.

And in the centre of the circle was a perfectly ordinary, if somewhat large, wooden chest. It was not even scorched. Someone on the far side of the arena started to laugh, but the sound was broken off abruptly as the chest rose up on dozens of what could only be legs and turned to face the Arch-astronomer. A perfectly ordinary if somewhat large wooden chest does not, of course, have a face with which to face, but this one was quite definitely facing. In precisely the same way as he understood that, the Arch-astronomer was also horribly aware that this perfectly normal box was in some indescribable way narrowing its eyes.

It began to move resolutely towards him. He shuddered.

'*Magicians!*' he screamed. '*Where are my magicians?*'

Around the arena pale-faced men peeped out from behind altars and under benches. One of the bolder ones, seeing the expression on the Arch-astronomer's face, raised an arm tremulously and essayed a hasty thunderbolt. It hissed towards the chest and struck it squarely in a shower of white sparks.

That was the signal for every magician, enchanter and thaumaturgist in Krull to leap up eagerly and, under the terrified eyes of their master, unleash the first spell that came to each desperate mind. Charms curved and whistled through the air.

Soon the chest was lost to view again in an expanding cloud of magical particles, which billowed out and wreathed it in twisting, disquieting shapes. Spell after spell screamed into the mêlée. Flame and lightning bolts of all eight colours stabbed out brightly from the seething *thing* that now occupied the space where the box had been.

Not since the Mage Wars had so much magic been concentrated on one small area. The air itself wavered and glittered. Spell ricocheted off spell, creating short-lived wild spells whose brief half-life was both weird and uncontrolled. The stones under the heaving mass began to buckle and split. One of them in fact turned into something best left undescribed and slunk off into some dismal dimension. Other strange side-effects began to manifest themselves. A shower of small lead cubes bounced out of the storm and rolled across the heaving floor, and eldritch shapes gibbered and beckoned obscenely; four-sided triangles and double-ended circles existed momentarily before merging again into the booming, screaming tower of runaway raw magic that boiled up from the molten flagstones and spread out over Krull. It no longer mattered that most of the magicians had ceased their spell-casting and fled – the *thing* was now feeding on the stream of octarine particles that were always at their thickest near the Edge of the disc. Throughout the island of Krull every magical activity failed as all the available mana in the area was sucked into the cloud, which was already a quarter of a mile high and streaming out into mind-curdling shapes; hydrophobes on their sea-skimming lenses crashed screaming into the waves, magic potions turned to mere impure water in their phials, magic swords melted and dripped from their scabbards.

But none of this in any way prevented the *thing* at the base of the cloud, now gleaming mirror-bright in the intensity of the power storm around it, from moving at a steady walking pace towards the Arch-astronomer.

Rincewind and Twoflower watched in awe from the shelter of *Potent Voyager*'s launch tower. The honour party had long since vanished, leaving their weapons scattered behind them.

'Well,' sighed Twoflower at last, 'there goes the Luggage.' He sighed.

'Don't you believe it,' said Rincewind. 'Sapient pearwood is totally impervious to all known forms of magic. It's been constructed to follow you anywhere. I mean, when you die, if you go to Heaven, you'll at least have a clean pair of socks in the afterlife. But I don't want to die yet, so let's just get going, shall we?'

'Where?' said Twoflower.

Rincewind picked up a crossbow and a handful of quarrels. 'Anywhere that isn't here,' he said.

'What about the Luggage?'

'Don't worry. When the storm has used up all the free magic in the vicinity it'll just die out.'

In fact that was already beginning to happen. The billowing cloud was still flowing up from the arena but now it had a tenuous, harmless look about it. Even as Twoflower stared, it began to flicker uncertainly.

Soon it was a pale ghost. The Luggage was now visible as a squat shape among the almost invisible flames. Around it the rapidly cooling stones began to crack and buckle.

Twoflower called softly to his Luggage. It stopped its stolid progression across the tortured flags and appeared to be listening intently; then, moving its dozens of feet in an intricate pattern, it turned on its length and headed towards the *Potent Voyager*. Rincewind watched it sourly. The Luggage had an elemental nature, absolutely no brain, a homicidal attitude towards anything that threatened its master, and he wasn't quite sure that its inside occupied the same space-time framework as its outside.

'Not a mark on it,' said Twoflower cheerfully, as the box settled down in front of him. He pushed open the lid.

'This is a fine time to change your underwear,' snarled Rincewind. 'In a minute all those guards and priests are going to come back, and they're going to be *upset*, man!'

'Water,' murmured Twoflower. 'The whole box is full of water!'

Rincewind peered over his shoulder. There was no sign of clothes, moneybags, or any other of the tourist's belongings. The whole box was full of water.

A wave sprang up from nowhere and lapped over the edge. It hit the flagstones but, instead of spreading out, began to take the shape of a foot. Another foot and the bottom half of a pair of legs followed as more water streamed down as if filling an invisible mould. A moment later Tethis the sea troll was standing in front of them, blinking.

'I see,' he said at last. 'You two. I suppose I shouldn't be surprised.'

He looked around, ignoring their astonished expressions.

'I was just sitting outside my hut, watching the sun set, when this thing came roaring up out of the water and swallowed me,' he said. 'I thought it was rather strange. Where is this place?'

'Krull,' said Rincewind. He stared hard at the now closed Luggage, which was managing to project a smug expression. Swallowing people was something it did quite frequently, but always when the lid was next opened there was nothing inside but Twoflower's laundry. Savagely he wrenched the lid up. There was nothing inside but Twoflower's laundry. It was perfectly dry.

'Well, well,' said Tethis. He looked up.

'Hey!' he said. 'Isn't this the ship they're going to

send over the Edge? Isn't it? It must be!'

An arrow zipped through his chest, leaving a faint ripple. He didn't appear to notice. Rincewind did. Soldiers were beginning to appear at the edge of the arena, and a number of them were peering around the entrances.

Another arrow bounced off the tower behind Twoflower. At this range the bolts did not have a lot of force, but it would only be a matter of time . . .

'Quick!' said Twoflower. 'Into the ship! They won't dare fire at that!'

'I *knew* you were going to suggest that,' groaned Rincewind. 'I just *knew* it!'

He aimed a kick at the Luggage. It backed off a few inches, and opened its lid threateningly.

A spear arced out of the sky and trembled to a halt in the woodwork by the wizard's ear. He screamed briefly and scrambled up the ladder after the others.

Arrows whistled around them as they came out on to the narrow catwalk that led along the spine of the *Potent Voyager*. Twoflower led the way, jogging along with what Rincewind considered to be too much suppressed excitement.

Atop the centre of the ship was a large round bronze hatch with hasps around it. The troll and the tourist knelt down and started to work on them.

In the heart of the Potent Voyager *fine sand had been trickling into a carefully designed cup for several hours. Now the cup was filled by exactly the right amount to dip down and upset a carefully balanced weight. The weight swung away, pulling a pin from an intricate little mechanism. A chain began to move. There was a clonk...*

'What was that?' said Rincewind urgently. He looked down.

The hail of arrows had stopped. The crowd of priests and soldiers were standing motionless, staring intently at the ship. A small worried man elbowed his way through them and started to shout something.

'What was what?' said Twoflower, busy with a wing-nut.

'I thought I heard something,' said Rincewind. 'Look,' he said, 'we'll threaten to damage the thing if they don't let us go, right? That's all we're going to do, right?'

'Yah,' said Twoflower vaguely. He sat back on his heels. 'That's it,' he said. 'It ought to lift off now.'

Several muscular men were swarming up the ladder to the ship. Rincewind recognized the two chelonauts among them. They were carrying swords.

'I—' he began.

The ship lurched. Then, with infinite slowness, it began to move along the rails.

In that moment of black horror Rincewind saw that Twoflower and the troll had managed to pull the hatch up. A metal ladder inside led into the cabin below. The troll disappeared.

'We've got to get off,' whispered Rincewind. Twoflower looked at him, a strange mad smile on his face.

'Stars,' said the tourist. 'Worlds. The whole damn sky full of worlds. Places no-one will ever see. Except me.' He stepped through the hatchway.

'You're totally mad,' said Rincewind hoarsely, trying to keep his balance as the ship began to speed up. He turned as one of the chelonauts tried to leap the gap between the *Voyager* and the tower, landed on the curving flank of the ship, scrabbled for an instant for purchase, failed to find any, and dropped away with a shriek.

The *Voyager* was travelling quite fast now. Rincewind could see past Twoflower's head to the sunlit cloud sea and the impossible Rimbow, floating tantalizingly beyond it, beckoning fools to venture too far . . .

He also saw a gang of men climbing desperately over the lower slopes of the launching ramp and man-handling a large baulk of timber on to the track, in a frantic attempt to derail the ship before it vanished over the Edge. The wheels slammed into it, but the only effect was to make the ship rock, Twoflower to lose his grip on the ladder and fall into the cabin, and the hatch to slam down with the horrible sound of a dozen fiddly little catches snapping into place. Rincewind dived forward and scrabbled at them, whimpering.

The cloud sea was much nearer now. The Edge itself, a rocky perimeter to the arena, was startlingly close.

Rincewind stood up. There was only one thing to do now, and he did it. He panicked blindly, just as the ship's bogeys hit the little upgrade and flung it, sparkling like a salmon, into the sky and over the Edge.

A few seconds later there was a thunder of little feet

and the Luggage cleared the rim of the world, legs still pumping determinedly, and plunged down into the Universe.

THE END

Rincewind woke up and shivered. He was freezing cold.

So this is it, he thought. When you die you go to a cold, damp, misty freezing place. Hades, where the mournful spirits of the Dead troop for ever across the sorrowful marshes, corpse-lights flickering fitfully in the encircling—hang on a minute . . .

Surely Hades wasn't this uncomfortable? And he was very uncomfortable indeed. His back ached where a branch was pressing into it, his legs and arms hurt where the twigs had lacerated them and, judging by the way his head was feeling, something hard had recently hit it. If this was Hades it sure was hell—hang on a minute . . .

Tree. He concentrated on the word that floated up from his mind, although the buzzing in his ears and the flashing lights in front of his eyes made this an unexpected achievement. Tree. Wooden thing. That was it. Branches and twigs and things. And Rincewind, lying in it. Tree. Dripping wet. Cold white cloud all around. Underneath, too. Now that was odd.

He was alive and lying covered in bruises in a small thorn tree that was growing in a crevice in a rock that projected out of the foaming white wall that was the

Rimfall. The realization hit him in much the same way as an icy hammer. He shuddered. The tree gave a warning creak.

Something blue and blurred shot past him, dipped briefly into the thundering waters, and whirred back and settled on a branch near Rincewind's head. It was a small bird with a tuft of blue and green feathers. It swallowed the little silver fish that it had snatched from the Fall and eyed him curiously.

Rincewind became aware that there were lots of similar birds around.

They hovered, darted and swooped easily across the face of the water, and every so often one would raise an extra plume of spray as it stole another doomed morsel from the waterfall. Several of them were perching in the tree. They were as iridescent as jewels. Rincewind was entranced.

He was in fact the first man ever to see the rim-fishers, the tiny creatures who had long ago evolved a lifestyle quite unique even for the disc. Long before the Krullians had built the Circumfence the rim-fishers had devised their own efficient method of policing the edge of the world for a living.

They didn't seem bothered about Rincewind. He had a brief but chilling vision of himself living the rest of his life out in this tree, subsisting on raw birds and such fish as he could snatch as they plummeted past.

The tree moved distinctly. Rincewind gave a whimper as he found himself sliding backwards, but managed to grab a branch. Only, sooner or later, he would fall asleep . . .

There was a subtle change of scene, a slight

purplish tint to the sky. A tall, black-cloaked figure was standing on the air next to the tree. It had a scythe in one hand. Its face was hidden in the shadows of the hood.

I HAVE COME FOR THEE, said the invisible mouth, in tones as heavy as a whale's heartbeat.

The trunk of the tree gave another protesting creak, and a pebble bounced off Rincewind's helmet as one root tore loose from the rock.

Death Himself always came in person to harvest the souls of wizards.

'What am I going to die of?' said Rincewind.

The tall figure hesitated.

PARDON? it said.

'Well, I haven't broken anything, and I haven't drowned, so what am I about to die of? You can't just be killed by Death; there has to be a reason,' said Rincewind. To his utter amazement he didn't feel terrified any more. For about the first time in his life he wasn't frightened. Pity the experience didn't look like lasting for long.

Death appeared to reach a conclusion.

YOU COULD DIE OF TERROR, the hood intoned. The voice still had its graveyard ring, but there was a slight tremor of uncertainty.

'Won't work,' said Rincewind smugly.

THERE DOESN'T HAVE TO BE A REASON, said Death, I CAN JUST KILL YOU.

'Hey, you can't do that! It'd be murder!'

The cowled figure sighed and pulled back its hood. Instead of the grinning death's head that Rincewind had been expecting he found himself looking up into the pale and slightly transparent face of a rather worried demon, of sorts.

'I'm making rather a mess of this, aren't I?' it said wearily.

'You're not Death! Who are you?' cried Rincewind.

'Scrofula.'

'*Scrofula?*'

'Death couldn't come,' said the demon wretchedly. 'There's a big plague on in Pseudopolis. He had to go and stalk the streets. So he sent me.'

'No-one dies of scrofula! I've got rights. I'm a wizard!'

'All right, all right. This was going to be my big chance,' said Scrofula, 'but look at it this way – if I hit you with this scythe you'll be just as dead as you would be if Death had done it. Who'd know?'

'I'd know!' snapped Rincewind.

'You wouldn't. You'd be dead,' said Scrofula logically.

'Piss off,' said Rincewind.

'That's all very well,' said the demon, hefting the scythe, 'but why not try to see things from my point of view? This means a lot to me, and you've got to admit that your life isn't all that wonderful. Reincarnation can only be an improvement – uh.'

His hand flew to his mouth but Rincewind was already pointing a trembling finger at him.

'Reincarnation!' he said excitedly. 'So it is true what the mystics say!'

'I'm admitting nothing,' said Scrofula testily. 'It was a slip of the tongue. Now – are you going to die willingly or not?'

'No,' said Rincewind.

'Please yourself,' replied the demon. He raised the scythe. It whistled down in quite a professional way, but Rincewind wasn't there. He was in fact several metres below, and the distance was increasing all the time, because the branch had chosen that moment to snap and send him on his interrupted journey towards the interstellar gulf.

'Come back!' screamed the demon.

Rincewind didn't answer. He was lying belly down in the rushing air, staring down into the clouds that even now were thinning.

They vanished.

Below, the whole Universe twinkled at Rincewind. There was Great A'Tuin, huge and ponderous and pocked with craters. There was the little disc moon. There was a distant gleam that could only be the *Potent Voyager*. And there were all the stars, looking remarkably like powdered diamonds spilled on black velvet, the stars that lured and ultimately called the boldest towards them . . .

The whole Creation was waiting for Rincewind to drop in.

He did so.

There didn't seem to be any alternative.

THE END

Visit

www.**terrypratchett**.co.uk

to discover everything you need to know
about Terry Pratchett and his writing, plus all
manner of other things you may find interesting, such as
videos, competitions, character profiles and games.

TURTLE RECALL: THE DISCWORLD COMPANION . . . SO FAR
(with Stephen Briggs)

NANNY OGG'S COOKBOOK
(with Stephen Briggs, Tina Hannan and Paul Kidby)

THE PRATCHETT PORTFOLIO
(with Paul Kidby)

THE DISCWORLD ALMANAK
(with Bernard Pearson)

THE UNSEEN UNIVERSITY CUT-OUT BOOK
(with Alan Batley and Bernard Pearson)

WHERE'S MY COW?
(illustrated by Melvyn Grant)

THE ART OF DISCWORLD
(with Paul Kidby)

THE WIT AND WISDOM OF DISCWORLD
(compiled by Stephen Briggs)

THE FOLKLORE OF DISCWORLD
(with Jacqueline Simpson)

THE WORLD OF POO
(with the Discworld Emporium)

MRS BRADSHAW'S HANDBOOK
(with the Discworld Emporium)

THE COMPLEAT ANKH-MORPORK
(with the Discworld Emporium)

THE STREETS OF ANKH-MORPORK
(with Stephen Briggs, painted by Stephen Player)

THE DISCWORLD MAPP
(with Stephen Briggs, painted by Stephen Player)

A TOURIST GUIDE TO LANCRE – A DISCWORLD MAPP
(with Stephen Briggs, illustrated by Paul Kidby)

DEATH'S DOMAIN (with Paul Kidby)

THE DISCWORLD ATLAS
(with the Discworld Emporium)

A complete list of Terry Pratchett ebooks and audio books as well as other books based on the Discworld series – illustrated screenplays, graphic novels, comics and plays – can be found on
www.terrypratchett.co.uk

Non-Discworld books

THE DARK SIDE OF THE SUN

STRATA

THE UNADULTERATED CAT (illustrated by Gray Jolliffe)

GOOD OMENS (with Neil Gaiman)

Shorter Writing

A BLINK OF THE SCREEN

A SLIP OF THE KEYBOARD

SHAKING HANDS WITH DEATH

With Stephen Baxter

THE LONG EARTH

THE LONG WAR

THE LONG MARS

THE LONG UTOPIA

THE LONG COSMOS

Non-Discworld books for young adults

THE CARPET PEOPLE

TRUCKERS

DIGGERS

WINGS

ONLY YOU CAN SAVE MANKIND

JOHNNY AND THE DEAD

JOHNNY AND THE BOMB

NATION

DODGER

JACK DODGER'S GUIDE TO LONDON

DRAGONS AT CRUMBLING CASTLE

THE WITCH'S VACUUM CLEANER